Dandelion Jane

Strawberry Jelly

A.R. STANLEY

Dandelion Jane

Strawberry Jelly

A.R. STANLEY

arstanley.com

© A. R. Stanley

arstanley@arstanley.com

Cover by J. Ryan Stanley

ISBN: 9781982911737

Imprint: Independently published

For my parents

You always stood by us no matter what crazy crap we pulled. You made me a better person, wife, and mother by watching that example. You just don't stop loving people.

1

The lock on my apartment door jiggled and clinked the way it always did when you tried to unlock it. The damn thing was old and stuck frequently. The key pulled out of the lock. I heard it jam back in, more jiggling and shaking. My head snapped up from packing, my heart rate accelerating. I was inside my apartment packing up the last of my belongings. No one else owned a key to my crappy apartment. I sprung up and went towards the door just as I heard the lock click. My foot caught the edge of a box, sending my body reeling towards the wall. My hands flung in front of my face, catching the full weight of my body against the wall next to the door. I watched as a hand pushed open the door, followed by his face that was inches from mine. Our eyes met, we both screamed.

"Who the hell are you?" I yelled.

"Why are you in my flat?"

"I think you mean my apartment!" My hands pushed my body away from the wall and my shoulders squared.

"Clearly mine or I wouldn't have a key." He held up the key ring.

"I am inside the apartment! Mine! Furnishings, see them? This is my apartment for another twenty-four hours." I cast my arms out towards the contents of the room. His eyes scanned the apartment, a puzzled expression creeping onto his face. My knee rose, preparing to crotch kick him out the door when he opened his mouth to speak.

"I am so sorry," his eyes noticed my leg. He dropped his bag and flung his hands into the air, "Oh shit, don't!" He took a step back. "You're totally right! It is clearly your flat. The leasing office made a mistake." I moved my leg, debating on lowering it, his hands instinctively moved to his crotch, "Please don't! Don't kick my balls!" He sounded pathetic. "This is seriously the worst day ever." The last part came out as a mumble. My heartstrings tugged as much as I didn't want them to. Against my better judgment, I lowered my leg, hands falling to my hips.

"Ok, spill it," I replied.

He stood, gazing at me from behind his glasses. Bug-eyed, and confused, he began to take in the surroundings behind me. The apartment was in that fun transitional phase of everything being half in a box and half out. Some of my things more than others, like my clothes, were lying on the sides of boxes and on the floor around them. "Spill it?"

"You sound like someone with a story. What's the story?" There were few things better in life than stories. They were on my Top 5 List. Most of my decisions I made by impulsivity and the knowledge they would make good stories later. I once robbed a frozen yogurt store knowing it would make the local paper. The worst parties were the ones you blacked out at, not because of the pounding headache the next day, but because there were no stories to tell.

"Well, I literally just flew in, and I must have lost my wallet after I exited the taxi. When I grabbed my mobile, I realized my wallet wasn't in my pocket. I looked 'round, but I can't find it." He told me as if he did not expect me to believe him. "When I went to the leasing office they literally just handed me the key and sent me on my way. I don't know what to do about the flat. I didn't expect to show up in the States and find myself homeless."

I bit my tongue. There was something about him. It reminded me of someone back home. I could not put my finger on it but decided to give him a chance. It's what my family was good at, taking in the strays, the ones no one else in town wanted to touch, that was us. Growing up I usually snuck my drunk friends through the window, but if

Pops had known he would have let them in the front. Why didn't I let them in the front? Because what thirteen-year-old kid is going to admit their partying to their parents? I was dumb, not that dumb.

"I know, I probably sound like a conman or something. I promise I'm not. I just don't know what to do. I need to ring my credit card company." He added, "I'm William Lovatt by the way, everyone calls me Liam." He shoved his hand at me.

He didn't sound like a fake, he sounded like someone down on their luck. A feeling I was accustomed to. I returned the gesture, "Dani,"

"Well, this is probably the worst impression I have ever made on a female," he laughed.

We stood in the doorway for a long moment. William adjusted his glasses.

"Do you mind if I come in and ring the bank?" he asked bravely, breaking the awkward silence.

"Sure. Why not. I mean you already have a key. Why not make yourself at home? I'm just going to call the manager and find out what's going on." I waved at the couch, half knowing I would have no luck with the manager. I grabbed my phone from the side table by the door and pounded in the number. I listened in on William while he verified his accounts to cancel his cards. I wondered if he flew in from England or somewhere else. His accent was decidedly British.

"Hey," a thick New York accent said into the phone.

"Hi, this is Dani Sanders in apartment 5D. I am moving tomorrow, but some guy just walked in with a key saying the apartment is already his. What's going on?" I hoped for an apology, an explanation of their blunder. I got anything but.

"Well, lookin' at your original lease agreement, we allowed you to move in before the beginnin' of the month a year ago, which means yesterday your lease was officially over." I could hear him typing away at a computer as we spoke.

It almost didn't surprise me. This was my life, one mistake after another. "Did it not occur to you that I hadn't turned the key in? Do you people not check the apartments before you lease them back out?"

"Usually, but things are movin' fast, and we didn't get around to it. Baby, people forget to leave the keys all the time."

"Do you have a different apartment this William something can move into? My stuff isn't gone." I tried, knowing it was useless.

"Considerin' your lease ended yesterday unless you want to sign a new lease and pay for it, that apartment ain't yours. So, I can either look the other way; pretend like I don't know you're still in there, or I can send you a bill. What do you think?"

"I'm not even here anymore, just packed the last box, and I'm gone."

"Good girl."

I clicked the phone off. My eyes flitted towards William sitting on the couch. He appeared more hopeful as he wrapped up his conversation.

"Congratulations, you just legally won your right to stay and I need to get the hell out. Also, you might want to ask them to change the locks."

"Listen, I feel like the leasing office has inconvenienced both of us. We can both stay the night, right? I'm happy sleeping on the couch. Hell, anything is better than sleeping on an airplane. I assume you're leaving tomorrow?"

The proposition did not surprise me, I had been expecting it. It would seem odd to some, but I had received far worse in my day. I knew when I let him into the apartment I would let him stay, it was only a matter of time for him to ask. After all, it would make a fantastic story when I was a grandma someday. The time I let a British stranger sleep in my New York apartment. What grandkid wouldn't want to hear that story?

"Sure, why not? You can crash on the couch and get your wallet situation figured out and I'll finish packing. I promise to be done tomorrow and head out." That would not be a problem. Most of my belongings had already made their way to the pawnshop.

"Brilliant." He flashed a smile at me for the first time. The left side of his mouth went up creating a crease that was almost a dimple on his round face. It made his almond-shaped eyes gleam. There went my heartstrings again and my resolve to make him sleep on the couch.

I quickly smiled and walked into the tiny galley kitchen. I began packing the cupboards up and hoped my head would clear. The conversation and niceties dropped, I packed, and he made phone calls. I had moved out of the kitchen and was finishing packing my bookshelf when I realized he only had one bag with him. It piqued my curiosity.

"So, where's all your stuff? You aren't taking an extended holiday with one bag, are you?" I dropped three books into a fresh box and heard them clunk before he answered.

"Sort of the worst day ever, the airline lost my luggage."

"Light packer?"

"What does that mean?"

"Most people bring junk with them, you know, furniture."

"Right. Well." He cleared his throat. "Just thought I'd get stuff when I got here."

"I get that. The only reason I have any of this is because my Pops made me bring it. Otherwise, I would have been the same. Anyway, I'm sorry. You sound like you are starting this new beginning out like how I'm ending it."

"Hopefully both our lives get better in the next twenty-four hours," he replied.

"Well, mine can't get that much better."

"Why's that?"

"Because I'm moving to a horrible, pokey, little town, in the middle of the Midwest. You, on the other hand, get to stay in the city that never sleeps and realize all your dreams. At least, that's what they try to sell you here." More books clunked into the box, falling from my hands.

"I'm not much in the market for dreams. What's the name of this pokey, little town?"

"Home," the small word slipped from my mouth with the same heaviness as the books. I turned back around to finish packing.

"Well, you know what they say. Home isn't a place; it's a feeling. Granted, it might be a feeling that makes you want to spew, but that's still a feeling."

I laughed.

"I knew I could get on your good side," he replied, pleased.

"You're a funny guy. What brings you to New York?"

"The girls," he winked at me, "Seriously though, my cousin twice removed grew up here and owns his own business. I needed a change from Canterbury, and he offered me a position. I figured why the hell not? If I would have stayed put I would have started eating second breakfast and growing hair on my feet."

"Did you just call yourself a Hobbit?"

"Did you just understand my reference?"

The banter paused. We both sized each other up.

"Have you been to the States before?"

"I have not. I'm looking forward to traveling while I'm here. Anything, in particular, I should see?" There was a tinge of something hidden beneath the question.

"Skip Florida and the Arch. If you like nature, you should make it out West. If you like the city, you landed pretty." I told him, finishing packing my box of books and folding the cardboard flaps down.

"What if I like pokey, little towns?" he teased.

There it was. I stood up and started to walk towards my room, "Then you should turn your key in and follow me home." I sauntered back through the French doors that separated the living room and bedroom and began packing my nightstand. William came into the room and threw his body down on my bed, leaning up on his elbow to watch me pack.

"Can I help you?"

"I would read or do Sudoku or something, but remember how the airline lost my bags? The best entertainment I have is to watch you."

"You could help me pack, the sooner it's done the sooner you get the apartment all to yourself."

"Ah, but you're forgetting that you are my sole source of entertainment. No real hurry for me to be rid of you."

Of course not, I thought.

"Why are you headed home?"

"I have PTSD. I couldn't cut it at Juilliard. So, I'm headed home with my badge of shame proudly displayed on my chest." The words tumbled from my mouth much easier with a stranger than they would with anyone else.

William looked at me perplexed. "Have you been in combat?"

"Girls are always in combat, didn't you know that? It's just a different kind." I stopped packing and watched his face.

"I'm sorry, Love, that's a shame." The playfulness in his green-and-yet-almost-blue eyes had vanished, replaced with genuine concern. His hand reached out towards me, squeezing my shoulder tightly, reassuringly. It brought me up short, his genuineness. Most boys like him did not care that much about girls' sullied pasts. The men who did were few and far between in my experience.

He slid off the bed and started to put books into the box with me. "Do you have family? How did they take it?"

Had I read this boy all wrong? The flirtations from a moment ago vanished from my mind. Perhaps William Lovatt was the kind of man who could handle a real conversation. "A simple question with an intricate answer," I mulled it over for a moment, did I respond about school, my condition? "Just my dad. For blood relations that is. He hasn't said a lot. He'll probably just be glad to have me back home." I paused, what the hell, "We don't talk much, about the bad things that have happened. It's hard for him to hear. Shit, it's hard for me to talk about. It's one thing for your Pops to know you've done shit, it's another to tell him details. He knows I've seen a shrink. He watched the meds backfire. But we don't talk about the other stuff. Do you have family missing you back in England?"

"Reverse from you, just my mum. She's not missing me so much though."

"You two don't get along?"

"She's ill; she hasn't known me for a couple years." His voice lowered. "I was away for a bit and when I came back I was a perfect stranger to her. Pills, I hate 'em. Your Pops probably does too. They can do crazy things to people, it's hard to watch. I hope you've had someone to talk to about what happened to you." He stood up and walked out of the room. "Is the toilet down this hall?" he called back to me.

"Yep," I twisted my lips up thinking about this flirty, kind, cute William who had waited until the day I was leaving to show up. It was typical though, people seemed to show up and leave at the oddest times of my life. My mom, Daisy Rivers, left when I was four. It always made me mad she did not leave the year before when I was only three. I had read someplace that memory before four did not stay stored in your brain well. If she would have hurried up and left, I probably would not be able to recall any memories of her. Like, the stupid one, of her teaching me to ride a tricycle that frequently played in my dreams. Sixteen years later and it still woke me up in the middle of the night when I went crashing into the creek and felt my lungs fill with water. Daisy Rivers wasn't the best mom. Then there was Cadmus Hall, he had arrived in town the first few months into my sophomore year. He got a job at my dad's hardware store and spent the next few months getting to know us. He ended up being the only person who could help save me from myself. I had always found it odd that he had not shown up one or two years earlier. If he would have, I might have never needed saving in the first place. It was his idea I go to Juilliard and his opinion was the only one that mattered to me when I lost my spot in the program. If he would have shown any disappointment, I would have decided to not go back home. I would have slummed it on the streets if I needed to.

"I have to say I love all the dark woodwork." William was saying while he came down the hallway and around the corner to my room.

I had not managed to pack anymore since he left, lost in my thoughts of home. "Right? I love it too. Most people just paint over it now. It gives some character to this crappy old place."

William yawned and sat on the edge of the bed.

"You're probably exhausted from jet lag. Do you want to take a nap or something? You can have the bed, I can pack something else." I asked, standing up and dusting my jeans off.

"No, no. I mean, I am. But everyone told me not to take a nap. That you have to stay up and reset your internal clock. I suppose I have to be a bloody man about it and push through."

A broad grin spreads on my face.

"What?"

"You just said 'bloody', it was amazing."

He looked at me in a way no one had looked at me in years. Like I had innocence and it was attractive.

"Listen, I'm starving. Is there a good pub close by I can grab a bite at?"

Thank god, a drink was exactly what I needed at that moment. "Two thoughts on that: one, we call it a bar here.

Two, you lost your wallet, and your good looks aren't going to get you free food."

"Oh shit," he mumbled.

"I'm starving too, and since I was apparently supposed to be moved out of your apartment yesterday. I'll buy you dinner. Even?"

"Even."

We walked down the busy New York street shoulder to shoulder. Well, his shoulder hit me about where my nose was. I pressed my arm into his ribcage. If the boy had already lost his wallet and luggage, I felt determined not to lose him. When we stopped at the end of the block for the light to change, I laced my long lean fingers in with his short thick ones and pulled him across the street behind me. The bar was just on the other side of the road. He firmly held on even after we crossed and entered through the green front door.

"Seat yourself!" The man behind the counter called. The old wooden bar hugged the wall, glass bottles stood on shelves in front of a mirror. The beer taps seemed to call my name when we walked down the narrow room towards the back. I wiggled my hand free of his. My palm smacked the top of the bar a few times, getting the attention of the bartender. I ordered a pint for myself and glanced back at William, he replied he would have the same. The glass mug felt icy under my fingers. I took him towards my favorite booth in the back.

"So, William," I began when we slid into the seats.

"Liam, no one calls me William but my mum."

"Okay... Liam," I pulled my satchel over my head and deposited it next to me on the seat. "What really made you run across the pond to us Yanks?"

He shifted his glasses up his nose. "What makes you so sure I was running from something?"

I narrowed my round, blue eyes, "Don't play coy with me. A runner knows a runner. What's the story?"

"There was a girl..."

"I knew it," I replied, pleased. Glad to sit and listen to someone else's tale of failure for once.

Before he could finish, our server came to take our order. Liam hesitated, I blurted out I would need another pint, and wanted a cheeseburger and fries. He raised his eyebrows at me but ordered the same.

"Continue," I told him when she had left, taking a large gulp from my mug.

"We've known each other for ages."

"Of course."

"I don't know what to tell you. It's a long story." He ducked his head.

I took another drink, licking my lips. "You knew her for forever, you dated on and off, but you couldn't settle, could you? Because what if she's not the one. What if there's someone better for you, something more exciting waiting around the corner." I told him.

He leaned back in the booth. "Exactly! What if I settled with Anne and regretted it immediately. There is a lot of world out there. And not just the world, I have a million and one ideas all piled up in my head waiting to come out."

We fell silent. Liam sipped his beer, mine was already a third gone. The noise of the bar, glasses clinking, TV blaring, a baseball game, people talking and laughing, faded to white noise.

"What are you running from?"

"What am I not running from? That would be a better question. I ran away to New York, and now I'm running from here. Maybe some of us are just meant to never stay still." I paused and took another drink, "I'm sure Anne was a great girl." I chuckled, "Of course she was. Have you ever met an Anne you didn't like?"

He smiled that crooked, almost dimpled smile, "She was the best. Sweet, kind, understanding, loyal. Beautiful."

I nodded my head. She sounded like the kind of girl boys ended up marrying.

"That's why I was going to tie the knot with her." He slung back his beer.

"Wow. I wouldn't have guessed you were running from the altar."

"I am the lowest of scum."

"You didn't for real?" I asked, hoping he had not let it go that far. Betrayal was a sin I could not forgive easily.

"No. Not the literal altar her in a white gown, all that. Very near it though. The date set for this autumn. But I couldn't do it. I couldn't let go of the field. I took the job with my relative. I packed my bags, told her I might come back someday but not to wait for me. I tucked my tail and fled."

He looked wounded, the color fading from his cheeks. His eyes that looked playful, teasing, and risky earlier now looked sunken and distraught. Turned out, I didn't have the same stomach for failure like folks back home.

I touched my glass to him, forcing his eyes back to mine, "Cheers. Cheers to all us terrible people who can't commit and ruin everything we touch."

He picked up his freshly filled glass and clinked it against mine, "Cheers, Love."

I drained my pint.

2

"No, no, no, I'm not making this up! He is out there every single day cleaning that driveway off. It is like a nervous tick or something for him. I once saw him with a toothbrush cleaning the cracks out. I swear to god." I crossed my heart and held my hand up. Liam could not stop laughing.

Three hours had passed since we entered the bar. The booth in the back, dimly lit, with high wooden backs, gave it the feel of its own private room. We had devoured the burgers and fries' hours ago, along with cherry pie an hour later. Liam wanted apple pie because it was "All American!" I convinced him cherry was better. Liam felt like an old friend. Well, friend might be the wrong term. Not a stranger, that much I was sure of. In my life, family were the people who helped you out, and friends were the ones wanting something from you. Acquaintance were the worst of all. They were the ones who stood on the sidelines and judged your life for you.

"Is this all you do? Sit around your pokey, little town watching people? Do I need to be concerned you are some sort of stalker?" Liam asked me with a grin.

"There isn't anything else to do! Also, everyone knows everyone and everything about them. It's creepy, but people try to tell you it's charming."

"What is the one thing about yourself you wish the lot of 'em didn't know?"

I paused. It was a tricky question. Depending on how I answered there could be more questions than answers I wanted to give. "Who I've slept with."

He nodded, knowingly, "That one I get. Blokes usually get a pat on the back. Unless you've been shagging the right one and suddenly shag an awful one. Which one were you?"

"Not the right one. God, I would love to be the right one for once." I took a drink. "There was this one guy, growing up, I slept with him a lot. Ruined my life. Him? Nothing. Everyone blames the destruction of Aaron Abbot on me." Another drink. "I never put a joint or drink in his hand, but as far as the town is concerned I took a nice boy and corrupted him. If it wasn't for me he would have never gotten clean."

"Poor girls always get the short end of the stick."

I rubbed my forehead, "Maybe they're right though. Maybe some of it is my fault."

"Like hell. How old were you?"

"First time or with nice boy?"

His eyebrows rose.

"Thirteen. It was a big year for me."

"I don't think I would have pegged you that young."

I shrugged, "What's one thing you wish no one knew about you?"

Liam took another drink. He mulled this question over, "Didn't I come to the States to get away from this tyranny?"

"Spill it. What happens in the booth stays in the booth." I replied, glad to not be the only one with a sordid past.

He cleared his throat, "That I killed someone."

A nervous laugh escaped my lips. "That's not a funny joke."

"You're the one laughing." He gave me a pointed look. "I'm being serious."

"What the hell happened?" my nervous laughter had turned to curiosity and concern; after all, I was letting him sleep in my bed tonight.

"I got drunk one night at a party. We were outside on this chap's roof. I was being ludicrous and showing off. Someone at the party started talking about how he was taking karate, and we started a dumb fight. It was all in good humor. Except that I landed a good kick on his abdomen and he lost his balance and fell off." He narrowed his eyes and stopped talking.

"That's horrible," my breath caught in my throat. "Did you go to jail?"

"I did, I served a year. The judge was lenient on me. I was only a kid, and it was a horrible accident."

"You were only a kid?"

"Seventeen."

"Is that what you were talking about, how you were away for a while and then your mum didn't know you?"

He took a drink, "Yeah. Ruined my life. People stopped talking to me, givin' me the side eye all the time, wantin' nothing to do with my mum. I had this thought that after the trial was done and I served my bit and went home everything would be normal again. But when I got out we were alone. I mean, I was completely alone. The person I lived with didn't even remember me. No one cared."

My hand found its way across the table, covering his palm. "You know what I think? I don't think hell is a place you go when you die. I think it's something that happens to you while you're alive. It's this thing that separates you from people. It leaves you alone. It's these terrible things that happen to us and people on the outside judge you for it or leave you." His eyes were clapped on mine, unmoving, "The only good news is that you aren't dead and that means you can walk out of hell. I think you did, by moving away. You walked out of hell."

His face sunk, "It's the only reason I asked Anne to marry me... She didn't leave. God, I don't think I ever even loved her. She just didn't leave. The whole thing was hell." He took a drink. "How come I feel like such a heel?"

"Because you finally did something for you. Let's get out of here," I replied, getting up and throwing my bag over my shoulder. I almost lost my balance as the beer rushed to my head. I grabbed the side of the booth. "Want to drunkenly wander the streets?"

Liam looked up at me inquisitively. I could see the dark circles forming under his eyes. It occurred to me he had probably gone without sleep in twenty-four hours.

"Dani, can I be totally honest?"

"Always,"

"I need to pee, and I'm about ready to fall asleep."

"Bathroom is that way. I'll wait here for you and take you back." I pointed down the hallway and crossed my arms over my small chest. There went my fun last night out.

Liam rose slowly and stumbled towards the restroom.

He emerged a few minutes later. He looked a little worse around the edges. "Come here," I told him, I held my hand out. He took it up, giving it a firm grip. "I'm not going to lose you drunk on the street."

"I appreciate that," he kissed the top of my head.

I pulled him behind me, again, until we got outside. Night had fallen on the city while we talked the day away inside. New York City in the evening was something I was going to miss. You could not see the stars over the lights. It was as if it was its own galaxy. Where I grew up, when night fell, everything became still and quiet, except the insects and bullfrogs. In New York, nothing stopped, ever. If anything, it was more alive now. Liam's body leaned into mine while we waited for the crosswalk. It felt like a brick pushing onto my shoulder. I pulled my fingers out of his embrace and threw my arm around his waist. His arm slung across my shoulders, pulling me closer and closer to his torso. I put my other hand on his taut stomach to help him keep balance.

"Here we go." The light had changed. I gave him a little push to start walking.

"Thanks for not leaving me on the curb."

"Why would I want to do that?"

"So, you could have your apartment back for the night."

He stopped walking and leaned against the brick wall of the building we were passing.

I stood in front of him, my hands on my hips. "I'm not so worried about that. I'm leaving regardless. New York can't handle me anymore."

"I have a feeling few can," that irresistible smile spread on his face.

"Yeah, well, I wouldn't say that is a great quality to have." I pushed my caramel brown hair out of my eyes. "Think you can make it back?"

He grabbed my hand and pulled me to his chest. "You could stay a few more days, show me 'round the city."

"I'm not sure that would be a good idea."

"Why's that?"

"Then I would just leave you with a broken heart," I smirked at him.

He leaned down and pressed his lips against mine. They were soft. It was a gentle touch. I pulled away. "Let's get you back to the couch." It had nothing to do with Liam and everything to do with me. My heartfelt raw. The wound too fresh. The irony of my soft spot for drunks and how it left me here in this situation. I couldn't stand on the street corner and kiss him.

A few minutes later, we were laughing and stumbling up

the steps of my apartment building. It was not much, but it was home since the summer after my first year at Juilliard. As hard as the last year had been, there were many good memories that floated around this shanty apartment. Before I lost my lunch on stage at Carnegie Hall and Juilliard said, "Thanks, but no thanks", my friend, Ruben Asaf and I spent many hours here. With me practicing the piano, while he danced, and occasionally cooked Ramen Noodles for us. After school ended, I kept myself busy. The more things I had on my plate the better I did, I tended to make poor life choices when bored, something Cadmus and Arty (my pseudo dad) incessantly reminded me of. I hadn't done the best job with that though. If I would have kept my shit together I wouldn't be leaving tomorrow for home.

I leaned Liam against the wall and fumbled with my keys until the lock decided to give, and the door swung open.

"Hey," said Liam, quietly.

I turned to look at him, "What?" I whispered back.

He tugged his head to motion me over, "Come here,"

If I was not such a sucker for drunk boys I would be coming home to a dancer right now. Instead, there were no dancers left in my life because of all the drunks, and here I was, bringing another one home. "I don't think I want to do that, friend," I replied, coyly, and walked into the apartment, leaving the door open behind myself.

"What?" he asked. Following behind me closely, "All drinks and no fun?"

"You are far gone, and I'm not a rebound kind of girl." At least I didn't think I was. It was a new sensation for me.

"You're drunk too," he gave me a sheepish look. His glasses were sliding down his nose. "That makes it all the more fun. We won't remember it tomorrow which means it never happened. And that doesn't make you a rebound, Love, that's a one-night stand."

"Who said I was the rebound?" I tossed my satchel onto the table by the door before walking into the kitchen.

He whistled. "Runner."

There was a bottle of whiskey sitting on the counter. I picked it up and swirled the amber liquid. There were a few shots left. I uncapped it and tossed it back while walking into the main room. Liam was still standing in the middle of it, a hungry look on his face. I tossed back the rest of the contents of the bottle. The liquid burned my throat on the way down. I closed my eyes tightly, feeling it hit my brain, and the world went off kilter.

I set the bottle down on the couch, crossed the few inches separating me from Liam. I leaned into him and wrapped my arms around his neck. His face tilted down. He playfully rubbed my nose with his, drawing my gaze up. His mouth pressed against my lips, gentle, soft. His lips parted mine, growing in intensity, his hands pressing my lower back closer to his body. Hot energy ran up my spine and ignited in my brain. Or maybe it was just the booze. My hands shot up and under his shirt, pulling it over his head. We clumsily pushed our way through the small living room and the French doors of the bedroom. A colorful mixture of blue, brown, and white clothing flew in the air. We fell onto the sheets.

Now, this is the way to say good riddance to New York. I thought to myself.

The light streaming in through the bare window woke me late the next morning. The inside of my head was trying to escape into the daylight by pounding against my skull. I rubbed my eyes and forehead. Liam pressed against me with his creamy white arm slung over my waist. I crammed my neck around to get a look at his face. He was out cold. I flipped his arm off me and slowly stood up. For about two seconds I thought I would be okay, and then I raced for the bathroom.

After my beer, fries, and pie had made their exit down the toilet, I brushed my teeth three times. There was a small box still open in the bathroom just waiting for my last few belongings. I tossed my toothbrush and paste in, quickly rubbed on some deodorant, and tossed it in next. I splashed some cold water on my sandy-colored-freckled-skin face and patted it dry with the last towel hanging in the bathroom. I peered at my reflection for the first time that morning. I ran my fingers through my hair, tugging out the tangles, and tried to make it look fuller than it was. I pouted my rosy lips trying to look seductive but only succeed in making myself laugh. There was no use in trying to be sexy the night after a drunken escapade. It just wasn't my style in the morning light.

I walked down the hallway and through the doors to my room. Liam still passed out, his arm slung across his face to block out the light, his dark hair poked up everywhere. Our clothes from the night before, strewn across the floor, except for his boxers that he had retrieved at some point. I scrunched my mouth up while I looked at him and the mess. I could not remember much. Except for the feeling of his lips pressed against mine. They had left me wanting more. I rubbed my forehead again; the jackhammer in my brain had restarted. I grabbed my jeans and flannel shirt, and folded them up, tossing them into the only open box and I grabbed the fresh clothes I had left out yesterday.

The apartment was bare, completely packed into less than eight boxes. The only thing left to do was tape the boxes down. The rhythmic sound of the tape gun filled the apartment with its: shruiipipp chhhhik. It did not even rouse Liam from his heavy sleeping. After an overseas flight, staying awake for twenty-four hours, and having a hangover, it made sense nothing would wake him. I was downright giddy when I found migraine meds in a box. I popped two pills and swallowed them dry. Shortly after, I realized I needed to catch a cab to take me out of the city to pick up a small moving truck.

The bedroom was warming up from all the afternoon sunlight streaming in. Liam was lying in the middle of the bed on his stomach, the sheet kicked off and hanging off the bed. I lingered in the doorway for a moment watching him sleep. His biceps created a nice curve where he had his arms pulled up under his head. It was a new feeling for me, to look down at the previous night with no regrets.

There is no use in feeling attached to this one, girl. I told myself. I took a few steps over to the side of the bed, ran my fingers through his short dark hair, leaning into his ear, "I will be back in a few hours". Kissed his lips lightly and left.

It did not take me long to wave down a cab and give the driver the address of where I needed to be. I settled in for a long ride, most of which would be trying to get out of the city. The traffic was one thing I would not miss by going home. I pulled my earbuds out of my satchel and slipped them in. My eyelids began to feel heavy the cabby cursed at the car next to us for not letting him over. I cranked the music up on my phone and closed my eyes, leaning my head back on the seat. I must have fallen asleep quickly and heavily, because the next thing I knew, he was shaking me awake at the truck rental facility.

"Huh," I sat up, disorientated for a moment. I shook my head and grabbed money out of my bag. I shoved it into his palm and crawled out of the taxi. I walked up to the small building in the middle of a parking lot surrounded by trucks. I yanked the earbuds out while I opened the door and walked in.

"Can I help you?" the lady sitting behind a desk asked.

"Yeah, I'm Dani Sanders. I reserved a truck."

"Let me look ya up. Have a seat." She smacked her gum and typed away at her computer. I sat in front of her desk and took in my surroundings. The room filled with desks piled high with paperwork, but the receptionist's desk was the only one with a computer on it. There was a large pegboard hanging on the back wall with keys.

"Okay, I found you. You were supposed to pick your truck up yesterday." She frowned at me.

"I must have written the day down wrong." I repressed a yawn. This better not take a long time.

"Uh-huh, well, I sure hope we still have a truck for ya."

"Your lot looked pretty full," I slung back with ample snark in my tone.

"Just because I have trucks out there, Sweetie, doesn't mean I have one left for you," She gave me a sharp look then continued to type. "Alright, I found one. It's smaller than the one you wanted. It's either that or you take a seventeen-foot truck."

"What? Where's my truck I reserved?"

"Gone. You didn't show up and we rented it out this

morning. So, you want the cargo van or the seventeen-foot truck, or do you wanna go someplace else?" she smacked her gum again and glared at me.

"Give me the cargo van," I said between gritted teeth.

"I need your license and credit card."

I dug them out of my wallet and handed them over.

"This says Dandelion Sanders; I thought your name was Dani."

"My full name is Dandelion, but I go by Dani. Is that a problem?"

"Not now," she told me while hitting the backspace several times. "Who names their kid after a weed?"

I shrugged my shoulders at her, biting down, hard, on my tongue.

She stood up and grabbed the keys off the pegboard. "A little advice, a smile and a good attitude go a long way. Try them out sometime."

I yanked the keys out of her hand and left without another word.

Two hours, 158 curse words, and a 36-ounce gas station coffee slushy later, I walked back up the steps to my apartment. I found myself braiding my hair and pressing my lips together before I walked through the door.

"Hey," I called, silence met me. How Liam could still be asleep was beyond me. He had not been that much drunker than I was. I peeked around the corner into the bedroom and found it was empty. I furrowed my brow and looked down the hall to the bathroom, but the door was open, and the light was off. I finally walked into the kitchen and found it empty. "Bastard," I pounded my fist against the counter. They were all the same. No matter how charming, how connected you felt, what a great laugh you had, in the end, they all just ran away. None of them could handle strings. What could I have possibly asked for? I was leaving the state. I felt as string-less as they came. Bastards all left after they got off. I grabbed a box off the counter and took it into the other room, dropped it on the floor by the door with a thud. It did not take long to empty the kitchen out, one angry thump after another.

The freight elevator (that was a piece of junk) was right across from my door. I propped the door open with a broom and slowly loaded all my boxes onto it. I had spent a few minutes staring at my bed and couch wondering if there was any way I could fit them in the van. I finally decided it was not worth the hassle even if I could make it work. It could be my last parting gift to Liam. First, he got my apartment, then my body, now my furniture. It seemed a little out of order, I mused. I yanked the broom out from under the grate and let it fall with a bang. I jammed my finger into the ground button. The elevator shook and groaned before it slowly started to descend. I instinctively put my arms out and braced for the impact if it did a free-fall. Wouldn't that be a great way to die? I could see the headline in my head:

Girl Dies in Freak Elevator Accident

She couldn't stop the inevitable freefall of her life

The elevator shook and groaned while it slowed and came to a stop on the last floor. "Thank god," I yanked the grate up and shoved the broom under it. "Here's hoping the van is still there," I said to myself. I opened the back door and looked out. The van was where I parked it illegally in front of the dumpsters. I found a dolly stashed in the corner of the storage room. I loaded up three boxes, took them down, and shoved them in the back. In no time at all, I would be cursing my way through traffic again. Longing for the open road and to head anywhere but back to where I was going.

3

72 hours, 43 minutes, 256 ounces of coffee, and countless curse words later I pulled up to Cadmus's cabin. I had
decided to take the scenic route home and stretched out the
driving. I stopped in Hershey PA and picked up more chocolate than I could ever eat. Jefferson National Forest was
healing after spending two years surrounded by concrete.
The last eight hours of driving west just felt like home. I
was eager to sleep in a regular bed tonight and not the back
of the van.

The sun was on its way down when I turned onto Cadmus's dirt lane. The headlights on the van turned on auto-
matically. The shadows stretched and lengthened across the
ground. The little cabin was a guiding light in the middle
of the dusk. The headlights swept across the front porch

where he was sitting in his rocking chair, he always was this time of the evening. I loved his cabin settled in the woods. The front had three windows looking out onto the porch where three rocking chairs sat. The steep roof was metal and painted a bright barn red. On the left side of the house stood a staircase that led up to a small attic room where September slept. She had slept there on and off, the last year her momma was alive. When Marie passed, almost four years ago, Cadmus took her in officially. It was months of negotiating, but ultimately no one else would take the responsibility of September.

"Hello Dani," Cadmus greeted me. He stood up from his chair and walked to the van. I instinctively threw my arms around his neck and pulled him close for a hug, inhaling his scent deeply. It was a mingling of vanilla, cedar, and leather. I buried my head in his neck. It was a space that felt like home and safety. He picked me up easily, squeezing me against his chest. "We've missed you around here," he replied, putting me down. I held onto his neck and looked intensely into his eyes. I wanted to soak up this moment. His brown eyes glistened as they considered mine.

"What's this friend?" I asked, mischievously, rubbing a closely cropped black beard. It covered his smooth dark skin.

"Well, come now, you can't mock me two seconds after you arrive. It was bitterly cold this past winter and a man needs to protect his assets." He pulled himself up straighter.

"So, to protect your beautiful face you hid it behind a beard that has not left with the warm weather?" I cocked my head and glared at him with one eye.

"What's the plan to get you moved back to New York?"

I threw my arms around him again and hugged him.

"Dee!" I heard September shriek from the top of the stairs. "Dee!" she hollered again. I heard her pound down the steps, and once she reached us, she threw her arms around both of us.

"Hey girl," I laughed, pulling her into our embrace. Sep had grown to be the little sister I never had. The smaller version of me. The one I could protect and save.

"Yer daddy didn't call and tell us yah got home yet." Her forest green eyes scrunched up into half-moons, from her bright and unstoppable smile.

"Probably because he doesn't know," I told them as we released each other and walked into the cabin. I slipped my hand into Sep's small-tawny-skinned one that reminded me of hay bales in the summer. "I wanted to come see my two favorite people first." I smiled down at her and pushed her unruly, dirty blonde hair out of her eyes.

I had always thought September had the sweetest freckled-face of anyone I had ever met. She squeezed my hand hard before dropping it and running into the kitchen to pour us all water.

The inside of the cabin could not be more than 800 square feet. The floor plan was open and well designed, all things Cadmus were. He had impeccable taste and liked everything neat and organized; which was the chief reason for September to have her room out of the main part of the house. Arty once described Sep and me as an erupting volcano surrounded by a whirlwind. I hated him for it, mostly because it was true.

"Are you hungry?" asked Cadmus, removing the lid from a large soup pot sitting on the stove. Steam billowed towards the ceiling.

"I am a little," I replied while I curled up on the couch that sat in front of the windows.

September handed me a glass of water and smiled, sitting on the coffee table in front of me. "What was the best part of drivin home?" she asked, leaning in closer.

I thought for a moment, "Jefferson National Park. I'll have to take you some time and we can get lost in the woods for a day. Scour for pinecones and acorns." It was an activity we had done often in a time that felt like a lifetime ago. I remember sitting at the coffee table in the funeral home doing leaf rubbings for hours with her when she was 8.

She giggled, "Let's do it!"

"Hand me my bag. I have a present for you."

She jumped up and grabbed it. Tossing it into my lap and sitting next to me. I flipped the cover open.

I pulled out the largest candy bar I had ever laid eyes on and handed it to her. "You better ask Cadmus before you eat the whole thing though." I winked at her.

"Soup is up," he had placed three large bowls of steaming liquid on the small metal table. I noticed Sep tuck the candy bar in the back of her pants and hide it with her shirt. I tried to not laugh and give her away. "Sep, when we're finished eating I need you to take your shower and head to bed."

She opened her mouth to protest.

"No protesting from you girl, we have to get up early tomorrow, and Dani isn't going anywhere." His voice was firm.

She shut her mouth then stuck a spoonful of soup in it. She gave Cadmus a death glare from across the table that he ignored.

"Why are you two getting up early tomorrow?" I asked. I took a bite out of the dense artisan bread he had set before us. It had thick layers of butter on it. Before I could stop myself a groan of pleasure escaped my mouth, I had not had home cooked anything in over two years. September burst out laughing. Cadmus closed his eyes and shook his head.

"I have to be at the hardware store early for your pops. He asked me to open up, so he could make you breakfast in the morning. I have a few errands to run beforehand." He shot a look towards Sep.

"What's that about?"

"What?" September asked with large eyes.

"That look," I glanced back at Cadmus, curious.

"Never mind," he scooped out a ladle of soup, "Here, eat more."

"I'm going to get fat fast with all these homecooked meals," I told him as I held up my soup bowl.

"It would do you some good. You look like skin and bones. Did you eat while you were away?"

"Most girls don't want to be told to get fat, Cadmus. I did eat. I have a petite frame, adding a few pounds isn't really on my radar." I took a bite out of the bread.

"You're a swimmer; you need some meat on you."

"I was a swimmer. Now I'm just a girl."

"Nobody is just a 'just.' Eating good food, having a few curves, there isn't anything wrong with that, and it would do you some good." He pointed his spoon at me. "To start swimming again."

"Well, you're the only man to ever tell me to gain weight so... I think I look fine."

"No one ever complained when they had something to hold onto."

Sep's eyes grew large, and she dropped her bread in her soup.

"Don't repeat that," we told her in unison.

"Did you get to go to Carnegie Hall when you were gone?" she asked me. The girls knew how to change a subject.

"I did. It was beautiful and so inspiring." My stomach twisted, remembering the nerves I felt when I walked onto that stage. I thought once I hit a note it would go away, it was my destiny, after all, to play in grand halls for hundreds of people.

"Did yah get to play while you were there?"

"Did I play in Carnegie Hall?" I asked. "Nope," I lied. I did not have the heart to tell them, the day I played at Carnegie was the beginning of the end.

"Maybe yah'll go back," she smiled at me, brightly.

"Maybe,"

"Yah still like to play, right?"

"I think so," I hesitated, knowing she would not be happy with what I was about to tell her, "I haven't been able to play in a year though."

"Why?" they asked in unison.

"I had to sell the piano."

September gaped open-mouthed at me.

"I'm sorry, I just... I had to do something to pay rent. I didn't have a lot of options."

"Why didn't you ask your pops for help?"

"I wasn't going to ask for more money because I'm a lousy waitress, and I couldn't cut school."

"It wasn't that you couldn't cut school. You have a condition."

"You just made me sound like a crazy person." After my winter break incident at Juilliard, I scheduled a visit with a shrink. It wasn't my first rodeo, and although meds backfired like a mother the first go around, I thought maybe it was time to try again. Before he would give me anything he upgraded my status from mere addict with depression to severe mental disorder. PTSD. Prescription? Cognitive behavioral therapy. I walked. It wasn't that I could deny I had something going on, obviously, my past had left me screwed over. But there was no way in hell I was going to sit in someone's office and complain about my lot in life again. That gig had happened the last two years of high school.

"Aren't yah?" Sep asked, innocently.

Cadmus and I both glared at her for a moment.

"What? Isn't that what... what... an... en... anxiety means?" she asked, trying to remember the right word.

"September Marie Woods, do I look like a crazy person to you?" I asked her. I sat down my spoon and rested my chin on my hands.

"Well no, but neither does ol' Bill, and he's got bats in his belfries. Everyone knows that. Same as Craig, I mean, how many times a day can yah clean your driveway off and not have people thinking yer a nutter?" her eyes were wide, innocent, and full of fight.

"Dani is not crazy, and I don't want to hear you saying that or questioning it. Anxiety is a condition that makes it hard for you to control your nerves; it makes her worry a lot and feel stressed," Cadmus replied.

"Well, worry is silly and yah just shouldn't think too much about stuff," she told me.

I repressed a laugh, "Trust me, there are plenty of things I don't spend much thought on." I avoided Cadmus's gaze, "And isn't it your bedtime?"

"Don't make me go to bed 'cause yer mad at me," she pleaded.

"Regardless of Dani's feelings towards you, you're done

eating, and it's time for you to run up to your shower and bed. I'm coming to check on you in thirty minutes. If you aren't clean as a whistle and tucked in your bed, I won't read to you tomorrow."

"Yes Cadmus," she replied.

I watched her, amazed, as she pushed her chair in, cleaned her dishes out, and kissed him on the cheek. While she hugged me around the neck she said, "Sorry I called yah crazy."

"Apology accepted. Love you, girl."

She smiled at me and took off to her room upstairs.

"I'm glad we could teach her about what boys like in the sack and mental disorders all in one dinner. Better us than kids on the street, I suppose. Honestly, she has grown up a lot in the last two years. You have done a great job with her. Better than I ever did. She's less like a wild animal and more like a tomboy." I pushed my chair in while Cadmus cleaned the dishes. I retreated to the couch and curled up on the far end of it. I tilted my head over to the windows; you could not make anything out now that the sun had set. If I twisted my neck and looked up, I could see a million stars in the sky.

"Thank you. She does keep me on my toes."

I turned back to him, he was sitting across from me in his leather chair. "How is school going?"

I detected a suppressed sigh from him.

"It's going. There has been a lot to catch up on. I am confident she has a strong foundation now. I just need to get her caught up to her grade level."

"Oh, Marie..."

September's mother, who was not of sound mind or body, had raised her on the streets. Most of the town's people let it go. They realized if they interfered, they could be responsible for Marie and ultimately September. They weren't kind-souled enough to take on such a task.

"You can't fault Marie for not sending her to school. She wasn't right in her mind. If I had to guess, whatever trauma she had in her life happened at school, which is why she was fearful to send Sep."

I bit my lip. My palms suddenly felt sweaty.

"I just wish Arty or your pops would have gotten her started younger. But she is settling down now and has decided she loves to read."

"Arty did try." My voice came out low and harsh. "That was the only reason he let Marie clean his house. So, he could try to teach Sep something. I tried. Pops tried. We all tried before you got here, Cadmus."

"Slow down, I wasn't implying no one tried."

I rubbed my hands on my jeans and looked back out the

windows. "I'm glad she likes reading now." I felt his eyes narrow at me. My heartbeat began to slow down. The last thing I wanted to think about was trauma at school.

"How did you do while you were gone?"

A chill ran up my arms and down my spine. I knew he would be digging. I had only hoped it would wait for a few days or a week.

"No relapse."

"But," he questioned.

"But nothing," I shot my eyes back to look at him. "Honestly, I was clean the whole time I was there. Maybe that's why I have anxiety now." It came out accusingly even though it shouldn't have. I wrapped my arms around my knees and hugged them close to my chest.

"That's good. I've always had faith in you that you could do it."

"But I didn't. I mean, not really. I fudged it up, again. Back home, a drop out from college, not a penny to my name. I'm stuck in this shit town when I should be traveling the world. I'm never going to dig out of this one again."

"You'll figure it out."

"Will I? I can't seem to do much on my own. I'm always going to need some kind of drug to function."

"Don't say that."

"But it's true. If it's not alcohol, it's drugs, and if those fail it'll always, always, always, be a boy. I just can't cope alone."

"How's the drinking?"

I rolled my shoulders, "It was college. I wasn't going to write off all the parties."

"I can understand that. But on a scale of one to ten how bad do you want a drink right now?"

I licked my lips, "I don't know... Maybe, like a three."

"Liar."

"Okay, maybe more like a six... or a seven..."

"Perhaps the number you are searching for is a ten?"

My silence answered him.

"Are you going to work on that, or are you happy with that? My Tuesday and Thursday evenings are still open."

"I'm not going back to those meetings. I've been fine for four years."

"You were in meetings for two of those. And it sounds like you had a lot of fun the last two."

I looked back out the windows. No one in college cared about my physical health, much less my mental health (that was not true, Ruben cared). The questions would take time to warm up to. Cadmus's chill attitude as well. How he could stay calm, interrogating me, and I felt like a ball of stress unnerved me even more.

"Enough about that though," Cadmus replied. "Meet any nice boys?"

I could hear the sarcasm dripping from his words. I laughed and looked back at him. "I can honestly say boys from the country and boys from the cities aren't that much different. They all want to buy you drinks and get you to bed before the buzz wears off."

"Not your friend though, Ruben?"

I wagged my head, "No, not Ruben." It still stung. The memory of our first kiss and the subsequent discussion of his "temple". He couldn't defile it with sexual intercourse. My arms had dropped to my sides, my face tilted back to gaze up at his before I started to take steps away from him. There was no trace of an accent in his speech, but I could have sworn he was speaking Hebrew to me. I hadn't kissed him again until the day before Liam showed up. We had spent the day arguing about my leaving New York. He begged me to stay; I told him there wasn't anything for me to stay for, washed up. "I'll be done in a year, we can go anywhere after that." He told me. I didn't know what to do with that, so I did what I did best. I reached up and took hold of his face, his stubble felt soft under my fingertips. I pulled him down close to me and kissed him with everything in me. I left after that.

"How'd that work for the rest of them?" Cadmus's question pulled me back to the present.

"Pretty good." flashes from a million parties flew through my mind's eye. "To be honest, it makes me glad to be home. I know it will be quiet here. It would be nice to rest and figure out what to do next."

"I'm glad you're home. I'm sorry that Juilliard didn't work. You'll figure it out though. You can come up with a new plan."

"I should probably head home. Pops will be staying up waiting for me, and you need to go tuck Sep in."

"I still have faith in you," he told me. "We'll see you tomorrow."

I grabbed my bag and let the door clap shut behind me.

4

Cadmus must have called my dad when I left his cabin. Dad was standing on the front porch watching the driveway when I pulled down it. Our Bernese-Mountain dog, Mazy was sitting alert next to him. I could detect her tail wagging while she obediently waited. My dad, Melvin Sanders was not a tall man by any means. He was a little rounder around the middle than he would have liked, but his presence was commanding. His white-gray hair rustled in the breeze.

"Hey Pops," I called. I slid out of the seat, ran up the steps two at a time, and threw my arms around his sun-bronzed neck. It knocked him a step back, and he hesitantly put his arms around me.

"Hey Girl."

I pulled away and held his shoulders, "I missed you, Pops." I surveyed his face. I could see the disappointment playing around the lines of his eyes and mouth. I realized he knew by the size of the vehicle that I sold things. I wondered if Cadmus warned him.

"We missed you like crazy, Girl. Did you sell the piano?" his bright blue eyes, that always reminded me of the ocean, were unrelenting.

"Well, you sure don't miss a beat, do you? Yeah. It was the piano or the street. I figured you would rather I sold the piano," I answered him, braced for his response.

"I would've rather you asked first," Dad said. He turned expressionless away from me and went inside. "Free Mazy."

"I'm going to grab my bags," I called after him. Mazy bounded over to me licking my hands. "Fudge," I mumbled under my breath.

About time I made it back into the house, Dad had gone to bed, and only left one light on for me, the one at the bottom of the stairs. It was his way of telling me he was glad I was home, but he could not deal with my drama. I was to turn the light out on my way to my room and not make any more waves for one day. That light had turned into our own personal beacon. When Dad would come down the stairs in the mornings, he would know if I had ever made it home the night before. The mornings he found it lit were a sure sign I needed help. If it wasn't for that light, I would have OD'd years ago. I gritted my teeth, twisted the knob on the lamp, and tromped up the stairs. Far as I could tell in the dark, nothing had changed inside the house, including my dad. I supposed tomorrow over breakfast would be a fun conversation. It would probably be better that way, the exhaustion from the long drive was settling around my shoulders, and my brain felt a bit foggy.

I dropped my bags in my room and went to the bathroom. Dad had bought all new toiletries for me and left them on the sink. I ripped open the toothbrush and toothpaste first. After I finished brushing them furiously, I yanked off my blue bandana and threw it in the wicker basket that sat on the shelves above the toilet. I caught a whiff of my underarms and decided a bath could not wait until the morning. I cranked up the hot water and stripped down. After four days in a van, I knew this would be a long one. The hot water relaxed my shoulders. I felt myself lean into it as my mind began to race, wondering how mad Dad was about the piano, to thinking about September and Cadmus. I loved how Cadmus would pick whom to love and then love them with everything in him. There was something about him, something about his energy, he managed to calm the hot storm of September and the whirlwind of destruction I caused, all in one swoop. The three of us were family in a way I never could be with anyone else.

The water began to cool. I turned the hot tap a few turns. The piano... I told him when he sent it with me that we should keep it at home. He insisted, he always did, that it was a great idea. Of course, once I arrived at school it was clear that I could not keep it. I found a storage facility and never told Dad. When I left school to set up my own apartment, I pulled it out of storage. That was the reason I pleaded with the leasing office to let me move in early. Ruben Asaf was free to help me move it in that day. After eight months of trying to make ends meet, I found myself with barely enough money to buy groceries for one month. I knew I should ask for permission or help, but I told myself I would never move home, and they would never be the wiser. How stupid could I get? I grabbed the shampoo bottle and squirted a large amount into my palms. I closed my eyes tight, the water and soap ran down my face, and down into the drain.

Ruben's piercing brown eyes with their long dark lashes flashed through my memory. A pain in my heart simmered. I remembered our painful parting with a strange new sensation, this was my penance, coming home. I hadn't expected to care as much as I did. He snuck up on me and I didn't want to let it go. Ruben was the only real love I ever had. We did not owe each other a thing. Or at least we hadn't until I fudged it up.

I wondered how Liam was. He had a heart too, even if it was a drunken one. I had a hard time resisting males. I was never sure what that said about me. I was sure Cadmus had an entire thesis in his head on this very flaw. The thing I was sure about, was that I just hadn't found the one that would fulfill me. I turned the water off and stepped out of the shower. Mazy was sitting on the rug, her head cocked, and her large brown eyes were looking up at me, wanting attention. I grabbed a towel off the shelf and wrapped it around myself.

"Come on girl, you can sleep with me tonight," I told her with a wave of my hand. I slept better with company. Mazy had been the perfect companion for years. A warm body, the presence of another soul, no demands on my body. When I slept alone, the nightmares crept in. The dark woods, the water. I snuggled my back next to Mazy, her fur tickled my bare skin. The warmth radiating off her eased my mind as my eyes closed.

The buttery vanilla smell of pancakes woke me the next morning. Mazy had already left. I was sure she was at Dad's heels hoping for a few morsels. I tossed the covers off my body, slipped on my clothes from the day before, and padded down to the kitchen. Dad's house was masculine, there was no other word for it. The furniture was dark leather with wooden frames, the wood floors stained a rich brown, and the walls painted navy blue. The one saving grace, Dad did not hunt, as every other man in town did, which meant our walls were taxidermy free. The main floor plan had a shape like a large backward C with the stairs coming down in the middle. They faced towards the front door. I walked through the family room and around to the kitchen where dad stood at the island flipping pancakes on the griddle.

"Good morning, Girl,"

"Mornin', Pops. Mornin', Mazy." I scooted onto a stool at the island. Mazy put her head on my lap waiting for an ear scratch, I obliged her.

"Did you sleep well?" he asked, pouring more batter onto the sizzling pan.

"Better than I have in a month," I confessed.

"Plans?" he continued and flipped three pancakes onto a plate, handing it to me.

"I only have one wild and free life." I took the plate with a smirk.

Dad sighed, "Thank you, Mary Oliver."

"I need to unpack the van and get it returned. No big plans outside of that. Are you working today? Cadmus said he was opening up for you." I replied around the pancakes in my mouth. The casual conversation, the old routine, it felt disconcerting.

"I figured I would go in later after we were settled."

"Pops," I paused, the words stuck to the roof of my mouth. "I'm sorry about the piano."

"I know you are."

"I couldn't ask anyone for money. I couldn't take a hand out."

Dad's eyes held onto my face for a moment. "You do realize the piano was not yours to sell, though. It was mine, given to me by my family. In a roundabout way, you took a handout, without asking."

"You're right." I pushed my pancakes around on my plate. "What can I do to make it up?"

"Nothing," he answered and poured more batter out, "What is done is done, and there is no fixing this problem."

We fell silent. I chewed my pancakes, they felt sticky in my mouth. I gulped down a glass of milk to wash them down.

"How will you practice now?" Dad asked.

"Pops," I set the cup down, "I haven't touched the pearly whites in over a year."

"That is unacceptable."

"Well, it's just a fact, and y'all are going to have to get over it." In less than a day at home, I had already returned to the country slang. I had worked hard to drop it from my vocabulary in the city. What other terrible habits would I pick back up by the end of the week?

Dad stopped making pancakes. He set the spatula down forcefully, "Excuse me, girl? I might not have had much say in your life for the last two years, but you are under my roof again. I suggest you change your tone. And you will start to play again."

"Pops, I don't want to play."

Dad threw a cold hard glare in my direction.

"Playing makes me feel... I don't know... I can't do it."

"Playing will help you heal. Wasn't it Chopin who said, 'Sometimes I can only groan and suffer, and pour out my despair at the piano!' That's what you need to do again."

I did not even try to argue with him. Dad was the epitome of stubbornness; I knew if he was quoting my favorite pianist to me, I had lost the argument. I would not fight with him if he were going to insist on finding a new piano. I did not have to play it, after all. It could sit in the family room, in the spot still empty from the antique piano now gone. It did not mean I had to mess with it.

"Maybe I'll go for a swim today," I changed the subject.

"That would be good for you; the water is still pretty cold though. Don't make it a long one."

We finished our breakfast in relative silence. Mazy did not take her head off my lap. I absently stroked her ears with my right hand.

"Before you take a swim or anything else I want to get you unloaded. I need to get into work at some point and give Cadmus a break." The clock was nearing 10:30, Dad was an early riser. I would guess he had awoken close to six hours ago. On a regular day, he would have worked for at least three hours already. It was mid-afternoon to him, and time to stop being lazy.

"Pops, you can head into work. I can manage my stuff. I mean I loaded it without any help. Also, you don't need to be doing all that lifting and up and down the steps." When the words left my mouth, I wished I could bite my tongue. Mazy even let out a growl and walked away from me.

"Girl, I may have aged two more years while you were away, but I'm not decrepit. Clean your plate and meet me at the van in five minutes," he told me, putting the plate of pancakes away.

"Yes sir," I scooted off the stool, rinsed my plate, left for my room and my shoes. There was nothing quite like coming home and realizing you were still a child and not an adult like you previously thought. A worse off child than when I lived here before. If it were still 2012 I would have a bottle of booze hidden in my closet. Now I had to go at it alone and dry.

I met Dad behind the cargo van a few minutes later. The back doors were open, Dad had his hands on his hips, looking at the contents. I sidled up to him, put my hands on my hips, mocking him, and looked angrily into the van. The crickets chirped in the field next to us.

Dad shook his head, "Where are all your belongings?"

"Right there."

"I left you at school with a bed, couch, piano, boxes of

household things. Where did it all go, Dandelion?"

"Well, you know I sold the piano. They didn't have a moving truck for me, I didn't know how to fit the bed or couch in. It wasn't as if anyone was helping me move. Everything else is in the boxes."

"Why didn't you ask someone to help you move them?"

"Who would that have been? My Chinese neighbor, who didn't speak English?"

"How about a friend from Juilliard?"

"I'm not sure who that is," I replied, grinding the dirt drive under my toe, wishing this conversation was over.

"You fit all your books, clothes, and household items into..." He pointed to each box and counted them, "Six boxes?"

"Seven, there is a small one over there." I pointed out, "I suppose I did. Pretty good packing, huh?" I smiled at him. Dad frowned. "What?"

"Did you sell all the kitchen items?"

I hesitated.

"Of course, you did." He picked up the box closest to him.

"Pops, that's full of books. Let me take it," I offered.

"Dandelion, most of them are going to be books, you didn't bring anything else back. Grab a different box."

I took hold of the next closest box and heaved it out of the van. Dad was already in the house when I made it to the steps. I lugged the twenty-pound box up to the second floor. I dropped it with a thud.

"Careful," Dad complained.

I turned my back and rolled my eyes on the way down the steps.

"Why are none of the boxes marked?"

"Because I didn't think about it? They're all going to my room anyway. If I find things that belong somewhere else in the house, I'll put them away, I promise."

"Organization is key to getting a task done."

"And efficiency." I yanked up another box and trudged up the steps.

We finished unloading in silence. My thighs and calves felt tight from the steps. I dropped down on the couch. Dad was unfazed by the manual labor. It was what he did all day.

"Where are the keys?"

"I'll take the van back." A drive sounded needed at this point, stranded at home sounded too 2011.

"I asked where the keys are. I'm going to go drop it off before I go to the store."

"Pops…"

"Dandelion, don't argue with me. Give me the keys. You go for a swim."

I got up from the couch with a sigh, dug through my satchel that hung on the peg by the front door. I retrieved the key and handed it over to my dad. "Thanks."

"I'll see you tonight. Don't forget, it's Thursday."

"Right. Bye Pops." I listened to the door slap shut, behind me. It reminded me of a prison. There had been plenty of them in my life, all different kinds.

5

The pond was my favorite spot on Dad's property, nestled back in the woods about 700 yards from his back porch. The body of water itself was rather large, close to 15 acres. The walk was peaceful through the oaks, hickory, and maple trees. The floor of the forest covered with fallen leaves, moss, and soft rich soil. Today Mazy was excited and running a few feet ahead of me scaring off all the wildlife. There were no critters to see, but I could hear them, scurrying in the trees and flying past my ears.

The woods ended a few yards from the water's edge, and the ground slowly turned from rich soil and dried leaves to a muddy, rocky outer ring. The far side of the water met up with a meadow. I slipped out of my denim canvas shoes and gray linen shorts, leaving them on a large rock baking in the sun. I tugged the aqua colored sleeves down on my swimsuit before I threw my arms over my head and stretched them out. My black goggles hung around my neck. I pulled them up onto my eyes, securing them in place.

The algae covered stones and rocks felt slick and soft under my toes. The water rippled with my movement distorting the reflections of the blue sky and white clouds into an abstract painting. My thighs submerged in the water, my hands out in front of me, I dove down into the deep middle of the water. The cold hit my skin and woke my mind up like a bucket of ice water thrown over my shoulders.

The water was clear, and the fish scurried out of my way while I dove down and up again. I broke into a stroke, taking each movement moderately. My muscles warmed back up to the excursion I had not participated in for two years.

After Daisy Rivers let me almost drown in the creek (the very creek that fed into this pond) and abandoned us two days later, Dad decided I should learn to swim. He took me down to the pond in my pink Minnie Mouse shorts and a white tank top. We played in the mud with rocks and sticks for a long while, all the time edging closer and closer to the water. It did not take me long to venture farther and farther into the water until it was up to my chest. Dad stood back from me, watching closely to see what I would do, sure to not make any sudden movements and startle me.

Dad took me to the pond every day for a week and just let me play and become accustomed to the water, rocks, fish, and mud. Then one day he took me in his arms and swam to the middle of the pond. It was a good ten to twelve feet deep there. I clung to his neck watching the fish skitter and scurry around his feet treading water. For the next week, that was what we did when we went to the pond.

One day, I let go of him. My arms flopped about, and my legs kicked wildly in the water. He chuckled and placed his large sun-bronzed palm under my stomach to keep me afloat. I figured out how to keep from going under on my own shortly after. Dad was not a man of many words; I do not remember him giving any instruction or encouragement during any of these outings. We simply were. Dad had a way of sitting back, leading, but not pushing me, through the things that I feared most.

Over the years, I fell in love with the water. The rhythm of swimming had a calming effect on my overly active mind. It gave me the freedom to focus on the movement of my arms and legs working together to propel myself towards a goal. The rest of my world would fall away. It was only the water and me. We did not work against each other but worked together to go farther.

The bottom rocks were getting closer where the pond rose to meet the shore on the far side. I popped my head above the water and slowed my stroke, falling into a paddle until my feet scraped the top of the rocks, and I found my footing. It was hard to believe I had used to swim back and forth for an hour in this pond. My stamina had grown weak. Mazy was sitting with her head cocked to the side watching me. The meadow sprawled behind her, full of bees buzzing and birds circling. This time of year, it was a vibrant green, dotted with tall white Queen Anne's Lace blowing in the breeze, and yellow Black-Eyed Susan that were my personal favorite.

"I made it out alive," I told her with a smile. The sun was high in the sky and had warmed the large boulders scattered around the edges. I yanked the goggles off my face and set them down before I peeled the wetsuit away from my small frame and rang out the water, laying it on the rocks to dry. I found a patch of soft grass surrounded by the tall flowers and sprawled out. Mazy snuggled next to my cold sandy skin, sending immediate heat to my torso. I watched the fluffy white clouds pass slowly along the bright blue afternoon sky. A sigh passed my lips, my eyelids closed. The slow pace of the country felt right in my soul at this moment.

When my eyes fluttered open, the sun was dipping down close to the tops of the trees. Mazy's head was resting on my stomach, I scratched her ear to wake her up, she licked my chin.

"We better head back before Pops starts to wonder where we are. You know he'll worry," I told her, walking over to my swimsuit, which had completely dried in the sun. I yanked my legs through it and pulled it over my small chest, slipping my arms through the sleeves. I wrapped the goggles around my wrist. Mazy followed close on my heels. We made the trek back around the shore to where I left my shorts and shoes. The sweet smell of the maple trees wafted on the breeze coming out of the woods. The sound of my feet treading on the squishy mud mixed with Mazy's soft padded feet stomping next to me filled my ears. I picked up a long thin branch and swished it back and forth in the tall grass to my left. It sent the crickets jumping and scurrying. Mazy tried to catch them in her mouth.

My linen shorts, hot to the touch, they smelled like pine and sunshine. I slipped them over my suit. I tucked my cold, muddy feet into my shoes. We plunged into the woods and bee-lined to the house. The shadows were growing with the long rays of the late afternoon sun filtering down through the trees.

When we came into view of the back of the house September bounded down the back steps hollering at us.

"Dee! Dee! Come quick! Yer gonna to be so excited!" she screamed running down the deck steps towards us, her long hair blowing behind her. She grabbed my hand and pulled me along with her. Mazy barked excitedly and ran with us. I noticed Arty's maroon vintage truck parked out front next to Cadmus's black one. We ran up the back steps and in through the back door of the kitchen. I could hear the men talking in the front of the house. She continued to drag me around. The old dark walnut upright piano sitting in the empty spot in the foyer caught my eye.

"What's this?" I asked Arty, who came over and embraced me.

"Just a little welcome home gift from us boys," he told me.

"We picked it up this morning," Sep added with a large grin, her eyes turning into forest green moons.

"So, this was the early morning errand?" my voice dropped.

"Guilty as charged," Cadmus responded.

"But... you didn't know the piano was gone until I came home," I replied. My eyes narrowed, I gazed from the piano to the three men standing around me.

"Let's just say I know you well, and we also know how much you struggled while you were away," Dad answered.

"Are you telling me you all assumed I had sold the damn thing before I came home and decided to replace it before I got here?" Sep squeezed my hand.

"Technically, I am the one who found the piano, and I told Mel about it. It just so happened to work out you had sold Mel's while you were gone," Arty said.

"And you assumed I had?" I asked Dad.

"Yes," he confessed, while Cadmus and Arty told me 'No'.

"Play something," Sep begged from my side.

"I'm not much in the mood, Sep." I pried my hand free of hers. "Thank you for the beautiful gift, Cadmus, and Arty," I forced a smile on my face and walked back to the kitchen. I grabbed a glass from the cupboard and turned the tap on. I guzzled the whole tumbler and slammed the cup down on the counter. Wishing it was something more, something harder than water. I exhaled heavily while looking out the window, holding onto the edge of the counter to calm my nerves. "There's no place like home." Where they all know what a screw up you are and how you'll never change.

"Dee," Arty said from behind me, "I want you to know that I didn't purchase the piano with the thought that you'd sold your dad's."

"I know, Arty. I would never blame you for being the bad guy."

Arthur Jones was like a dad to me. For over thirty years, he and Pops had stayed friends. Most of my childhood memories had Arty in the background of them. After Daisy left, Arty stepped up to help my dad raise me. Makayla Fowler once asked me what it was like to have two dads; the implication not lost on my young thirteen-year-old mind. I replied that it was fantastic because while one was getting me in trouble the other was grilling steak outside. It did not seem like a likely rumor to be passing in our town, but if it was, I wanted everyone to know that I did not care, and my head held high.

"Are you going to be alright?" he asked. His furrowed brow showed the wrinkles more prominently from what I remembered. His face, older, weathered, and full of stubble.

"Honestly, I don't know. Coming home to the same old same old. It isn't going to be easy."

"The whole gang will be here over the summer. How are you going to handle that?"

My heart beat a few extra times at the mention of my old friends. Something like a Snapdragon Popper popped in my chest. It made me jump back slightly. Arty did not seem to notice.

"Don't block us out, Dee." His eyes reminded me of the smooth gray-blue stones you would find along water banks, cold, hard, yet smooth and silky to the touch.

"I'm not planning on blocking anyone out, okay? I just got home for Pete's-sake."

September began playing Heart and Soul on the piano. We stood silent, looking at one another while the notes filled the air.

"You need a plan,"

"I have a plan." I lied.

"You never have a plan."

He was right, but I didn't want to think about that now. I wanted to postpone the inevitable as long as possible.

"Man, her note inflection sounds so much better! Doesn't it? Don't you agree?" I cut him off and walked back around to the foyer. "Sep, that sounds lovely," I told her, leaving Arty in the kitchen.

She turned around and smiled, "Thanks! Cadmus had me practice the entire time you were gone."

I glanced at Cadmus sitting across the room, his legs crossed and his hand resting in front of his face. He dropped his palm and smiled at me, "I wasn't going to let what you had started go to waste. I'm sure she would much rather learn from you than the computer, though."

I sat next to her and began playing the upbeat accompaniment. She started to play along. The three men settled into the family room and chatted in hushed voices as we continued. Sep showed me her scales and arpeggios she learned and one short song she memorized. I taught her another two-line song from memory and worked on her finger placement. Time passed slowly. It would take time for that to feel normal. I began to smell roasted carrots, potatoes, and beef cooking from the kitchen.

"You girls getting hungry? There's a roast coming out of the oven," Dad told us, he stood up from his chair and walked towards the kitchen.

"I'm famished," I replied, catching a pleased glance from Cadmus. "What?"

"Nothing," he replied amused.

"Don't 'nothing' me," I teased.

"What are you carrying on about?" Dad asked, setting a large roasting pan full of vegetables and meat on the table.

"Nothing, Cadmus is just giving me trouble about my eating habits."

"Nothing to worry about there. We'll have you good and fat again in a month." Dad replied.

Cadmus laughed.

"What is it with you guys wanting me to be fat?"

"Isn't that how men like their girls, soft?" Arty added, humorously.

"September Marie, be happy with the body you have no matter what it looks like. Please, do not listen to these fools."

"I never do listen to them," she answered me, grabbing a potato out of the pan and shoving it in her mouth.

"September," Cadmus chided her while everyone gathered around the table. She stopped chewing and slowly swallowed the lump in her cheeks.

I watched my dad clear his throat and lower his head. Cadmus, Arty, and Sep followed suit. I stood watching them while Dad spoke,

"Have no fear for what tomorrow may bring. The same

loving God who cares for you today will take care of you tomorrow and every day. God will either shield you from the suffering or give you unfailing strength to bear it. Be at peace, then, and put aside all anxious thoughts and imaginations. Amen."

"Amen," the rest said in unison.

"Since when do we pray?" I asked.

"It's Saint Francis," Arty replied.

I glanced around the table, met with the same surprised look from everyone. "Are we doing the program because I'm home?"

"A little God around here brought to us by good ol' Saint Fran ain't going to hurt any of us. Now stop making drama and eat your damn dinner," Dad told me.

"Pass the rolls," I asked Cadmus, between gritted teeth. He handed me the bowl from across the table, our fingers touched. I tapped his nail with the edge of mine. He looked up at me. I shot him a piercing, betrayed look.

His shoulders rolled back, he inhaled. "Dani,"

I shook my head at him. "No excuses."

"There are none to give."

Arty looked from me to Cadmus and back again, piecing together the glances. "Don't go thinking Cadmus gave away some secret of yours."

I passed the rolls to September, averting my eyes from them all.

"Dandelion, I know I'm an old man, and it is impossible for you to think of me as younger than ancient," Dad began, "But there was a time that I was a teenager. And in those days, I never said 'no' to a good drink."

My chin popped up, looking over at him.

"Cadmus never spills your secrets. It's just that I'm not a stupid old man. I know you fell off the wagon while you were gone. It's time to get back in it."

I kept silent.

"It's Thursday night by the way…"

"Oh, for the love of God. I'm not going to a meeting!" I shoved a carrot into my mouth.

Arty laughed, rattling the table, "Family dinners just got entertaining again. Dee, I missed your stupid face."

I didn't want to, but I started to laugh.

"Were you a teenager in the 40's?" September asked, her eyes wide with wonder.

Arty spewed his lemonade back into his cup. Cadmus looked like he would rather be dead. I almost choked on the roll I was still trying to chew.

"Good lord, Cadmus, work on September's math skills

this week," Dad replied.

"What? Didn't I figure it out right?" she asked, she sounded hurt. I rubbed her back while I choked down the roll.

"September, how old do you think Mel is?" Cadmus asked.

Her cheeks turned a rosy pink, "Well, how old are yah?"

Dad folded his hands in front of his face, looking at Sep with patience in his blue eyes. "Do you not remember how old I turned back in April? That was just a little over a month ago, girl. I turned sixty-three. I wasn't even alive in the forties."

"Oh." The blush in her cheeks darkened.

"Now, you're smart as a whip. When would I've been a teenager?"

September closed her eyes and scrunched up her face, "Yah would've turned thirteen in... in... 1966!" she beamed at Cadmus.

"Well done," he nodded at her. "Now, pass me the rolls, and tell me how delicious my dinner is, to make up for your blunder."

She handed him the bowl of bread while stuffing a carrot in her mouth, "It's delicious, Mel! Thank you!"

"Did you make a lot of friends in New York? Any of

them going to come down for a visit?" Arty asked.

I hesitated, turning my fork over and over in my fingers, watching the potato twirl around. "Not so much."

I did not need to look up to know the look the three men were passing between them. I had never wanted for friends when I was a child. In my teenage years, people followed me wherever I went. At least they had, up until my junior year.

"I'm sure there are some who would want to come visit," he prodded.

I popped the potato in my mouth. "I don't think so, Arty. There weren't many friends. There were people around, but we all know that doesn't mean friends. They were just people. Certainly, no one who would want to come to this place."

"Anyone you are going to go back and visit?" he tried.

My faltering was answer enough for him.

"Does this person have a name?"

"Yes. But... I don't think I'll go visit." The idea of going back to New York to see him had not even crossed my mind. What an odd thought, to get off a plane and see him again. Would he walk towards me or turn and run?

"Because why?"

"Because we didn't part that great. I don't know that he

would want to see me. I'm not sure." The same look passed between the three men again. I rolled my eyes. "It isn't what you think. I can just be friends with people of the opposite sex. I'm just friends with Cadmus," I offered.

Dad cleared his throat.

Cadmus looked back at his meat.

"Well yeah, but he's thirty-five years old," Arty interjected.

"Thirty-four," Cadmus corrected him.

"Excuse me," Arty put his hands up, defensively.

I looked around the table at them. Dad giving Cadmus a hard time on his correction of Arty. September giggled over Arty turning her scraps of meat and potatoes into funny faces on her plate. Mazy was lying on my feet, snoring contentedly. I could hear the voice of my old demon, reminding me I would tire of this soon. The quiet, the simplicity, it could never hold my captivation. Give it a few months and I would be climbing the walls. I tried my best to stuff the voice down. Telling myself it could be different now, I had changed, I had grown, hadn't I? things did not always have to go back to how they had been. One could form their own new destiny.

6

The town of Greenside Missouri consisted of 1,523 people, 6 churches, and 4 stores: two for groceries and basic needs, one for farm equipment, and one hardware store, that my dad owned. The main drag had a row of small shops, frozen yogurt, sandwiches, canoe, and boat rental to name a few. There was one funeral home that Arty ran, and zero things to do.

Main Street was narrow and lined with tall, old brick buildings from the early 1900's. A face-lift had happened a few years back. They painted each building a bright new color, slapped a few black awnings on, and the sidewalks extended into wide brick patios. I had to admit, they had done a beautiful job. The bright yellow, green, and blue buildings stood out with the rolling mountains in the background. Well, they weren't mountains like the Grand Tetons or anything, in fact, most people would probably call them hills, but if you look up the Ozarks it calls them mountains, and as far as I'm concerned, 'mountain' sounds better than 'hill.' The new black light posts added a little class to the otherwise country street. I made note of the newly renovated hotel on the corner with its curved oriel windows jutting out over the sidewalks. If I looked up small towns in the US to visit and saw a picture of this street with that hotel, I would book a trip. There was a lake on the other side of the mountains, where Dad lived. It offered hours of entertainment. On the other side of the lake was another town. That town drew most of the lake traffic in. The Mayor of Greenside's plan to draw the tourist had worked, I noted unfamiliar faces milling around the stores. However, once off the main drag, the streets opened up to the wide lanes, with angled parking in front of the stores. The buildings slowly began to look shabbier the farther away you went. This was the Greenside I grew up with, small, grubby, unassuming.

I parked my vintage, steel blue and eggshell-colored scooter in front of the smaller general store. My own little rebellion against this town. It would always be a rite of passage I refused to walk through, to get your own truck. Small towns were like that, new seasons had rites to go through. Once you were around 7 years of age you learned to shoot and hunt. It tended to be more of a boy thing, but Arty made sure I did it. I hated it as much as Dad. We just weren't predators by nature. I took off my white and brown helmet and attached it to the handles. I slipped the key into the pocket on my denim button-down dress and adjusted my small leather backpack. My hair hung in a loose braid down my back. I peered up at the large unpleasant building in front of me. It was comparable to a house with the large front porch and garret windows in a line on the roof. The Fowler family had lived above the store for generations. The porch, filled with wooden pallets stocked with vegetables and fruits, from the local farms. There were racks of garden equipment on the ends full of shovels, rakes, and hoses. I scrunched up my mouth before taking my first step towards the door.

A memory of being six or seven and running up and down the wooden planks of this porch with my best friends swam through my mind. I could feel the warm summer sun on my face while the breeze whipped my hair around my neck, it felt like yesterday. We would sit on the stoop and drink ice-cold lemonade while we shared our secrets and told stories. "It's gonna be a sister." My friend had told us long ago. Wonder and mystery ran through my veins with the words, siblings, an experience I continually felt jealousy over. "I think I like him." She had told me. I had forced a smile on my face as apprehension sprang into my stomach. "Where'd that bruise come from?" I had asked, my hand reaching for his cheek. "Never you mind, Dee," he replied with a shove to my hand. I wondered if Makayla Fowler would be working today or not. My back stiffened with the thought. I tried to roll my shoulders to relax, but it did not help.

The bell above the door chimed when I entered the store. I quickly grabbed a basket from the holder. A quick glance to the right confirmed my suspicion that Makayla was here. She was checking out Ol' Bill. I could see his hands tremble from here. He painfully counted out his change, one small coin at a time. I pretended to overlook her presence. She glowered at me from behind the register.

The interior was similar to a convenience mart instead of a grocery store. The shelves were lower, although I still had to stand on my tiptoes to see over the top, the perimeter lined with closed refrigerator cases. The far-right corner of the store had a selection of miscellaneous household goods and a self-serve soda fountain.

My eye caught the back of a medium-sized man getting a drink. Sheriff Ritter stood next to him chatting. His laughter filled the air. When the Sheriff laughed it shook the building. Craig Fisher was stocking up on frozen pizzas by the look of his basket. Mrs. Cooper and CeCe were walking down the same aisle I was going up.

CeCe waved and said, "Hey Dee," when they scooted past me. Mrs. Cooper was careful not to make eye contact.

"Hey, CeCe," I replied, ducking my head down, pretending to be attentive to my list:

Strawberry jelly

Granola bars

White bread

Mac and cheese

Milk

Eggs

Frozen waffles

The smell of cigarettes unexpectedly filled my nose. I wheeled around on my heels, knocking the basket into his stomach.

"Oy," he rubbed his abdomen, "I thought that was you." He reached up, brushing my fly-away-hairs away from my face, his fingers glided down my cheek. I shuddered at the touch but felt paralyzed to move away. "When did you get back from the city?" he flashed his perfect white smile at me.

"You scared the shit out of me, Aaron," I complained while I looked him over. He looked better than he had looked in a long time. The dark colored t-shirt made his ivory skin appear cool and smooth. The weight he had gained in senior year had turned to muscle over the last two. Perhaps he had joined the wrestling team again. Or worse, football. God, that sure would make his daddy proud. "About a week ago," I replied. "Why are you here?"

"Because I wanted a soda," he responded snarkily, shaking his cup at me.

"I think you know what I mean."

"Summer break, everyone should be flooding into town within the next few weeks. Shit Dee, I knew you could be dumb, but you do know what season it is, don't you?

I ignored the rib, "You always come back for break?"

"Why not? Some of us know our place in this world."

I ground my teeth together, scowling at him. Aaron's famous parting words to me revolved around how I would end up back here, just like the rest of them. I could never shake the dirt of this place off me.

"Should be fun now that you're here. That brings the whole gang back together."

"I'm not part of the gang, Aaron. Please, tell me you don't get home on breaks and start up again. You look good, really good. Don't start."

"Who says I haven't?"

"You look too good. No way you're on something." My eyes ran over him again, making sure I had not missed telling signs the first time.

"I just wanted to hear you say that again," he laughed at me. "I do look good, don't I?" he raked his fingers through his short dark hair. "You look pretty good yourself. Although you lost some of your curves, Mel better start feeding you again and getting you swimming." His small, russet brown eyes, rolled over my body.

"Shut up, Aaron." I pushed past him. He followed on my heels. Things in this town never changed.

"Don't be a stick in the mud, Dee."

"I'm not a stick in the mud. I just have self-respect," I replied, grabbing the jelly off the shelf.

"That is the biggest lie you've ever told me. Let's go wash that mouth out with some soap." He tried to grab my hand, I quickly turned and grabbed a box of granola bars.

"So, what? You go off to Juilliard and come back too good for the rest of us? You know I'm only giving you trouble," he continued.

I stopped walking and turned around to face him, his downward tilted face jolted up to my eyes with a coy smile. He pulled on my hip, drawing me closer to him. I hated myself for letting him. The smell of cigarettes grew in intensity. "You wanna go have some free fun?" his warm breath tickled my neck.

I pushed his hand away, "No. Things have changed." My senses were blaring a different story to me. It would be easy to go with him. Ease the tension of being home. I couldn't do it, I couldn't do it to September. I had to stay strong for her.

I pushed the craving down inside me as far as it would go.

"Why do I find that impossible to believe?" he pushed my body away, walking down the aisle to the front door, flashing a smile at Makayla. I noticed her cheeks flush light pink. Things never changed. Aaron wanted me. Makayla wanted Aaron. I wanted... I wasn't sure what I wanted. I glanced around. None of the patrons seemed to have noticed our interaction. A more likely story would be they chose to look the other way. They had grown accustomed to, what should I call it? Shenanigans. Ignoring us would be easier.

The soda fountain was calling my name. I placed the last item in my basket and yanked a large 32-ounce cup out of the slot and filled it with crushed ice, added in some cherry flavor, and hit the cola button. I slurped down a few ounces, walking over to the register, stiffening my spine.

Mrs. Cooper was standing in front of the counter checking out. She turned her body to block me from her view. CeCe hid, wrapped in her mother's skirt, poking her head around her legs to see me. I made a funny face to make her laugh. She waved again. I slurped down more of my cola before they left.

"Find what you wanted?" Makayla asked, curtly.

Before I can answer, Sheriff Ritter comes from behind me, dropping exact change for his soda on the counter. "Dee Sanders, it has been a piece since I saw you last."

"Sheriff," I nod at him, one of the only men in town I had any respect for.

"I saw you talking to Abbot, best if you two keep some distance. Wouldn't yah agree? Let's not repeat old tales."

"Yes, sir. Trying my best, sir."

"Thata girl." He walked out, leaving me alone with M.

"Doesn't seem like you guys have changed the store since I left."

"No need to, it makes it easier when the Little Weeds show back up," M smirked as she scanned each of my items as slowly as possible.

"Well, at least I tried something new, it just wasn't for me."

She laughed, "You've been trying something new since we were twelve. None of them seem to... what... fit you just right? When you think you're going to figure that out? Your place is working in a hardware store and fucking in a storage unit."

I had almost forgotten how vile it had made her. To go high or to go low. "I screwed him in every locker and he fit just fine. Problem was, I just didn't like him." Low it was.

"Your total is thirteen seventy-two." She flipped her long copper hair over her shoulder.

I dug the money out of my wallet and slung my bag

onto my back. I grabbed the plastic bags, slurping down more soda, furiously. I shoved my hand into my pocket to grab my key and realized it was missing. A few curse words slipped out as the door snapped closed behind me, making me jump. I saw Aaron sitting on my scooter drinking his soda, with my key dangling from his finger. "Why are you such a bastard?" I asked him.

"I'm not. My mom had married my dad before I was born."

"We aren't in middle school anymore, Aaron. Stop being a child."

"It's just so much fun. Your entire life gives me so much material."

"Give me the key," I replied, trying to grab it. My insides were churning, I felt hot.

He quickly stood and held it above my head. I dropped the bags at my feet and jumped up to grab it. It made me feel like a little kid. I yanked the key down with his finger still laced through it.

"One kiss and I give you the key,"

"Go to Hell."

"Already planning on it. I think we have seats next to each other." His fingers looped around my hand. With one swift tug, he pulled my body next to his, brushing his forehead against mine.

My breathing accelerated and sweat filled my palms. "Please give me the key, Aaron."

His lips were an inch from mine. "You'll be asking for it again before the summer is out." He whispered, dropping the key off his finger into my palm and walked away.

I stood frozen to the pavement listening to him leave. It did nothing to calm my nerves. The street was quiet and empty now. My stomach turned once too many times, I lost the soda I had chugged. I stopped heaving, kneeling next to my scooter, I buried my face in my arms. You are safe. You are fine. You need to get up. My mind told itself over and over. My body refused to listen. My strength gave, I fell back onto my butt, like a heap in the street. My stomach flopped, I leaned over, but nothing came this time, just pain in my abdomen. You are safe. You are fine. You are safe. You are fine. The sound of his shuffling feet hit my senses before his shaky arms pulled me up.

"There, there, girl. All's well. No need to stay in a lump. Yah go to your daddy's store and drink some water." His gravelly voice told me.

I stood eye level with Ol' Bill. His coke-bottle glasses gave him the appearance of a bug. I muttered something incoherent.

"Not my first episode to see. Yah'll live, we all live." He patted my shoulder and started back down the street. I stood gaping at him until he was out of sight. I hadn't had an episode as bad as that since winter. Something about Bill finding me felt comforting, or maybe it was convenience, who would he tell after all? I realized the only thing to do, was exactly what he told me to, go to Dad's store.

A few minutes later, the small white building came into view. The front of the store had a large window with hand-painted lettering that read, "Sanders' Hardware". The small concrete patio had a planter made out of an old whiskey barrel sitting next to the red wooden door. I could see September sitting on the counter cross-legged as I came inside. Her overalls only snapped on one side. Her brown boots covered in dirt, and her button-down green shirt wrinkled where she kept pushing the sleeves up over her elbows. A decent-sized book was sitting on her lap that captivated all her attention. I noticed Cadmus stocking nails close to the door.

"Hey Dani," he leaned over and hugged me.

I grabbed ahold of him as if there were no tomorrow.

"What happened?" he asked as I began to release him.

"A whole lot of nothing," I lied, giving a quick glance in Sep's direction. He nodded, understanding. I walked over to her, pulling myself up onto the counter. "Whatcha readin'?" I asked her, pressing into her shoulder. She could not peel her eyes away from her book.

"It's about a girl who got shot cause she went to school," she sort of mumbled, pushing her hair behind her ear,

"Yah ever read about her?"

"Malala Yousafzai? I did. What do you think?" I could never be as brave as her.

"How can people be so cruel?" she looked up at me with tears in her eyes.

I put my arm around her, grounding both of us, "You know everyone has a million voices talking to them every day. The voices come from all around us, like our school, our friends, our enemies. They are our inner workings telling us who we are, how we should act, how we should process information. Sometimes people have more evil voices in their heads than good. It makes them do terrible things. But you always have the power to change those voices and change your life." I smiled at her, hoping my words could be true, even for me.

"Why would voices tell yah to hate someone cause they're a girl?"

"Men have always been afraid of strong women."

"Why?"

"Because we don't need them," I caught the look of satisfaction on Cadmus's face.

"I hope the people who shot her learn to listen to different voices."

"We must all face the choice between what is right and

what is easy." I told her, "As Dumbledore taught us." I kissed her forehead and jumped down off the counter.

"Come with me out back?" Cadmus asked. He walked past me and through the back door.

Out behind the store were three rows of storage lockers and a few more rows of junk. That was just how it was in the country. People did not get rid of anything and for one reason or another, some of it found its way here. When I was little, I loved to come and sit in the old rusted-out pickup truck that sat close to the building and watch people haul in their junk. You just never knew what sort of things they would bring or what type of people would bring it.

Cadmus leaned against the old truck, I stood with my arms crossed in front of me. "What happened?" he asked.

"I had to go to the grocery store. I figured M would be there."

"But who else was there?" he pried.

"Aaron Abbot."

Cadmus waited for me to elaborate.

"He was an ass. He doesn't know how not to be."

"What did he do to you?"

"He made some bad innuendos, but other than that, he didn't do much." I wasn't even sure if it was truth or lie.

"We need to have a plan, or it is going to be a really long summer. You know that." I watched the late morning light filter through the broken windshield on the truck. It cast patterns onto Cadmus's blue shirt and up his arms. A small piece of me wanted to go pull his arms apart and hide against his chest.

"Everyone wants a plan, a spreadsheet, new and tidy. That isn't life. God knows it isn't Greenside. I ran into old friends and I tried my best to deal with them. That's all I can do with them. He'll be gone before we know it." I always fought when I felt vulnerable.

"You ran into your dealer. Let's call it how it is."

"Okay, fine. I saw my old dealer today, and if you want to pat me down to make sure I didn't buy, feel free." I raised my arms up over my head and frowned at him. Why couldn't I just tell him the truth? Why did everything need to start at zero again?

"I'm not patting you down because I trust you. Do you realize that I trust you, I have faith in you?" he placed his large dark palms on my shoulders, "I ask you because I care. I want you to have a plan so that we succeed and don't fail. I have trust in you to succeed."

"Well, we can all see how my track record is with that."

"You need to let us back in, Dani. You don't need to be alone in there." He tapped my forehead with his finger.

"I wish I was alone in there." I pulled away from him. "There are so many people yelling at me in my mind. I just want them all out."

"If you don't want me to be a voice in your head anymore I don't need to be."

"That isn't exactly what I meant. It is all the baggage from years past that is hollering at me. Your voice might be the only one of sanity in there. Lord knows mine isn't."

"Then I need you, to be honest, and blunt with me. Call things what they are. I can't help you if I have to guess at what we are talking about."

"Yeah, I sort of had to learn some social niceties in New York. I was hoping to make friends you know. I tried to drop words like, 'addict', and 'going to my meeting'. That last one really scares people away." I paused. "By the way... Aaron is still clean. That makes my life easier."

Cadmus shifted his weight, "He told you that?"

"Mostly, I mean, you can tell by looking at him. Maybe this summer won't be that rough." I turned away from him, going into the store. I knew there were no easy things about Aaron Abbot, though.

"We can say that, but let's plan for the crap to hit the fan," he answered.

I walked down the small hallway lined with photographs back into the main part of the store. September's laughter flooded my ears. She and my dad were standing behind the counter eating cheeseburgers and fries.

"Where the hell have you been?"

"I woke up and went to the store. I needed my food. Your pantry was lacking."

"First of all, I was asking Cadmus. Second, my pantry is fully stocked. Frozen waffles and strawberry jelly are not real food."

"Strawberry jelly is its own food group, old man. Where's my burger?" I stole a fry from September's Styrofoam container.

"I wasn't sure you were going to be around. Cadmus, yours is by the microwave." Mel pointed the box out.

"Dani, you want half of my burger?"

"No, I'm alright. I think I'm going to head home with my groceries. I want to take Mazy on a walk."

"Think about what we talked about, huh?" Cadmus nodded at me.

"Sure thing..." I slipped my helmet back on, going out of town and back up the mountain. Back up to the safety of the woods filled with daylight and away from town.

7

The room was white, floor to ceiling. It was the only space with a touch of feminism in the house. The ceiling was 9 feet high and came together in a peak. There was a large square window at the top without a curtain, letting the light continually flood the room. The two windows closer to the floor hung with long, white muslin curtains. Flower boxes attached to the windowsills with purple and yellow pansies. A small desk tucked in the corner, a nightstand that stood by my double bed on its wrought iron frame. The walls were planks of unfinished wood giving the room a rustic feel.

I was lying in the middle of my bed with my white down comforter bunched around me. Mazy was sleeping next to me. Her black and brown coat added a beautiful contrast to the room. I absently petted her with my right hand while my left held a book up over my head. I had picked up a biography on Amelia Earhart from the library a few days ago, inspired by September's reading choice. I could not wait to pass the book on to her. Amelia's childhood adventures reminded me of September's own spirit and intensity.

I heard my dad's slow heavy tread coming up th e stairs before he knocked on my door. I lowered my book, "Come in."

He pushed the door open through a heap of clothes on the ground, "Good lord, girl. You've been here for less than two weeks and your room is a pigsty," Dad criticized. He stepped over a pile of towels lying on the floor.

"Is it considered a pigsty if I know where everything is?"

"I'm sure the pigs know where all the shit is. You still call it a pigsty. What are you reading now?" he kicked my boots out of the way and sat on the end of the bed. Mazy wagged her tail while Dad gave her bottom a pat.

"Biography of Amelia Earhart. I'm gonna loan it to Sep when I'm finished."

"Did you talk to Cadmus about taking her lessons back up?"

"Not yet."

"Haven't you rested enough? I think it's time you start doing something with your time. Like cleaning your room."

"Pops, my room is just how I want it." I pushed my body up unto my elbows, setting the book on the night-stand stacked high with books.

"You need to make yourself useful."

"Doing what?"

"A job." Dad stood and paced to the other end of the room, gazing out the window.

"Ah, a necessary evil." I bemoaned.

"Any thought to your potential prospects?"

"Nope. Does Mara Wagner still own the Sno Cone Cart? Maybe she would give me my old job back." I smirked. "Or I could mooch off you longer."

"No way in hell you're mooching your whole life. And Mara Wagner still refuses to sell me snow cones. I don't think she'll give you a job again."

The Sno Cone Cart operated out of an old bus. Mara had cut a service window out of the side, attached an awning to the roof, and painted the whole thing bright green and pink. She liked to keep it parked close to the lake, but it was a fully operational vehicle. One night, my best friend and I decided it would be a great story to take it for a joy ride. I lifted the keys from Mara when I took over my shift, waited until closing time, and took off in it. The miracle was how we drove it all around town without causing any damage. We were high off our asses.

Mara fired me the next morning when the sheriff found us thirty miles out of town, parked in a field, sleeping in the back.

"Well, I have given it a lot of thought." He turned around, arms folded across his chest.

"That's not surprising. What do you want me to do?"

"Work at the store."

"No." it flew from my mouth like a cannonball.

"Dandelion,"

"No, no way in hell." I sat up, ready for a fight.

"You have no plans, Cadmus and I made a plan."

The wheels in my head began to spin a mile a minute, "I can ask Jo for a job. How about Mary? I can go work for Arty. Just let me go to work there."

"What is so horrible about the store?" he had started to look offended. "I would think we beat out dead people."

"It's what they all expect from me." My hand cast out from my side.

Dad rubbed his forehead, sitting next to me on the bed. "Screw them all, Dandelion."

"Pops," my voice turned to pleading, "Please, please don't make me."

"Girl, I am tired. I don't want to work forever."

"I know. Just don't make me take over the store. Please."

Dad's head popped up, "Hell no. I'm not leaving you my store. My baby is going to Cadmus. I need you to take over his job. Good lord girl, do I look like a fool to you?"

"What? No." My mind faltered to catch up, "You just want me there part-time?"

"Yes." He sounded frustrated and tired.

"Oh," that was a different spin on it. "And if I say 'no' do I get kicked out?"

"Probably," he smirked at me while giving Mazy another pat.

There it was. My future outlined by a sixty-three-year-old man and his thirty-four-year-old counterpart. Dirt roads, small shops, and customer service had replaced the glory of Juilliard, performing at Carnegie Hall, touring the world with 88 keys.

I needed to change the subject before dad handed me a schedule for the rest of my life. "I saw Aaron the other day,"

Dad visibly flinched. "Why didn't you tell me about that?"

"You were too busy hollering at Cadmus for leaving the store unattended for five minutes. I don't know.

I forgot about it." I leaned against the headboard.

Mazy rolled onto her back for us to pet her stomach. We welcomed the distraction.

"He looked good. He looked really good." I added.

Dad looked up at me, a storm brewing in his eyes, "You need to stay away from him. You hear me."

"I'm not an idiot, Pops! I've got this." If one more person told me to keep my distance from Aaron Abbot I would flip a gasket.

"You better. Keep it together, Dandelion."

"Planning on it."

"Sure, you are. I've heard that one before." He stood and left.

I kicked my legs out from under me and let out a low moan, Mazy looked up with curiosity in her large brown eyes.

"Is it possible to dig yourself out of the same hole twice?"

She snorted.

"I think I'm gonna be sick."

She jumped off the bed and sat by the door watching me expectantly.

Dad's voice carried up the steps, "It doesn't look like

you ate today, come get some lunch! I'm making BLT's."

Mazy raced down the steps, I swore she understood English and knew the 'B' in BLT stood for bacon. I swung my legs off the bed and set off down the stairs. Arguing with everyone could wait. When I hit the landing on the steps, I heard the dog bark and went for the front door before I even heard the knock. My neighbor, Cricket, stood in front of me, looking as fresh as ever. "Dani!"

Two things I knew immediately, she would hug me, and she would have a better conversation with my dad than I ever would. A small part of me wanted to slam the door in her face, her showing me up didn't feel like something I wanted right now. The larger part of me welcomed some estrogen into the mix. I braced for the on coming hug as she stepped into the house, her smile large, her personality larger. As her arms wrapped around me, pulling my face towards her chest, I began counting to seven. I had learned a few years back that if I counted to seven during a hug by the time I finished it was safe to pull away. Too soon and people felt snubbed, longer and I thought I would suffocate. Cricket smelled good, her clothes felt soft, it still puzzled me that we were friends.

I pulled away, "Hey, we were just getting ready to eat lunch."

"Smells delicious." She replied, following me around to the kitchen.

"Look who showed up."

Dad looked up from his bacon, "Well, well, if it isn't my favorite insect. How are you, Cricket?"

"I'm good Mr. Sanders. I've missed you. Whacha cooking?" she peered over the counter at the griddle.

"BLTs. Dandelion, this is the kind of friend you need to hang out with this summer." He pointed the spatula at me.

"Thanks, Pops."

Cricket laughed, "What's that mean?"

"Oh, Pops and I were just discussing my options earlier. You know how he is."

"Controlling."

"Bossy."

"Big-hearted."

"The best cook this side of the Ozarks," we finished together, smiling at him. Cricket wasn't so bad. Mainly she annoyed me with her perfection, but it was something I could overlook when I needed a listening ear besides Cadmus.

"So, I noticed the new piano on the way in. Beautiful. Did you bring that back with you, Dani?" We sat at the table, grabbing sandwiches off the plater, I pulled a handful of grapes off the vine.

Dad laughed, "Dandelion brought a whole lot of nothing back."

"Not true."

"Books. You brought all of those back. Am I right?" she asked. I nodded. "Why didn't you bring the piano back?"

"Couldn't move it."

"Sold it." Dad corrected.

Cricket opened her mouth, then decided to keep it closed. She even knew when to keep her trap shut.

"Arty and Cadmus bought me that one."

"How is Cadmus?"

I tossed a grape into my mouth, "He's Cadmus."

"You two should play together again. It would give you something to do." Dad told us. Cricket could sing, better than anyone in town, better than anyone at our high school, good enough to get into some college in L.A. It was the whole reason we met. Our high school put on a musical once a year, the first year she was at our school she blew all the competition out of the water. It sure didn't win her any friends with the girls who had been the leads every year since they were 5. It turned all the heads of the boys, too. I had been playing the piano solos for every production since freshman year. We spent a lot of time together, getting ready for the play, and having no friends.

"You know I learned to play this last year at school."
Of course, she had.

"How's your mom?" I asked.

"She's good," Cricket stole a piece of bacon off a sand-wich. "She's glad I'm home. I thought about traveling this year, and then didn't."

"How come?"

"I heard a rumor you were going to be home," she shrugged. I wondered if it was a nicety. We barely spoke once we went away to school, her to one end of the country and me to the other. She used to text me, I tried to write back. I was never very good at communication though. Dad had asked her some question, something to do with California, I think. I didn't really listen to them as they chatted away. I caught snippets of the ocean, beauty, peo-ple. My mind was busy putting together what this summer was shaping up to look like. Working in Dad's store. Spend-ing time with Cricket. Teaching September piano. Staying away from certain people. Having zero fun. For all the rea-sons New York turned distasteful, there was one thing it had that this place never would, freedom. Liam. Why did he have to come into this? I wished I would have gotten his number. Then I reminded myself he had darted off the first chance he got. Runners. The sound of a chair moving across the floor pulled me back to the table.

"Well, I'm going to make some sweet tea, would you

girls like some?" Dad asked, standing.

"That sounds delicious," Cricket replied.

"Let's go sit on the deck," I needed some fresh air. Cricket cleared our plates off and followed me onto the deck. It was the length of the house and a good ten feet wide. There was a hammock on a stand, a tall wooden patio table, and stools. Arty had made five Adirondack chairs a few years ago. We sat on them and looked out into the dense wood teeming with life. The air was thick with the sounds of insects and birds. The trees were full and green.

"I missed this."

"I didn't think I would, but once I got back I realized how much I had," I confessed. "Stars. I knew how much I missed the stars."

"Yeah? There is something New York and Los Angeles have in common, too much white light."

"If you get up on a roof and wait until the wee hours of the night, sometimes you get lucky. It isn't anything like here though." Instinctively, I looked up at the bright blue sky. There were hardly any clouds.

"Did you spend a lot of time on roofs?" Cricket asked.

"A decent amount..."

"What all happened in New York?" I suddenly remembered the last message I had sent to Cricket.

I told her I wanted to come home. That New York had been a mistake. Something I had never told anyone else, not even Cadmus.

I scrunched up my mouth and wondered how to answer, "A lot. A hell of a lot." I knew why I told her I wanted to come home. I also knew I never wanted to talk about it.

"Meet anyone special?"

It felt like a million emotions flooded my senses. The feel of the cool, hard, ivory, piano keys under my fingertips. The smell of beer and chips at late night parties. Sitting in Central Park for hours reading. My eyes focused on a particular maple tree that was on the edge of the wood. The branches hung low, making the trunk look squat, even though the tree was over thirty feet tall. It was the same tree I spent most of the autumn in when I was fourteen. Two of the branches made a nice little crook. I would sit in them for hours and hide from the world. Some weeks I would spend entire days in those branches, skipping out on school, meals, anything, and everything. There was quite a lot to hide from that year.

"Dani?" Cricket pulled me out of my head and back to reality.

"Yeah, sorry. Special? Just one. Just one friend," my voice trailed off.

"Name, details?"

The name stuck to the roof of my mouth before exiting. "Ruben, Ruben Asaf."

"Okay..." Cricket was craning her neck trying to read my mind. "Is he your roof friend?"

"He was... For a couple months, we would wind up at the same parties. Once we crossed paths, we would grab some drinks, find the nearest exit to the roof, go and hang out for hours."

"He sounds nice." She was prodding. "Was he a student?"

"Dance." The wind the day we met was a force to reckon with, it nearly blew me off my feet as I walked. The wind, trying to stay on schedule, carrying my necessities, all of it had jumbled my brain. I stopped walking to gather my thoughts before entering the building. When I picked up my feet to move again, I tripped and started to fall. It seemed providential. Ruben walking by at the exact moment my arms flung in the air, and sheet music went flying on the wind. It seemed that his mind did not even need to tell his body what to do as his arm swung down and caught me around the waist. His eyes locked on mine. He smiled. Then he uttered a few words before righting me and left with his friends who were laughing.

"Are you going to have him come for a visit?"

"No. We didn't part so well."

"Oh…"

"I know, I know, why must I ruin every relationship? I didn't mean to. "

"That isn't what I was going to say. Maybe you should call him," she offered.

"Not him. He's not the kind you call after you hurt him. He's the kind that you give space to. Maybe one day he'll call me."

"How'd you hurt him?"

The birds seemed to grow in their squawking, drowning out our conversation. Dad placed sweet tea next to us and went back into the house. I chewed the tip of my finger.

"Dani, maybe you should call him. He sounds nice. It probably isn't as bad as you think."

I dropped my hand into my lap. "I don't really want to talk about it right now." Knowing it was bad, even for me.

8

The inside of the hardware store smelled like wood chips and oil. The walls lined with floor to ceiling drawers and cubbies. Each spot had held the same merchandise for over fifty years. My dad knew where every bolt, nail, screw, and bracket were stored in those three hundred compartments. The rich brown wooden floors were creaky. Old whiskey barrels held rakes, hoes, and shovels. Feedbags and hoses hung down from the ceiling.

Dad moved to Greenside from Kentucky when he was just thirty. He had done some traveling in his twenties and by thirty, he was ready to call it a rest and settle down. In Kentucky, he grew up on a horse ranch and did not know a day without a ride. After seeing most of the States, he decided someplace quiet and out of the way was what he really craved. It was never a conscious decision to be a bachelor for his entire life; it just happened to work out that way. He worked at the hardware store until the owner, Jonah, decided retirement was knocking. He bought the store outright and changed the name to Sanders. That was the only change he made.

Back then, Dad would have never thought that one day he would be without horses because his daughter had needed the attention. That his best friends would be a somewhat artistic bachelor\funeral director and a thirty-four-year-old kid from California. Or, that he would be helping to raise the town's deceased, semi-crazy, semi-homeless lady's daughter. If there was one thing Dad had learned in his thirty plus years in Greenside, it was to expect the unexpected. Like the day Daisy Rivers showed up on his front porch with a chubby-legged, round-faced girl, with blue eyes like the cornflowers that grew in his front yard. She called her Dandelion and claimed she was half his. Planning the future was for people with too much time on their hands because you never knew what tomorrow would bring.

The night before, we ate dinner with Cadmus and September, I, of course, agreed to take the job at the store. It was my understanding you never looked a gift horse in the mouth. Dad was right after all. I needed something to do with my time other than read, swim, take naps, walk through the woods all summer. Eventually, I would tire of it and drive myself crazy from being alone that much. I needed interaction like I needed air in my lungs. I let out my hundredth yawn while slipping the canvas, off-white apron on over my head and tied it around my hips.

"You better stop that, girl." Dad gave me a hard time as he dropped the money drawer in the register.

"When I agreed to take the job, I didn't know that meant coming in with you at the crack of dawn," I complained.

"Well, normally it won't. Cadmus shows up closer to nine and you can come in around then from now on. But this morning I'm going to show you where the inventory is kept."

"Can I please make coffee first?" I begged. My eyes flit to the 300 compartments covering the walls.

"Make it strong."

"I still remember how y'all like your coffee," I walked behind the counter and grabbed the carafe. "Black like your souls, right?"

"You know it."

After I added the ingredients to the machine, I stood impatiently in front of the coffee maker, watching the dark liquid slowly drip into the pot. The rich aroma filled the small building, mixing with the wood and paint smells.

"Aren't you hungry?" I asked while I poured a mug for Dad and myself.

"Not yet. Cadmus usually goes out and picks breakfast

up at the diner. Are you hungry?" Dad asked, surprised.

"A little," the mug felt like gold under my fingers, precious.

"Well, the diner opens at seven; if you want you can do the breakfast run in an hour. First things first. Nails. A good hardware store carries every size, and a good employee knows where to find each one." Dad walked over to the small cubbies closest to us and started opening each drawer, naming each nail, and showing me the difference in size. It was going to be a long morning.

After what felt like a college course on construction nails crammed into one hour, my stomach was growling. Dad not only showed me where each nail belonged in the cubbies, but he had taught me the name and use of each. There was a quiz at the end of it all. Even if I had never wanted to know the difference between a common nail, galvanized, and box nail, now I knew and would never be able to forget.

"Am I allowed to go grab us some grub now?" I asked.

"I guess. After you get back we can tackle screws."

"I can't wait. What do you want?"

"Whatever the special is. Here." Dad handed me the ring of keys from his pocket. I hung the apron up on the back hook and took off out the front door.

When I backed the truck out onto the road, I saw Craig

Fisher come out of his open garage with a broom. He meticulously started to clean the white cement, brushing leaves and grass away. I thought about how the definition of insanity was doing the same thing over and over again and expecting different results. I watched him get smaller and smaller in the rearview mirror while I went down the road towards the diner. I made a right onto Burch Street. Jo's Diner was at the end of the block. Already every truck in the town sat parked out front. Each truck had a layer of dirt covering it and I knew who belonged to each one. The morning crowd at Jo's consisted of the farmers and their boys filling up before a long morning of work. All of them dressed in jeans, work boots, button-down shirts rolled up over their elbows, dusty hats on the tables, and jokes flying out of their mouths. It was not the only restaurant in town, but it was the most popular. The breakfast menu was by far the best: fluffy waffles, hearty omelets, bacon with every-thing, and fresh-squeezed orange juice. My mouth began to water as I parked the truck and walked up the steps. Mr. Young and Mr. Sampson were walking in front of me and they stopped to hold the door for me, something that rarely, if ever, happened in the city. I thanked them and walked over to the counter, grabbed a menu to browse be-fore Archie could take my order. The hum of the chatter lulled for a few seconds. The men were making note of me standing at the counter. The hairs on the back of my neck rose as I felt them all look me over before going back to their breakfast.

"Hey, Dee, nice to see you back in town. Whatcha getting this mornin'? Doing the mornin' run for Cadmus?"

"Hi Archie," I said, looking up from the menu with a smile. Archie's mom, Jo owned the diner, and he had started working the counter since he was old enough to see over it. We went to high school together and hung out occasionally. Archie happened to be one of the boys I had never slept with in town. I figured that was the reason he still treated me with decency. When I had asked Archie where he wanted to go to college at the end of high school, he looked at me confused and asked why he would need to do that when he already had a business to take over. It was the typical small-town way – following in your parents' footsteps.

"I am. Pops has me working at the hardware store over the summer. Just for the summer. It isn't really a permanent thing." I rambled.

"Dee," Archie cut me off, nodding down the line of hungry men waiting to order.

"Right. Sorry. Pops said he wants the special, and I want pancakes. Can I get extra bacon and two large OJ's?"

"Yep, I'll have it ready to go in ten minutes." He clicked his pen closed, tucked it behind his ear, and shoved the ticket in the kitchen window.

"Thanks, Arch. Good to see you, too."

"I'll see yah around," he replied. He walked down the

line away from me, taking more orders.

Ten minutes later I had to break my stare down with Sean McCall's dad to pay Jo at the register. "Do you have any openings, Jo?"

"Openings for what, Hun?"

"Never mind." I paid her and grabbed the two boxes and orange juices. I carefully poised the food and drinks in my arms and pushed the front door open with my back. Just when I turned to take one step down, I felt her body slam into mine before I saw her coming. Makayla Fowler shrieked and jumped backward down the steps, the orange juice tilted and toppled on the boxes and came landing straight back onto my chest. The bright yellow liquid exploded from the cups and ran down my torso while pancakes, bacon, and eggs splattered on the steps and pavement below. I heard a collective gasp from the inside of the diner and felt at least sixty eyes trained on me. Makayla started yelling that I should watch where I was going. Aaron Abbot stood next to her, his hair ruffled in the back, laughing at both of us. My stomach twisted. A small eternity passed while I looked back and forth between them. How could this be where we ended up? Her forever yelling at me, Aaron finding a joke in it all, me standing dumbfounded. When my senses came back, I directed my anger towards her.

"How the hell was that my fault, M?" I hollered, tired of listening to her frenzied yelling.

"Because most things are," she slung back. "Dammit Dee, every stray dog within a block of here is going to come running to eat all your damn bacon off the ground." She pushed past me into the restaurant. Aaron walked over to me, looking from the food to my front splattered with juice. For one stupid moment, I thought he would pity me. Instead, he ran his finger up my arm, leaving a trail in the coat of orange juice. He smiled, licking his finger, then followed Makayla into the diner.

My cheeks burned. I stood looking at the food around my legs. My t-shirt clung to my torso, and my arms felt sticky. I pushed my bangs out of my eyes with the back of my palm, the only part of me that did not feel wet. I shook my brown boots off, pancake bits flying onto the pavement. Makayla was right; every dog in the neighborhood would be here any second to scarf down the food. It didn't take me long to grab up the food strewn all over the steps and pavement, shoving it into the boxes, tossing them into the dumpsters. The last thing I wanted to do was walk back in that diner and wait for more food. Aaron's face caught my attention before I did. Makayla and he were sitting in a booth, she was laughing her ass off watching me, Aaron's expression was hard as stone. My left hand rose and flipped them the bird. That cracked a smile on his face. Dad would have to wait for Cadmus to do another run. There was no way in hell I was going back in there now.

"I didn't figure you would want to come in and order all over again," Archie said, coming down the steps with 2 boxes and two cups. His white apron stained with ketchup and coffee. The white paper hat sat crooked on the top of his head. He smiled an apologetic smile at me.

I took the food from him, avoiding his eyes. "Thanks, Arch. You're the best."

"Do you think you and Makayla will ever bury the hatchet?"

"It isn't from a lack of trying on my part."

"Well, keep your head up." He turned to head back inside but stopped and turned around, "Just so you know, I never did believe M's version of things."

I looked up at him, "Thanks,"

"See yah around," he ran up the steps and disappeared into the diner.

The small hairs on my arm slowly pulled away from the sugar plastered on my skin. Each pull and tug sent a prick of pain up my limb. A spew of curse words left my mouth. The pistachio green truck door groaned when I pulled it open and placed the boxes on the floorboard. I shoved the cups into the holder by the radio. Time to go home for a shower. The drive to get out of town and up the mountain would take me twenty minutes. I wasted no time once I was out of town. I had been known to pull a sixty going up and down the mountain. If no one came around a tight bend I would be fine navigating the narrow roads at that speed.

Once I got to the top and the trees cleared for a moment I stole a glance out my window at the town. The buildings, cars, people, looked like play things from here. I told myself to not let such little creatures get under my skin. Yeah right. Down the other side of the mountain, dipping into the valley. The tires thudded across the bridge leading over Johns Creek I had almost drowned in when I was four. Then the truck skidded down the rock drive to the house, Mazy ran along the side, barking at me. I jumped from the truck and pounded up the steps, Mazy tried to keep pace and lick the dried juice off my arms. I stripped the wet clothes from my torso, leaving them on the floor in the hall. Knotting my hair on top of my head, I got into the shower. The soap came out in a long thick stream onto the washcloth I held. Furiously I scrubbed at my arm. Aaron's face overwhelmed my senses. His smugness in the diner. The way he touched me every opportunity he had. I knew what he was doing, he was reminding me who owned who. He couldn't let me forget who had been in charge all those years ago.

"2,195 days." The skin turned pink and raw. "He doesn't own you anymore." A piece of skin broke, a thin line of red blossomed under the water. "Dammit," I murmured, stopping myself. My arms leaned into the shower wall. You are safe. You are fine. You are safe. You are fine. You are safe. You are fine. The litany streamed through my consciousness. The water washed away the sugar and my shame down the drain.

"Where the hell did you go?" Dad blustered when I came through the door with the food balanced on my arms an hour later.

"I had a little accident at the diner," I replied. I set the food down on the counter. The sleeve on my black button-down road up on my arm, I yanked it down over the raw spot.

"Are you in different clothes?" he asked, eyeing me.

"Yeah. Funny story, as I came out of the diner someone ran into me and all the orange juice and food landed on me. I had to run home to take a shower and change. I'm sorry, but we are going to have to heat the food back up."

"No matter. I'm just glad you're all right. Who ran into you?"

"I don't know," stupid, what a stupid answer. I put the food on plates and tossed them into the microwave next to the coffee maker.

Dad set his jaw.

"It wasn't done on purpose, Pops," I told him, impatiently.

"Sure, it wasn't," he replied, going to the front of the store to unlock the door. I heard him let a few obscenities fly out on his way.

9

The blonde and cherry colored Chris Craft Capri boat cut through the clear turquoise water. It made a white, foamy wake behind us. Cricket sat next to me on the minty-green leather seat drinking a beer and watching the waves. The bottle in my hand felt almost empty, an empty one sat in the cup holder by the wheel. The night before, I had made a run to the gas station about fifteen miles outside of town. The owner was a sleazy old man who never employed the most standup characters. When I was fourteen, we found out they would sell us beer. They didn't even ask for an ID. Cricket would drink beer and only beer. I had grabbed two cases. A cheap plastic barrel sat next to the counter enclosed with Plexiglass, small plastic bottles of hard liquor called my name. I tossed a handful onto the counter. The guy behind the glass smirked back at me, "Looks like you know how to have some fun."

"That's what they tell me."

It had taken some convincing on my part, but eventually Arty agreed to let us take his baby out if I would treat her with respect. The lettering close to the stern read, 'Doris' in a beautiful script font. When I had asked Arty about the name, he told me she was a sea nymph of bounty in Greek mythology. I drove Doris out to the middle of the lake where you could open up the engine and cut loose. The wind whipped our hair around our necks. I tossed my empty bottle into the small trashcan Arty kept nestled by the passenger's seat. The hills around us cut into the water. I guided the boat around one and, coming out the other side, found the quiet little alcove I was looking for. I slowed the boat until we came to a stop. I dropped the anchor and killed the engine. Cricket stretched her arms overhead and smiled.

"Ready for a refill," she tossed the empty beer bottle into the trashcan.

"Thank god," I gave her a high five then jumped over the front seat. I was glad she had managed to toss one back while I drove. She was always more fun after a few drinks. A red cooler sat on the floor behind the front seat. A bag of towels, sunscreen, Solo cups, and my mini bottles sat next to it. I grabbed a beer from the cooler, a red cup, and a bottle of clear joy (as I liked to call it). I popped the beer open, handing it to Cricket before pouring mine into the cup.

"What happened to sobriety?" she climbed over the seat, pulled out her beach towel and laid it on the stern.

"Sobriety is overrated. I mean, I'm glad I did it to finish high school. But, college, sobriety..." I shrugged. "They don't really go together."

"What does Cadmus say about it?" Cricket laid a towel out next to hers.

"I've got this under control. I'm not going boating without some clear joy." The breeze rocked the boat gently on the water. I took a tentative step out and sat quickly, crossed my legs, and took a sip from my cup.

We touched our beverages together, "Cheers."

We laid back, propped up on our elbows, drinking and taking in the sun for a few moments. When I finally closed my eyes, hat over my face, I drifted off for what felt like only a few minutes before Cricket woke me with the sound of her chirping voice.

"Okay, so I was going to let it go, but I can't," she told me, "What happened with this Ruben guy?"

"Cricket, why?" I asked, from behind my cap.

"I can tell there is a story there that needs to be told. So, tell me."

The air under the hat felt stale, I flicked it off my face, letting the bright sun warm my skin and blind my eyes. The memories of how we would spend our Sunday afternoons curled up in bed, me reading to him while he lay next to me. We would only leave the bed to refill our coffee or make noodles. The words of Kerouac, Tolkien, Palahniuk, and more had filled the space between us.

I pushed up on my elbows, "Ruben was the first friend I made in New York. We were a strange pair." I chuckled, tossing my empty Solo cup into the backseat.

"How so?"

"Ruben is the most straight-laced person I have ever met. I am suspicious that he ever drank any of the beers he carried around at the parties we went to. He hasn't done anything out of the lines. He calls his parents and sister on a regular basis. He calls his body his temple and won't let anything in it to defile it." I leaned down over the backseat, pulling another beer from the cooler.

"Whoa."

"I know. He should have never even talked to me. He should have stayed away from me by 100 yards. But for some reason he didn't, he wanted to get to know me. He sort of chased me down." I smiled thinking about the first party I saw him at after he caught me. A handful of junior boys had an apartment. It was the scene of the never-ending party. One day I got invited and went. I stood dancing on a coffee table when Ruben and his friends, Jaxon and Malik, walked in. Ruben bee-lined it for me, I made note of Jaxon shaking his head and walking away from his friend. Those first few times we talked he just listened to me ramble about music, on and on. He just got it; how it was all I could think about. When I finally got him to talk about dance, he was the same way."

"Kindred spirits,"

"Yes!"

"He sounds like the kind of friend you needed."

"What does that mean?"

"Your friends growing up helped you crash and burn. Not real friends. You were sort of a loner the rest of high school. I mean, I love you, but you don't exactly connect easily with people, Dani."

"Thanks." I didn't need reminding of this.

"Sorry. So, what happened? Why the painful parting?"

I watched the breeze play with her hair. The light glinted off the water, casting reflections on her face. "Want to take a dip and cool off?"

"No. I want you to answer the question."

"Fine. He wanted to move in together." I wasn't sure why this was the story I told. His wanting to move in together had nothing to do with our separation.

"And?"

"And I would have fudged that up. We weren't dating. We were friends. I would have gotten drunk and jumped him and then he would have hated me and… It was complicated. The boy couldn't taint his temple with me so… I don't know."

"Dani?"

"What?" I relaxed my clenched palms.

"Did you know you don't have to have sex with someone to date them?"

The waves rocked the boat. But you sure could end it by having sex with someone else.

"Are you ready to take a dip yet? I'm getting hot."

Cricket heaved a sigh, "Yeah."

We slipped our cut off jean shorts off, Cricket jumped into the water. I stood at the edge of the boat, glaring down into the depths. When I was thirteen, I trained my lungs for freediving. On more than one occasion, I had made it to the bottom of the lake and back up, over 100 feet deep. It wouldn't be in me any longer, seven years and too many bingers had passed from then until now. The depth didn't appear that bad here. I took in as much oxygen as I could, threw my arms in front of myself and pierced through the water. It coursed around my body while I propelled myself further down, feeling it close in around me, the light began to wane, and the fish grew larger. The air in my lungs began to give out when the bottom came into focus. A burning sensation swelled in my chest, my hand reached out for the dirt at the bottom. I grabbed a handful and turned quickly, kicking my legs vigorously, fighting for the surface with each pull of my body. Cricket's legs came into focus. I aimed for her, releasing the dirt just when I grabbed her feet, pulling her down under the water. When I popped above the surface, she came up splashing, screaming how I scared the shit out of her. Water flew between us as we splashed back and forth.

We had stirred the quiet water with our excitement. It took me a moment to notice the waves were growing. I heard the engine of a speedboat getting closer to us. We stopped splashing and looked around the lake until our eyes landed on it, a large white speedboat, with red pin-striping down the sides and the name 'Julia' close to the bow of the boat. I felt our happy energy sink to the bottom of the lake, the boat closed in on us. The two boys sitting on the bow of the boat were recognizable immediately. They were the same two boys Aaron Abbot had hung out with since freshman year of high school. Rob with his light brown skin, his closely cropped black hair glistened with water spray. Graham sat next to him with his bright green swim trunks on; his blond hair did this amazing gravity-defying poof on top. Even with the wind from the boat and the splashing of the water, it still stood tall on the top of his head. The silver ring through the left side of his lip reflected the sunlight; he saw us in the water first and stood to point us out to Aaron. The boat slowed to a stop next to Arty's, dwarfing his in size.

"Don't stop the girl fight on account of us," Graham yelled, the three of them walked close to the edge of the boat to look down at us.

I tapped Cricket on the shoulder and nodded towards our boat. She followed behind me. We pulled ourselves up onto the stern.

"What do you guys want?" I asked, grabbing a towel, getting ready to wrap it around my waist.

"I would prefer you not do that," Rob taunted me, "I'm really visually enjoying this." He framed us with his hands and smiled.

I glowered back at him and wrapped the towel under my arms, covering my entire body. Cricket followed suit.

"Come on Little Weed, don't be like that," he said, watching our movements.

"Since when did you get a modesty card?" Aaron chimed in, "I think we've all seen more of you then you are showing in your bikini anyway." He bit his lip and let his eyes run down my body and up again.

"Come on Dani, let's just go," Cricket said to me, nudging me towards the front of the boat.

"Aaron, leave her alone."

I turned back to see the face of the newest voice speaking. Thomas Abbot appeared from behind the driver's seat. He was taller than I remembered him; his dark hair was the same color as Aaron's, only longer and messier. Their ivory skin was the same, Thomas was tall and gangly while Aaron was muscular and wide. Thomas's voice had changed since I left. I remembered he must be close to fifteen now. There was always something about him that drew me in, a sadness he tried to hide. Well, to be honest, he tried to hide his entire being.

"Hey Thomas," I called.

"Hi Dee," he answered without a smile. He tapped his brother's broad shoulder, "Come on, just leave them be. Let's go."

Aaron threw his arm around his brother and pulled his head down, giving him a good noogie. Thomas tried to pull away, but Aaron overpowered him. "Since when did you turn into a knight in shining armor?"

"Leave him be, Aaron." I regretted the words as they left my mouth. It was a reflex, to protect the younger ones, especially the ones I owed. I hated having people who one-upped me. I spent the first year of sobriety angry with Thomas, I was sure he had done us no favors. Once my life started fitting into place I realized I did owe him. He had done the right thing by us. The least I could do was protect him from his brother.

He let go of Thomas's neck, "What's this? You got a thing for my little brother, Weed?" he teased us. Thomas' cheeks flushed. "I can see he has one for you. Come on, and make his day by going out with us. We promise to be nice." Aaron flashed his smile that made most women do whatever he wanted.

"Not on your life," Cricket piped up.

"Oh, watch out, the insect is getting ready to bite," Graham laughed. Rob patted him on the back and joined in his laughter.

"Come on Aaron, let's go," Thomas pleaded again. His brother was too preoccupied staring down at us and if he was trying to intimidate me, he was succeeding. The feel of the moment shifted from annoying to threatening. Rob and Graham had stopped their laughter and stood flanked on either side of Aaron.

I moved closer to the seats of the boat but realized under Aaron's gaze that he had parked his boat in such a way to block us in. I anchored too close to the shore and with the size of his vessel next to mine. Stuck. Blocked in. It would take great effort to maneuver out, and he would not give me the chance to do that. The pace of my heart quickened, my palms broke out in a sweat. My eyes flit towards Graham. Then I did a quick scan of the visible water. I did not spot another boat. I did another quick scan of the land closest to us but was not happy with that option either. The rolling hills came down into the water at a steep angle. Even if we could out swim the three boys (which I knew I could) we would not outrun them in the woods. Rob had at least a foot of height on me. He would be on top of me in a matter of minutes once we were on land. The thought was enough to freeze me in my spot. Instinctively, I reached behind myself for Cricket's hand and gave it a squeeze. Aaron watched us closely, something in that moment broke his gaze and energy. I heard him laugh under his breath, and he smiled at us again. Rob and Graham looked at him. I saw a tinge of disappointment in their eyes. They stepped back.

"Alright, fine, if you don't want a ride on a real boat, that's your loss."

My heart began to slow when I saw that even Thomas had relaxed. "Thanks," I heard him mumble to his brother.

"Thanks? What are you thanking me for?" Aaron asked him, turning to look at him. "Thanks for not forcing your girlfriend to do something?"

"She's not my girlfriend." I watched Thomas ball up his hand into a fist and wondered if he would really start a fight with his brother over this.

"That's right, she's not." Aaron planted his feet, and I noticed his hand form into a fist as well.

"Stop it!" I screamed. Real fear surged through me,

I had seen Aaron fight, he could break Thomas's nose with one hit.

Aaron whirled around and laughed. "Look at you! Did you think I would really hit my little brother over something like you?"

"Something like me?" I asked confused.

"Yeah, something like you, a poor, trashy, Little Weed."

He turned away from me to look back at his brother and that's when it happened. Thomas's balled up hand cracked right across his big brother's jaw. Aaron did not even lose a step on his feet. He grabbed Thomas by the top of his trunks and around his shirt collar and threw him over the side of the boat into the water. Graham and Rob roared with laughter. Thomas popped up to the surface gasping for breath. Aaron turned the engine of his boat on and pulled away, leaving the three of us in his wake. I found myself slightly exasperated when I walked over to the side of the boat, sticking my arm out for Thomas to grab a hold.

"I guess you're coming with us, kid," I told him, he grabbed for me, steading his shaking body.

He spluttered more water, hauling himself up and into a seat. "I'm dead when he gets home."

"No, you aren't," Cricket comforted him, throwing her towel over his shoulders.

"She's right. You'll be just fine. You know he couldn't

let you show him up in front of his buddies." I paused, and caught Thomas eye, "It really wasn't worth all the trouble, but thank you."

He smiled and dropped his gaze, "You're wrong. It was worth it." He held my gaze until I could not look at his piercing eyes any longer. "You're welcome."

10

The boat felt smooth under my guidance as I neared the dock. Arty stood on the shore, waiting for me. His hands in his pockets, his gray hair rustling in the air. I hadn't expected him to be there, I was glad my buzz had worn off, once Thomas was aboard I stopped drinking. Drinking in front of minors was sloppy and classless after all. I cut the engine and pulled up to the dock, tossing the rope to Arty. In a few quick movements, he had the boat anchored and me out of the boat.

"Did you have fun?"

"Not at first, but it got better." I tugged my hat down around my eyes.

"How so?" he took the bags out of my arms while we walked towards his truck.

"Aaron showed up with his buddies and little brother."

"Does his dad still have that Sea Ray 350?"

"He does." I tossed the cooler into the truck bed.

"That's one hell of a boat." I could hear the envy in his voice.

"Maybe you should look into getting one," I teased him.

"Right. Well, once I own an entire town like the Abbot's I'll look into it. maybe I'll buy two, one for me and one for you." Arty turned the key in the ignition.

"You're the best," I kissed his cheek playfully.

"Aaron or those other two assholes give you any trouble?"

"Yeah. Mostly he gave me his brother for the day." I pulled the seatbelt across my chest.

Arty watched the review mirror as he backed out. "That's a trade I would take any day." He turned the truck down the road. "You know, you really need to stay away from that son-of-a-bitch."

"There it is," I replied, the truck picked up speed, heading up the hill towards Dad's house.

"There's what?"

"Cadmus and Pops already gave me what-for about staying away from Aaron. Did you guys think I came back from college dumb as a rock? It was the fudging lake, Arty. What am I supposed to do when he shows up?"

Arty's foot got a little heavy on the pedal, his anger showing, "Don't 'fudging' me. You know what the hell I'm talking about."

"And I wish someone would listen to what the hell I'm saying! I live here now which means I'm going to see these people on a regular basis. If y'all are that worried about it, send me back to New York, or off to some other place. I'll gladly go."

Arty had a death stare that could put even me in check. "Do not humor yourself by acting as if your tragedies are new to the world. People learn to live in these circumstances every day."

Yeah right. The popular term for those people are 'addicts'. I kept it to myself. Arty went on with his lecture. I tried to tune it out, it was a hopeless endeavor. I knew from years of experience though, the longer I stayed silent the sooner he would stop. He loved arguing with me until we were blue in the face. He hated to lecture. The truck turned a bend, Johns Creek came into view. I craned my neck to get a look at the water. It cascaded across the rocks, smooth and pure. Arty was saying something about things in my blood. I kept my attention focused outside the vehicle. The water seemed shallow, the embankment leading down to it dry, full of rocks and foliage. In the springtime when the rain fell the heaviest the creek could swell to almost six feet deep. It had never occurred to me how far my tricycle must have flipped when Daisy tried to drown me. The bike lost for good that day, Dad only had time to retrieve me from the current and get himself out. I wondered if I suffered any head injuries. There were a lot of rocks on the embankment. I realized Arty had grown still. I kept my face looking out the window. Odd that Dad spent so much time after that teaching me to swim. Swimming would have never saved me, the current would have still drug me down and under, swimming had never really saved anyone around here. The truck turned onto one of the three wooden bridges that crossed Johns Creek. Thump, thump, thump. The tires on the wood filled the cab. The one advantage to keeping Arty talking, he had less time to formulate his thoughts into a pointed attack. The tires hit the gravel road, they had never paved the rest of the mountain. The closer we drove to Dad's property the more my muscles tensed, waiting for what he had coming. Dad's long drive came into view, Arty turned down it, perhaps I made it home free. No dice.

"Dandelion Jane," full name, it would not go well for me, "I have loved you since the moment your daddy introduced us. You know this. I have never met a stronger woman than you. You've got the grit to do what needs to be done. That being said, you self-sabotage faster than a McDonald's hamburger. I know your mind hasn't figured it out yet, but I can see what's happening and what will come of it. You need to start going to meetings. This casual drinking thing you've got going on isn't going to work. It's in your DNA. You keep going down this path and soon you'll be back where you were before. And I sure as hell don't want to find you on my table one morning."

"Arty! I've lived it. I know what happens. I've got this under control."

Dad kneeled on the ground, pulling weeds from the front garden. A pile of green and yellow sat next to him.

"Do not patronize me, Dee. It's just as hard to be on the outside of this shit and watch it go down. Don't light yourself on fire again to keep him warm! If you start hanging out with him again, it's going to happen, we all know it!"

"I'm not hanging out with anyone! I took your boat out on the lake, and oh my god, other people happened to be there. Jesus Christ Arty, get over it! I never started using because of him, I started because of all the goddamn voices yelling at me. I needed to escape it!"

I pushed the door open and slammed it shut in one fell swoop. The cooler and bags scrapped on the side of the truck as I hauled them out. Before Dad could get a word out I had stomped over his weeds and up the steps, slamming the front door. I hauled everything up to my room, locking the door behind me, letting it all fall on the ground. I angrily stripped my swimsuit away from my body and collapsed to the bed. My hands balled up into fists. I hated fighting with Arty. It bothered me more than anyone else. Dad had every right to holler, lecture, plead, Cadmus never yelled, he listened as much if not more than he talked. But Arty... he had a way of digging into me, hitting me where it hurt, smacking me with the truth. Telling me about things I didn't want to hear about, like his pain when I screwed up.

I wanted to shut this out, stop my mind from running, I didn't want to think about how close I had come to winding up in Arty's backroom. There was no way I would fall that far again. Drinking on a boat was a long way from drugs in a barn. I'd dealt with those demons... right? I did my time, sitting on the couch, talking about my feelings, telling the doctor what they wanted to hear. What was happening now had nothing to do with that. A person can drink for no better reason than liking the taste of a beer. They didn't own me anymore. I rolled over onto my stomach, letting my eyes flutter closed, the heat and confrontation of the day taking its toll on me. Yet, even sleep would give me no respite. The imagines in my dreams swirled together: Aaron, boats, frigid water, falling. The sensation of lake water filling my lungs, the dead eyes glaring back at me. It woke me with a start. I gasped for air as my eyes popped open. The dark of the early morning pressed into the room. The emptiness next to me sent a painful ache through my body. Alone. Scared and alone. My life on repeat. I raked my fingers through my knotted hair. There had been a reason I had filled my bed as often as possible for years. The sense of another soul close to mine held the nightmares off. I found not all were created equal, some one-night-stands provoked worse dreams, some banished them for good. On cue, my phone lit with a message. I reached over and grabbed it off the nightstand. The number had no name associated with it,

Reminded today how much I miss you...

I jumped from my bed and ran to the window, it was instinct to look down in the yard and see who was playing the trick. Even through the darkness, I could tell the yard lay empty. My eyes strained, looking into the edges of the wood, but no one was there. I glanced back at my phone.

"What the..." I muttered. I swiped the message into the trash folder, must have been a wrong number. Who would text me at five in the morning? They would figure it out soon enough. I paced my room, picking at my fingers, wondering about it still. I wanted to crawl under the blankets and sleep a few more hours. Not going to happen though, that damn dream would never allow me more sleep. The waded-up material of my swimming suit caught my eye, better that than any other options. I yanked the material over my body, hoping I wouldn't regret it. I spent longer than I should have looking for shoes. I found some under a pile of laundry and books.

The light at the bottom of the steps cast a glow onto the steps as I came down. Dad sat in his chair, reading a book, drinking coffee. "You're up early."

"I couldn't sleep. I'm going for a swim."

"Good idea. There's some toast on the counter."

I grabbed a piece on my way out, Mazy on my heels.

A flock of blackbirds rose into the air when we made our appearance on the back porch. Mazy didn't even bother running after them, her nose had found a trail, stuck down deep into the grass. She rooted around in the yard for a moment while I came down the steps, heading towards the path to the pond. Before I knew it, she took off into the woods. I nibbled on my toast while I went down the dirt path. I had worn the lush green foliage away when I was 10, swimming every day, every moment I could.

The muddy shore soon met my feet. I slipped my shoes off, feeling the mud under my toes, the last piece of toast popped in my mouth, I adjusted my goggles on my eyes. The humidity felt like a wet blanket draped over my shoulders. It would be a hot one for sure. A whistle left my lips, piercing the stillness, Mazy did not reply. I stretched my arms while wading out into the water. I dove down into the depths, the fish scattered in front of me. My tired limbs felt like dead weight as I forced them to move through the water, my kicks shallow and useless. Come on. I told myself, forcing my legs to move more. They slowly obeyed my command, growing in strength, propelling me across the water at a stronger pace. The last 20 plus days had been long. They shouldn't have felt that long. I tried to remember when I had left for college. Mid-August, right? That gave me 45 some days at the minimum before kids went back to school. The water grew shallow the closer I drew to the other side, I bobbed in the water, turning, and swimming back. Not all the kids. Not Makayla. Not Graham. Not Sean McCall. I snorted under the water, almost inhaling a mouthful. I gasped for air on my next stroke. The thought of Sean in college warranted a laugh, swimming or not. At least Sean would not give me trouble during the winter months. He would just be a constant reminder. Although, I realized I hadn't laid eyes on him since making it back. There was no question where I could find him though. I bobbed in the water and turned again. Could I last 45 days with Aaron? I lasted the last two years of high school, why couldn't I hold out for two months? Arty did not give me enough credit. I had this under control. I swam for another twenty minutes, my mind quiet, enjoying the calm of the water rushing past me.

"Mazy!" I hollered when I emerged from the water. The dog was nowhere in my sight. I shook the water from my limbs, wrapped my goggles on my wrist, whistled again. There was a rustling sound coming from farther into the woods towards the east. "Damn dog better not be eating a rabbit," I said, trudging towards the sound. The woods were thicker here. Berry bushes crowded together, vines climbed the trees, pulling the branches down low. I found myself pushing foliage out of my face and trying not to trip over limbs that had fallen and begun to rot. "Mazy!" I called again. I could hear her growling now. A flick of brown and black caught my eye, her tail. The rest of her body hidden from my view by a berry bush. The closer I drew the better I could hear her growling, low, and mean in the back of her throat. It made the hairs on my neck stand on end. I stood on my tiptoes to peer over the bush that obstructed my view. There in the brush, flat on his back, lay Graham. I jumped back. Mazy growled again. "Mazy, come on," I whispered forcefully to her. She would not move. I quietly took a few steps around the bush, grabbed her collar, and tugged with all my might. Her body did not budge. The smell of vomit and alcohol filled my nose. I started to gag. Well, he would not wake anytime soon. I dropped her collar.

"Fine. You want to stay?" I swore she nodded her head. "I'm walking back, I'm not waiting around for him to come to." She licked my hand. I took one more look at Graham. His swim trunks and shoes covered in mud. I wondered if he had walked or crawled through the woods. His white t-shirt showed sweat stains around the collar and armpits. He was a sad, sorry, familiar sight. I sighed, turned, and walked towards Dad's. Once I made it to the path the foliage cleared, making it easier to navigate. Behind me, further back in the wood, a branch snapped, a bush rustled, a tingle ran up my spine. With everything in me I wanted to run, but I forced myself to walk, Mazy had him under control, it was only a critter. You're safe. You're fine. You're safe. You're fine. The litany kept me company as I walked to the deck. I stopped, holding onto the railing, repeating the words over and over. You're safe. You're fine. The back door slid open, Mazy bounded past me up the stairs, it startled me, making me jump and look up towards Dad.

He looked down at me, concern on his face.

"You look like you saw a ghost."

"I think I did."

"Don't be ridiculous. I told Cadmus you would fetch September for a lesson. Get a shower and go get her."

I tried to catch my vacillating breath, "Right. Just got done swimming."

"Doesn't count as a shower, Dandelion. When you start the week out right the week turns out right. Come on now." He turned and went back to the kitchen.

The extremes of Graham passed out and Dad telling me to start the week on a good foot couldn't coexist in my mind. I sat down, hard, on the step, my forehead falling to my knees. I wanted a drink. I needed a drink. A drink could help numb this confusion. That propelled me upwards. When I went through the kitchen Dad tried to tell me to eat, I muttered something in return, driven only by my desire to numb this feeling. The cooler and bags sat on the floor in my room. I pulled the top off the cooler and rummaged through the bottles. They all appeared empty. I dug down deeper, frantic. I reached the bottom and found not one full of even a mouthful. I grabbed an empty beer bottle and hurled it across my room. It hit the wall and burst into pieces. My palms balled up, clutching the side of my head, I wanted to scream, but nothing came. 25 days, Dandelion. 25 fudging days and you already can't handle it. Get your shit together. I couldn't have a buzz and go pick up Sep. What was I thinking? What was wrong with me? Swallow it. I gritted my teeth, pushed myself up, and went to the shower. I could scrub away what clung to me and get over it. I had to, there were no other choices.

The cabin Cadmus lived in on Dad's property stood about half a mile away from Dad's house. If you cut through the woods, straight across Dad's property it took about 17 minutes. If you wanted to avoid the woods, you had to walk down Dad's drive, up the road, and down Cadmus's drive. It added a solid 15 minutes to the hike. It was 15 minutes I was glad to add today to stay clear of Graham asleep in the woods. About time I arrived at the cabin my body felt like it had another shower from the humidity clinging to my arms and neck. Cadmus's brow furrowed, watching me walk down the long drive, not coming through my normal spot in the woods.

"Morning Dani," he called, putting his book in his lap.

"Morning. Pops sent me for Sep, said I was to give her a lesson before work." As the words left my mouth September emerged from the inside of the house, eating a bowl of oatmeal.

"Heya." She replied.

"Sep, I found the music I wanted to teach you. Want to come over and learn some?"

"Can I, Cadmus?"

"Absolutely. Dani, I'll come pick you both up in an hour. Before you go, Sep, bring your dirty laundry down from upstairs. And finish your breakfast" September shoveled her oatmeal into her mouth before darting up the stairs to her room. "What's with avoiding the woods?"

"Thought I needed to burn the extra calories." I patted the small pouch forming on my middle.

"I know a better way to lose that."

"I'm sure you do." Of all days, today I needed lecture free.

"I remember you being a lot more likable sober. You got a hell of a lot more accomplished."

"Two things I'm just not worried about right now." Who did I need to be likable to? And what the hell could anyone accomplish in this town? No one and nothing.

Cadmus glanced to the woods, back to me, recognition spreading on his face, "Who's in the woods, Dani?"

My shoulders shrugged, like a reflex to deflect the question. No way I could talk now and take Sep home for a lesson.

"Should I walk you back?"

"No. Everything is fine. I wanted the extra walk." It sounded convincing, even to me. He looked back at the woods, second-guessing his assumption.

Before he could counter September pounded down the steps with a basket overflowing with laundry and her empty oatmeal bowl balanced on top. "I'm ready! Can we go now?"

"Sure thing, let's go, kid." September fell into step next to me. Her voice filled the woods as we made our way to my house. I had to prove Cadmus wrong, and Sep would never agree to walk the long way. Occasionally, I could hear something scurry away from us, but my eyes could never find the source. She rattled on about her weekend, where she went in the woods, what book she had read, what food Cadmus had made her. The sound of a twig cracking rung through the air. Without any thought I grabbed Sep's hand, taking off at a run. I ducked under branches and jumped over logs, pulling her with me. To September's credit she flew through the woods with me, no questions asked, no complaints made. She simply picked up her feet and went for it. I wasn't sure if it was pure trust in me or sensing my fear spike, perhaps it was both. I did not slow down until I hit the bottom step of the deck. I cast a glance over my shoulder, back to the woods, but nothing was there. We both clutched our sides, catching our breath.

"That was weird." Sep managed to get out over an intake of breath. I could tell she was searching my face for an explanation. What could I possibly tell her? That PTSD hijacked my startle reflux? That someone I didn't trust with my favorite book happened to pass out on our property last night? I couldn't laugh it off. September's eyes bore into mine, knowing it was no joke.

"Not for me... not anymore."

"How come?" she prodded.

"Promise me something."

"Ok..." her eyes narrowed.

"Don't do drugs."

"Are yah ok?"

"I'm fine." I straightened my spine and went for the steps, pushing all the memories away.

"Did yah go to the lake yesterday?" she asked. September was great at changing subjects.

"Uh huh, Cricket and I took Arty's boat out."

"How come I never get to come?" she asked while we ascended the steps.

"Don't say 'never'. Arty has taken you out before. I'll take you out sometime. I'm glad you weren't there yesterday. I had to take Thomas Abbot home."

Sep pushed her hair behind her ear and ducked her head. "How come?"

"Aaron was a jerk. Anyway, let's go look at this music. I think you'll really like it." I opened the back door and walked through the kitchen and family room, around to the foyer where the piano sat. "Here," I handed her the music, "look it over while I get us some water."

September's playing floated through the house. It sounded forced and choppy, my mind started seeing in black and white. It was an odd quirk of mine. I heard music and saw it as color. I only realized not everyone did this when I told Arty something sounded purple to me. I was four or five at the time. She missed three notes in a row. I walked up behind her, holding the water. Her body crouched over the keys. Her knees were pushing into her stomach. I noticed her feet pushed up on tip-toes. Her long blonde hair hung in her face. I set the water down, and tapped her on the lower back, pulled her hair behind her neck. She straightened up and pushed her feet down. I touched her shoulder lightly, making her pull them back.

"That looks better. Feel better?"

She nodded.

"Try again from the first bar."

Her hands were flat against the keys, making them fumble with each attempt. I tapped her wrist with my finger. It sprang up, curving her fingers properly on the keys.

"Better. Try again."

This time she managed to hit the notes correctly. It still had the choppy feel of learning something new.

I let her play until the end of the page without further interruption.

"Thoughts?" I mused.

"Play it fer me? I want to hear what it sounds like, fer real," September pleaded.

"Nope. You need something to work for, I'm afraid those online lessons made you lazy. This will give you a good goal. You won't know what it really sounds like until you practice it."

"But that ain't fair!"

I sat next to her on the bench. "It will be a good exercise for you. I believe in you that you can figure this out. Try it again, from the top."

She slouched at the bench, and I tapped her back. She groaned but fixed her posture before beginning. It went on like that for another thirty minutes. When Cadmus arrived to take us into town the music had begun to look slightly purple, it was an improvement. September bolted for the door when he arrived, still miffed at my refusal to play it for her.

"How'd it go?" he asked, I stood, let my hands fall to the keys, gliding across the tops of the ivory.

"Alright. First lesson back is always hard. She'll get it."

"Play it for me?"

"What?"

"What's in your mind right now."

"Maybe later…" I grabbed my satchel off the peg by the door. I wasn't sure I could let that out right now.

11

I sat on the dusty floor of the hardware store with piles of small retail bags filled with electrical plugs sitting all around me. The sound of Cadmus's deep rhythmic voice filled the air while he read to September, perched in her usual spot on top of the counter. A notebook was on her lap and she took notes with a pencil hopelessly chewed on the end. Seasons didn't matter to Cadmus if he had to be at work five or six days a week, that meant September could learn five or six days a week. School was not something he did with her; it was a way of life. She soaked up every word that came from his mouth like a sponge. A few hours ago, I was listening attentively as he read to her about the Revolutionary War. In the last forty minutes, my mind had wandered.

The sound of a truck pulling up to the store came through the open screen door. I glanced up from my work, Cadmus's voice dropped away. I saw three sets of boots hop down out of the cab of the truck and walk to the door. Tall, dark-haired, good-looking, Don Abbot came through first, followed by Aaron and Thomas.

"Hello Don, boys," Cadmus said from behind the front counter where he laid down his book. "What can I help you with today?"

I saw Thomas peering around his dad and brother at me. I was still sitting on the floor surrounded by bags. I smiled at him. He waved.

"I ordered a large amount of lumber from Mel last week. Did you get it in?" Don asked.

Cadmus checked the books by the register. "We did. It must be out back. If you pull your truck around, I'll help you load it up."

"Meet you in the back," Don replied. Aaron busied himself looking at tools. Thomas flipped through seed packets. Don left them behind which was just what Aaron wanted.

No sooner did the back-door close behind Cadmus than Aaron crouched next to me. "Whacha doing there, Dandelion?" he flipped my hair over my shoulder.

"Work," I answered.

"Sounds boring," he replied, not taking his eyes off my

face. His dusty, black, work boots sat on top of the bags.

"Well, it is. Thankfully, that's not what I'm living for." I tried to push his boot away. He slowly moved it over, just enough for me to grab the bag it was sitting on.

"What are you living for, Dee?" he ducked his head down, trying to force me to look at him.

I turned my face towards him. His eyes looked serious, but there was always a hint of mischief playing behind them. The skin around his eyes was clear. Free from the redness I feared would be there. "Red Vines."

Aaron smiled broadly at me, "I'm throwing a party on the boat this weekend. Want to come out?"

"Nope." I slipped a baggie onto the hook.

"Come on. I'll let you bring your Cricket." He picked up a baggie and handed it to me.

"Nope, I found some of your left-over party in the woods. I'm not interested." I yanked the merchandise out of his hand and hung it up.

He dusted his jeans off and stood up, "I'm not really sure what that's supposed to mean."

I looked up at him, "Graham..." I let it hang in the air.

Aaron shrugged, "What do I have to do to get you to come out with me?"

"Oh, I don't know, start being the man you were 8 years ago?" I focused back on my work, shoving bags onto hooks. I heard Thomas clear his throat. Aaron scowled at his brother. September watched them from her perch, catching Aaron's eye.

He walked over to her and picked up the book Cadmus left on the counter. "This looks a little above your reading level, little girl."

"Aaron, leave her alone." I stood up, pushing my way between him and September.

He dropped the book and held his hands up defensively, "Just making an observation. By the way, thanks for bringing my little brother home after his swim."

"That wasn't funny," Thomas replied, crossing his arms defensively over his chest.

"I'm always happy to help your brother out," I answered, directing it towards Thomas.

"Boys, let's go!" Don called from the back door.

Thomas gave me one last smile, "See you around, Dee. Bye, September."

"Bye Thomas," September's mouth spread into a wide grin.

Aaron brushed up against my side on his way out. He let his arm slingback and slapped my butt. "See you around."

September jumped down from the counter ready to holler after him. I grabbed her by the shoulders and stopped her. "Don't you dare, September Marie."

"But why, why do yah let him get away with that? You should go kick him in the balls."

"It wouldn't help anything," I told her.

She made a sound like a growl, "I just don't understand it."

"Just don't ever treat people like they are objects for your consumption."

"That's not what I don't understand."

"What then?"

"You." Her green eyes filled with fire. They clapped onto mine. "I don't understand you. If any other person on this planet treated yah the way he does, well, you'd probably murder 'em."

"No girl, I wouldn't murder them. That would be more your style or Arty."

"Well," she paused, "yah sure wouldn't put up with 'em."

I slowly walked back over to my bags all over the floor. Taking a moment before telling September what came to my mind. "Did you know Aaron had a little sister?"

I began hanging them on the pegs as she mulled this over.

"No."

"He did. I guess she would be about ten now."

"What happened? Where is she?"

I stopped hanging bags. Time seemed to stop, remembering that day. "She drowned."

I could hear Sep suck her breath in out of horror.

"We were about your age when it happened. Most days when I see Aaron, that's all I can think about. I remember him doing CPR on Katie. I think about him in his black suit standing in the funeral home." I shook my head to clear the memories that were always there just under the surface.

September was quiet for a long while. "Yah would think he wouldn't be so cruel."

"You don't know what happened to them after that. He changed. I changed. Everyone changed. I know you won't believe me, but there was a time when we were friends."

Sep shook her head. It made her hair fly into her face. "Yer right, I don't believe that. No way yah could ever have been friends with someone so mean."

I looked away from her and smiled. There weren't that many years between us, but the life I had experienced since I was her age, until now, it built a chasm.

"You never told me that's how you see him." I heard Cadmus say. He was coming down the hallway from the back.

I glanced over my shoulder at him, "I don't like to talk about it."

"I can see why," he stood next to me. I slowly stocked the pegs.

I hung the last merchandise up and walked away from him. The inquisitive gaze he gave me when he wanted me to open up was on his face. It was neither the place nor the time for memory lane.

The rest of the afternoon was quiet. Few customers were in and out. Cadmus continued to read to September while I stocked shelves. By four in the afternoon, Cadmus was ready to stop for the day and closed shop.

The three of us crammed into the cab of Cadmus's truck, heading out of town and up the mountain. The vent blew icy air on my face, fanning my hair and September's. I stuck my finger into the vent and pushed it towards the window and away from my face. The summer air felt thick and humid. Sitting up against the door of the truck, I could feel it trying to press its way in on me. The humidity was something I was glad to say goodbye to up east. The cicadas seemed especially loud this year. I could hear them over the engine of the truck as if I were sitting in a field.

"Do yah think my momma ever did drugs?" September broke the silence. She was sitting between Cadmus and me.

On cue, we both turned our heads and looked at her.

"Excuse me?" Cadmus asked, keeping one eye on her and one on the road.

"What is going on inside your head, girl?" I added.

"I dunno know. I was just thinkin' about her and havin' me and how that happened."

"I don't follow," Cadmus replied.

"Well, she made it all them years without getting knocked up. Then when she's old she gets me stuck in her, and out I come."

I groaned.

Sep looked at me, "Don't yah think maybe she took drugs and then got knocked up? Yah know, all crazy outta her mind like?"

I took a deep breath before turning to look at her. "You know what I think, September Marie? I think your momma was brave to have you when she was old. I think you are beautiful and add life to our family. I don't honestly care how you came to be, as long as you came to be with Cadmus and me."

She grew quiet for some time before piping up again, "Dee?"

"Yes?" I asked while I rubbed my forehead.

"Did yah ever get a baby in you when you were on drugs?"

I wanted to open the truck door and fall down the mountain.

"September," Cadmus chided.

"It's alright," I cut him off. My mind filled with memories. Ones I would rather cut out of my past, like the one where I took my first line of coke. My stomach turned, remembering how a little Sep could have grown inside of me after that night. The drugs did not help the sex go any better or the memories of it afterward. The only thing they did help with was removing what inhibitions I did still have. Just thinking about the high kicked in the craving, even now, years later. I rung my hands that had broken out in a sweat. "Thankfully no, I never had a baby grow in my belly," I paused, "And I don't think your momma took drugs when she had you."

"How come?" she looked at me, full of curiosity.

"For the reason that you came out too sweet to have ever had that poison in you."

She smiled at me.

I tried to smile back at her, to hold off the memories that were now tripping over themselves in my mind. It was just like that old folktale of the little Dutch boy and the dike. My thumb usually smashed into the dam, but just one mention could release the floodwaters. Unfortunately, I was not much of a hero in my life. The one time I tried to be a hero backfired on me like there was no tomorrow. A week after that first line of coke, I found myself standing in the field outside his window. The pebbles were not hard to find, they were probably from the gravel driveway. It was aiming right in the dark to get it to hit his window that was the hard part. The first three were shallow throws, one I managed to send over the roof. Finally, I hit the glass pane, sending a nice ping into the still night air. The sudden sound sent a chill up my spine. I grabbed my arms and hugged myself. I wondered if I should dart off to the road that leads back home. It was at that moment that the light flicked on and he stuck his head out the window.

"What are you doing?" he called down, groggily.

I faltered, looking up at him, "I... I don't really know."

"Are you drunk?" he rubbed his face.

"No." I dug my toe into the grass. Running away was sounding better and better. If only it was not for that cold sweat that had started to break out every time I thought about that high. "Listen, I don't know how to do this..."

"Do what?"

I forced my face up and looked him square in the eyes, "Do you have any more?"

The mischief in his face, replaced with a hardness

I would come to know well, met my gaze. "Are you sure you want to do that? You could just leave now, and no one would need to know."

"I'm pretty sure." I shoved my hands into my back jeans pockets.

"I can see that." He disappeared from the window for a minute. When he came back, he had a shirt on. "Give me a minute."

Once he came down, he grabbed me by the hand and ran into the barn. The option to duck out offered again, but my adrenaline was pumping. I knew there would be no turning back that night. What was one more hit? I just needed that feeling of invincibility one more time. That feeling that everything was great, and I could do anything I wanted. One more time would not hurt either of us. He pulled a bag out of his pocket. He worked the white powder and plastic around in his fingers. Then he flipped a barrel over. A few minutes later, I rolled up a dollar bill and snuffed a line of white powder into my nostrils. It felt like ecstasy hitting my brain.

The oddest part about that night was how it was playing in my head over a year later, the night Cadmus found my best friend and me on the floor of The Barn with seven other teenagers passed out around us. The smell of vomit filled the air. When the high wore off that night faster than it ever had before, I remembered that second time. How it seemed like it would never end, but I told myself

I would never touch it again. It made me laugh that night. If Cadmus would not have found us and drug us to the hospital, we would have sold our souls for one more hit. Just one more. It was always going to be just one more.

September touched my face. I jerked back to reality. I thanked the god that Saint Francis prayed to that a baby never got stuck in me. The world did not need more abandoned babies, like September, and shit moms like mine.

12

The three of us were standing behind the counter with our lunches in front of us. Dad had finished eating ten minutes earlier and was busy doing inventory. The smell of greasy cheeseburgers and fries had filled the store. I was telling September the story of Liam busting into my apartment on my last day there. It had become one of her favorite tales of mine. Her favorite part was how he jumped back from me and we stood screaming at each other for minutes before yelling actual words. Her cheeks packed with fries she couldn't swallow, she was laughing so hard. Even Cadmus was chuckling, although he had heard the story at least five times now. Every time I told it, my face grew more animated, my gestures more exaggerated, I put my whole body into it. A personal goal of mine was to one day have Sep rolling on the floor over one of my stories.

I pushed harder hoping today would be the day.

"I was near kicking him in the balls," I raised my leg, just as I had that day almost a month prior. Before I could finish, Arty came in, slamming the door behind him. We all stopped laughing, Sep choked down her fries, Cadmus wiped his eyes, and I took a slurp of my soda. Arty never came to the store. He was always busy during the day at the funeral home or his house.

"Mel," he called.

Dad turned on the step stool he had perched on, balancing himself while he held a notepad and pencil. "What's up?"

"I've got to make a run all the way to St. Louis." Arty looked breathless, his gray hair windblown. He must have walked the eight blocks rather quickly.

"Who's dead now?" Dad asked while he climbed down.

"Ed Miller's sister passed. They want her brought home and buried in the family lot."

"You leaving today?" Dad set his pencil and notepad on the counter next to me.

"Hoping to leave within the hour."

"Well, what do you need from me?"

"I hate to pull that drive alone. I'm getting too old for that shit. Want to run it with me?"

"Sorry Art, I need to get this inventory done. It's not that bad of a drive." Dad stole a fry from my container.

"What the hell are you doing inventory for? Isn't that what Cadmus is for? What happened to retirement?" Arty looked like he could slug Dad. I stifled a laugh behind my hand. "I'm looking at not pulling back in until close to midnight and that's without stopping. I figure I'm going to have to piss and eat at some point. An extra driver sure would be helpful."

"I'll go!" I piped up. Dad and Arty looked at me.

"You really want to go on a run?"

"Sure, why not? It gets me out of here for the day. Can we do anything while we're in St. Louis?" The days had turned to weeks the weeks into monotony. If I did not escape it soon I feared my mind would go.

Arty mulled this proposition over. "I suppose we could grab supper and walk around for a bit. Do you promise to do the driving back though?"

"Hell, I'll do all the driving if you let me go."

"Alright, I have to go make a few calls and get the van ready. I'll come pick you up within the hour. Got it?" he turned and left the building as quickly as he had come.

"Got it," I yelled after him. I smirked at September, "Want to bet five dollars I come back with an even better story than Liam?"

"You're on." She shook my hand.

I parked my scooter next to Sheriff Ritter's patrol car and ran up the steps to the store. There were two things I needed for a road trip. 1: Music. Thankfully, I did not leave the house without my phone. 2: Junk food. That was something I would need to load up on before Arty came back for me. When the bell knocked back on the door, I darted my eyes over to the counter. Makayla was not there; her mom, Mrs. Fowler, had replaced her. A wave of relief passed over my body as I grabbed a basket and moved down the aisles. By the time I finished, there was a selection of chips, granola bars, cookies, drinks, gum, and pretzels in the basket. Sheriff Ritter paid for his soda.

"Dee, how's your summer coming?"

"Alright," I replied.

"Staying clean?"

"Yes, sir."

"Keep it that way." He tipped his hat to me and left.

I dropped my basket onto the counter with a thump.

"How are you, Dee? I haven't seen you all summer." Mrs. Fowler never stopped being pleasant to me. Even after her daughter decided I was the spawn of Satan. "I thought fer sure I would see yah at fireworks on the fourth. The Abbot's sure know how to throw a party, don't they?"

"I'm alright. Yeah, I think we missed the invite for that." I busied myself looking through a magazine. I knew perfectly well the Abbot's didn't send invitations. I also knew we should not show up. Our invitation had gotten revoked 7 years ago, the year after Katie died.

"Goose, you know you don't need an invite to show up for the biggest bash of the year." Mrs. Fowler had a way of taking a two-minute interaction well into five or ten.

"How come M isn't working? Seems like she's always working when I'm in here." I turned a page, avoiding eye contact.

"She does work a lot now. Her daddy is getting her ready to take the store over one day." Mrs. Fowler scanned my chips.

I nodded. Of course, she would take over the store, just as Archie would take over the diner, Aaron would run the town, and so many kids would take over their parent's farms.

"Now that you're back for good, is your daddy going to let you take over his store? It really should stay in the family and not pass to that Cadmus fella."

"What?" my brainwaves seemed to stop mid-thought. I shelved the magazine. Had she just asked me if I was taking over the store? "I think Cadmus is better at management than I am. Where's M today?" The last conversation I wanted to have was about my personal goals with Mrs. Fowler.

She smiled and pushed her copper hair away from her face. "We gave her the day off. I think she went out with Aaron and his friends on the boat. I'm surprised you aren't out there."

"Yeah, well, I don't much get along with Aaron anymore." I twisted my brown hair around on my finger.

"That's a shame. He is such a nice boy. The three of you used to be so inseparable."

I tried to smile, but my face felt more like a nauseated scowl.

"It'll be twenty-six dollars and thirteen cents, dear." She pushed the bags across the counter towards me.

I pulled my money out and gathered the bags of junk food. "Thanks, Mrs. Fowler. Have a good afternoon." That was the thing I hated about Aaron; the way he could weasel his way into the hearts of the adults in this town. That pearly white smile, spiked up dark hair, nice clothes, and charming personality he could pull out, it always snagged them. There was only a handful that had seen his true colors. People who thought Aaron Abbot was another nice kid weren't paying attention.

By the time I made it back to the hardware store and unloaded my scooter, Arty was pulling in. I kissed Dad on his cheek, told Cadmus and Sep goodbye and ran out the front door. I opened the passenger's door and tossed in my two bags of junk food before getting in myself.

"Hell Snot, I thought I was taking you out for dinner."

"You are," I replied, confused.

Arty glanced at the bags, "Are you planning on eating all of that?"

"I have enough to share! You need a good variety when you're on the road."

"Oh, good lord, I can tell you were raised by Mel."

I yanked my phone out of my bag, jammed the jack into the radio, found a playlist, and turned the volume up.

"I haven't even made it off the street, and you already need the tunes going?"

I shot Arty a look, "Um, yeah, music is life, old man."

"Does this mean I don't have to talk to you for the entire drive?"

"I promise to not make you talk the entire time. Chip?" I tore open a bag of potato chips and popped three in my mouth at once, holding the bag across the empty space between us. Arty shoved his hand in and pulled some out. I knew Arty loved going on runs because it meant seclusion for hours on end. I also knew he would have never asked me to go with him because of that. It seemed fitting I try to give him what he wanted. Even though we were only four hours from the city, we never went. I remembered looking at pictures from when I was a toddler. My chubby legs and arms stuck out of cotton shorts and a spaghetti-strap tank top. I was in front of a fountain that looked like Sea Lions, there was a blue train going by in the background. The only time I saw the zoo. I had vague memories of going to the Art Museum when I was older, probably closer to ten. It seemed every summer, I begged Dad to take me back, and he never did.

The music, endless snacks, and watching the scenery kept me occupied for longer than I would have guessed. It was a pretty drive this time of year. Once we were past the hills, the pastures popped up with their vibrant wildflowers and horses grazing. The cattle fields dotted with hay bales stretched on for miles. The highway was relatively quiet. I supposed being in the middle of the week helped. There was not much tourist traffic until the weekend.

"Why does Pops hate the city so much?" I blurted out.

Arty considered this for a moment. "I wouldn't say he hates it."

"Okay. Hate is a strong word. He doesn't like it though. I've asked him about it and he just brushed it off."

"At one time in our lives, we ran to St. Louis on a regular basis," Arty confessed.

"So, there is a story. I knew it. Why did you come so much?"

"It was a place to go. We were young once, I know you forget that. Your daddy has always been a country boy, but I do enjoy the city on occasion. I started dragging him with me. We would come up on the weekends, do some bar hopping, go to some concerts, your dad had to eat at as many restaurants as he could. Then we would head home."

"Well, that doesn't sound like anything to be resentful of."

"I think he would agree all those are happy memories. It was the last time we came together. I had to do a run and Mel agreed to come with me. At that time, he came on most of my runs. On our way back, we stopped at a bar. The bartender was this tall, long-legged, blonde hair, green eyed, beauty who would not leave your pops alone. I could smell trouble a mile off. You know how your dad is with beauty. It blinds him. After thirty minutes of her attention, I came out of the bathroom to find them gone. It took me two seconds to do the math in my head. I found a booth and waited for him to get back."

"Daisy," I grumbled, listening to the tale I had never heard but often imagined.

"The one and only. Your pops thought he made off nice on that trip. I couldn't shake that pit in my stomach though. I warned him she would be trouble. He laughed at me. How could she be? He would tell me. When she showed up two years later with you, I wanted to laugh."

I swallowed hard, "So, Pops won't go to the city because last time he knocked up a crazy girl?"

Arty looked over at me and grumbled. "Eat another bag of chips. It'll make you feel better."

I took Arty's advice, ate another bag of chips, and drank an iced chocolate coffee drink. We kept quiet for another long stretch. I decided I did not want to hear any more of Arty's stories from before I was born. The hours had passed more quickly than I anticipated. The rolling hills were slowly turning into civilization.

"The plan is to press on to Forest Park, grab some grub, and walk around, then go pick up the body."

"That works for me. I'm starving."

Arty sighed at me.

Another forty minutes passed before we exited the highway and made our way slowly down a busy city street. Arty began cursing at each car that pulled in front of him. He was sure everyone was cutting him off. The shrill sound of an ambulance siren howled behind us. He pulled the van over to the side of the road. It came barreling down behind us. Just as the ambulance passed, Arty floored the gas and took off behind it. I gripped the side of my seat and the door, bracing for inevitable impact, either into the back of the ambulance or another vehicle. We crossed over another highway and met with construction and tall hospital buildings. They all blurred together while Arty sped behind the red ambulance. A blue car on our right swerved out of the way of the sirens and our van, their bumper only inches from the side of our vehicle when we went past. Just when the ambulance slowed to turn into the ER entrance, Arty jerked the wheel and crossed three lanes of traffic to make a left turn into the park. Cars all around us honked, I heard the distinct sound of someone skidding behind us. My knuckles went white while I gripped the upholstery for my life.

"What the hell was that?" I screamed at him.

"Just some city driving."

"You're a lunatic. Do you know that?" I unclenched my hands.

"Indeed." He grinned at me. "Now you have a story for Sep. I give you permission to exaggerate it as much as needed."

"Not sure I'll need to."

"No one barfed or died. Couldn't have been that bad." Arty made a right at the stop sign.

He pulled into a small parking lot next to a body of water. The building facing us had a large deck on the back that went out over the water. There were couples and families leisurely peddling in paddleboats up and down the channels of water. Gondolas skimmed the lake while their passengers ate grapes and sipped wine.

"After we eat, I'll walk you over to the Grand Basin. It'll be beautiful in the evening light."

"This place is magic," I said when we walked up to the restaurant.

"I wouldn't go that far. They do make a mean fish sandwich and have some excellent local beer on tap though," He replied, opening the door for me.

I relented over dinner and allowed Arty to reminisce over his younger days spent tromping around this city. It was the most I had heard him talk since being home. Of course, with September around it was hard to get a word in edgewise. When she was asleep, Cadmus and Dad were usually trying to get me to make plans for my life. He had not had much time or opportunity to converse with me.

"How is it you and my Pops were allowed to live life, make your mistakes, and go on living without adults jumping all over you?"

"Mostly because we made all those mistakes when we were thirty-year-old men. Back in our day, you just got cut loose and had to figure things out on your own. I wish I would've had someone knocking me on the back of the head telling me to get my act together. One day you might thank all of us."

"How am I supposed to learn if I don't make mistakes?" I shoved a piece of fried fish in my mouth.

"You've done plenty of learning already. Hell, you've learned more about life in your twenty years than I did in my first thirty-five. Some of your lessons I don't want to learn."

I pushed the crumbs on my plate around with my fork. "What if I don't come up with a plan? What if I just take each day as it comes?"

"No good."

"Why?"

"You'll get bored. When you get bored, you find trouble. Or trouble finds you. You need to stay busy. Make a plan."

"Can we go see the Grand Basin now?" I set my fork down.

"Sure thing." He tossed money on the table and stood. I followed close behind him.

13

When we made it to the Grand Basin the sun was setting, casting purple, orange, and vibrant pink hues across the sky. The lights on the fountains illuminated, bright, I watched them mesmerized. The Art Museum sat ceremoniously at the top of the hill in the background. There were people sitting on the grass, looking like dots from where we stood. Arty threw his arm across my shoulder and pulled me in for a side hug. I wrapped my arms around his waist and pulled him closer.

"Thanks for letting me come," I told him.

"Thanks for always driving me nuts, Snot," he replied. "We better head back soon and pick up our dead body." He gave my shoulder a firm squeeze, my bare arm rubbed against his soft cotton button down.

"She's probably wondering where the hell we are." I nestled my head against his chest.

I felt Arty's body shake with a laugh. "Let's get out of here, kid."

When we got back to the van, I realized we were picking the body up from the hospital across from the park. Arty had me stay in the vehicle while he went in to do the honors. I busied myself with a candy bar and music until he came out followed by a tech pushing a gurney. It hit me how I'd be spending the next few hours with a dead body in the backseat. Arty climbed into the passenger's seat and slammed the door.

"Ready?"

"Does it ever creep you out?" my nose wrinkled.

"Nah. I spent my entire childhood around death if it bothered we I wouldn't have taken it over. I don't think about it much. One time I even took a nap back there." He jabbed his thumb towards the rear.

"You did what?" I asked disgusted.

"It was an out of state run. I was tired on my way back and decided to take a quick nap." Arty clicked his seatbelt.

"Wait, you slept with a body back there?" I gripped the steering wheel and turned towards him. I must have heard him wrong, I told myself.

"Well, it sounds sort of dirty when you say it like that." He chuckled.

"Arty…"

"Finish your chocolate and get moving." He turned the music up.

Arty fell asleep with two hours left in the trip. I kept awake by cranking up the music and munching on potato chips. With less than forty minutes left, I glanced down at the odometer to see the needle pushing past 80. I slammed on the brakes, fearful of a cop with a dead body in the back. The seatbelts snapped our shifting bodies back against the seats, thankfully, before Arty's sleeping head met the dashboard.

"What the hell was that?" he screamed at me half asleep.

I could not even answer him, I was laughing too hard.

"What? The late-night-slap-happies kicking in? Get us home without killing us." A slew of foul words passed his lips while he dozed back off.

At 1:35 a.m. I pulled the van around to the back of the funeral home. I gave Arty's shoulder a firm shake. "Wake up old man, we're here."

He slapped my hand away, sitting up. "I'm awake, I'm awake." He rubbed his weathered face for a moment before exiting the van.

I walked around to the back where he was pulling the doors open. "Can I help with something?" my hands knocked against my hips.

"Here," he tossed the keys to me, "go unlock the back door and flip the lights on."

I pushed open the large metal door at the back of the funeral home. A shiver ran up my back when I entered. I ran my hand along the tiled wall until I found a light switch. I flicked the overhead fluorescent lights on. They blinded me for a moment. When my eyes come back into focus, they met the sterile, cold, room in front of me. The room looked, as you would expect it to. There were cabinets lining the walls. Long counters ran down the length of each side of the room. The walls covered with large white ceramic tiles. The floor and ceiling were white as well. There was a large metal table in the center of the room.

My mind filled with faces of those I knew who had laid on this table. Most of them were old. They had filled their days with family and friends, time had simply come knocking, it always did. However, my knees stiffened when I thought of September's momma lying there, Marie was not young, but she was too young to pass. I often wondered how a mother's heart could give out like that when it contained a great deal of love for a child. Shouldn't love keep it beating for years to come? Then little Kathryn Abbot walked through my mind. Most two-year-olds' were cute, bossy, a handful. She was beautiful though, just like her mom.

Her skin was perfect, like a porcelain dolls. Her cheeks and lips were a rosy pink. Her eyes were large, round, and the same russet brown as Aaron's. Her hair was dark and wispy, it framed her face perfectly. When I had to look at her, in the tiny casket, she looked just like a baby doll. My small twelve-year-old heart broke when I looked at her. I wanted to reach out and pick her up. Mrs. Abbot sat in a chair weeping, the two boys and Mr. Abbot standing around her. I realized now Arty would have had to prepare her tiny body.

The gurney pushed through the door followed by Arty. "Did you get lost in an empty room?"

"Huh?" I turned around and looked at him. "Did you need more help?"

He glanced at the table and back at me. "It's alright, I managed. You okay in here?"

"Just realizing all the people you've seen on that table." How could Arty do it? I ran away from pain every chance I got, he watched it every day in its worst form. Not only did he observe it, he handled it with dignity, he took care of people through their pain.

"It has been quite a few." Arty pushed the gurney over towards the refrigerated cases.

"Was Kathryn Abbot the youngest?" I gripped my arms around my chest, holding onto my elbows, thinking about the worst pain I had ever felt. I couldn't escape it even now and Arty had embraced the entire town through it.

"I believe so. The young ones are the hardest." He paused. "There was a time when my greatest fear was having you on that table." His face turned towards mine, the wrinkles seemed to deepen around his eyes, and his mouth set in a thin line.

"Uh..." I cleared my throat. "I only made it to Step 6, mostly because Step 7 and 9 scared the shit out of me. But... I am sorry for making you worry about me dying."

Arty turned away and pulled open the door of the case, the table rolled out into the room. "Step 9 is about making amends, not just saying a shallow sorry."

"I really didn't mean to put you all through hell. Do you know that?" It sounded shallow.

The gurney wheel squeaked on the floor. Arty pushed it up against the table. He gingerly picked up Ed Miller's sisters body and placed her on the ice cold, metal table. The rollers rattled when he pushed the table back into the refrigerated case. The door closed with a loud snap, my shoulders jumped. "I think you weren't thinking during those years. All you were doing was running as fast as you could away from your pain. Unfortunately, you just ran into more and more."

I wet my lips, "Well, I'm a little older and wiser now. I promise to make better choices. Scouts honor." I saluted him.

"Don't make promises you can't keep, Snot."

I sighed. "Can I crash at your house tonight? I don't want to have to drive up the mountain and I'm supposed to work tomorrow anyway."

"Sure, sure, we can head to my house." He flicked the light switch off and followed me out the back door. Arty parked the truck on the drive next to the house under a large maple tree. I followed behind him. He opened the front door and flipped the lights on.

"You can sleep in the extra room downstairs. Do you want a pair of sweatpants?" he asked, dropping his keys on the side table.

"Nah, I'm just gonna crash like this. Thanks for letting me stay."

"Not a problem. I'm heading right to bed. I'll see you in the morning." He trudged up the steps.

I walked down the hallway to the small guest room in the back of the house. I slipped off my shoes and jeans, turned the covers down and fell asleep once my head hit the pillow.

The sensation of falling overtook my body, falling swiftly through the air, knowing impact was inevitable, and hitting the water with a crash. The water turned from clear liquid to black around my body while I fell deeper and deeper towards the bottom of the lake. It felt like the water gripping me and pulling me down. The sting in my back from the fall growing in intensity, my legs and arms flailed around me until cramps seized them. The black water filled my lungs and quieted my screams. I sat bolt upright in bed. Choking, coughing, on nothing more than my imagination. My hands grasped my throat and chest until the coughing stopped. I sat, arms trembling, trying to calm my nerves. You are safe. You are fine. You are at Arty's. No strangers, no harm. I kicked the covers away, sitting in the middle of the bed, taking small measured breaths. You are safe. You are fine. It took me another ten minutes to swing my legs out of bed and shimmy into my jeans. I slipped my shoes back on, sticking my old socks into my back pockets. My hair hung in tangles around my face. The house was quiet when I emerged out into the hallway. I crossed the hall to the bathroom, listening for any sound of Arty. None met my ears. I squirted some of his toothpaste onto my finger and rubbed my teeth down.

"Arty?" I called when I came out into the main part of the house. He did not respond. I glanced out the window and saw the truck was gone. I noticed a white piece of paper stuck to the front door.

Needed to get to work early. There's cereal in the pantry and milk in the fridge. Help yourself.

- Arty

I crumpled up the note and tossed it into the black wastebasket. The dark insides of the container reminded me of the blackness closing in around me in my nightmare. I shook my head to clear the feelings. I walked to the pantry and yanked it open, surveying the contents. There were three different kinds of cereal in his otherwise bare pantry. I pulled one out that had raisins. Two bottles of Jack Daniel's and several cans of Guinness sat in the back of the cabinet. A tingle ran down my fingers. I grabbed a can of Guinness and popped the top, slurping down the dark liquid until my nerves calmed. My reoccurring nightmare of almost drowning always unsettled me. *You aren't really breaking any promises. You're just taking the edge off. This is ok. I'm just coping with a bad night.* I told myself, dumping a large helping of bran flakes into a bowl and found the milk in the fridge to pour over it. *Breakfast of champions.* The crunching of the cereal helped to calm my shaking hands, but those bottles of whiskey kept staring back at me in my mind. I rinsed my empty bowl and went back to the pantry. I hesitated in front of the closed door. What would it mean if I took one? That I was a thief? An addict? The word left a bitter taste in my mouth. *It just means you're thirsty.* I opened the pantry, looking at the bottles again. One of them was almost empty. I estimated there were less than five shots left. I contemplated if Arty would notice it missing. I stopped my brain and grabbed it. I shoved it down into the bottom of my bag. I glanced at the clock on the microwave: 9:03 am.

"Fudge," I mumbled. The Guinness sat half drunk on the counter. I picked it up and chugged down all I could muster. The trashcan was empty besides the crumbled note; I took the can with me as I went for the door. I estimated it would take me fifteen minutes to walk to the store. It was surprising Cadmus had not already called to find out where I was. I threw my bag across my shoulders and pulled the front door closed, an hour and a half late for work was not all that bad, right?

The humidity had started its' full-on assault for the summer. Overall, the first few weeks of June were mild. I tried my best to stay in the shade, walking down the street. If I had to guess, I presumed it was pushing 90° already. The stray dogs of the neighborhood barked at me as I passed them on the other side of the street. They were too busy nosing around the trashcans to do more than make a racket at me. I kicked some pebbles in the dust, took the last drink from my beer. The Cooper's five kids, Cole, Charlie, Christy, Calvin, and CeCe came running out their front door. Cole pushed through the gate of their white picket fence, his four siblings bunched up behind him. Each had a bath towel thrown over their shoulder. The younger boys had fishing nets. Off they all ran, down the road towards the woods and creek. I smiled and waved at CeCe, the only one who noticed me walking, she took a long glance at the beer can swinging in my hand.

"Hey Dee!" she called, waving, and not slowing her pace after her brother.

"Shit," I muttered as I flipped open a neighbor's trash can on the curb and tossed the can inside it.

I could tell I was almost to Jo's Diner. The smell of bacon and sausage wafted through the air, hitting my nostrils. I decided to stop in and find out if Cadmus had already made the breakfast run. The street was emptying out, although there was still a fair amount of trucks parked around the building. Most of the farmers would be back at work now, trying to beat the heat. I skipped up the steps.

"Hi Dee," Archie said to me when I came in the door.

"Hey Arch, was Cadmus already in for the breakfast run?" I asked him, leaning against the cool counter.

He pulled his pen from behind his ear and clicked it open. "Uh, yeah, he and Sep left over an hour ago."

I glanced down the diner and noticed Mr. McCall and Mr. Young sitting in a booth watching me. I smiled nervously, "Okay cool. I'm late for work and wanted to make sure everyone was fed."

"Are you alright?" Archie asked, leaning closer to me over the counter.

"I'm fine Arch, why would I not be?" I pushed my hands away from the counter, careful to not exhale close to him. I wished for a mint to turn up in my bag on my way to the store.

"Just checking," he shrugged and moved away.

"Cadmus had just asked if you had been in for breakfast yet. It didn't sound like he knew where you were."

I glanced back down at the men with a scowl. They turned their heads away from me. "I sure hope I look sober enough for y'all. I sure would hate for any nasty rumors to get started," I ranted at their turned heads. "Thanks a lot, Archie." I frowned at him and went out the front door. I cursed Cadmus, picking up my pace.

As I walked up to the front door of the store, September ran smack into me. "Oy girl," I complained, my patience already shot for the day.

"Sorry Dee," she exclaimed, taking a step back. "Where were you?" she pushed her unruly hair out of her face.

"I slept at Arty's. We didn't get back until almost two in the morning. Where are you going? No school work to-day?"

"That makes sense. Well, you weren't here and so Cadmus told me to scram, so he could watch the store. He got yah food. I'll see yah later." She said in a rush taking off down the road.

I shook my head at her and walked into the store. "Cadmus James Hall!" I hollered, walking down the aisle.

"Dandelion Jane Sanders," he called back, sarcastically. "You're late."

"Yeah, yeah. Why did you ask Archie where I was this

morning?" I caught sight of him at the back of the store. He was going over the logbook of orders.

He glanced up at me, "I didn't. I asked him if you already picked up our breakfast. He told me you hadn't. I ordered our food and left. I assumed you were here opening up." He replied, matter-of-factly.

"Well, all the farmers were listening in. When I showed up Archie asked me if I was alright, while all the men eyed me up and down, trying to determine where I'd been and who I'd been with."

Cadmus sighed, "I'm sorry. I don't know why something as small as that would start a rumor."

"You know how hungry these people are for gossip."

"I'm truly sorry."

"It's alright. Let's forget about it. Where's Pops?" I asked, shoving my hands into my pockets and looking around.

"Remember how he isn't supposed to be here every day?" Cadmus replied, pushing a Styrofoam box in my direction. "Eat something. You get crabby when you're hungry."

I opened the go box and picked up a piece of bacon.

Cadmus and I spent the morning quiet and busy, he organized orders, I restocked and cleaned. September came back in time for lunch. She filled me in on how many trees she climbed, how warm the creek water was, how crazy the

Cooper kids were when adults were not around, and how she had finished the Amelia Earhart biography I had lent her the night before.

"I learned a new word. She liked to say 'tenacity' a lot."

"That's a good word." I smiled, pushing boxes of bolts onto a shelf. "That sort of describes you."

"And someone else in this room," Cadmus added from behind the counter.

"Maybe all of us?" I smiled. "The most difficult thing is the decision to act - the rest is merely tenacity." I quoted.

"Which is only a good thing if you are making the right decision." Cadmus clarified, looking hard at September.

"Anything fun happen in the city?" September asked, pulling herself up onto the counter.

I shared the stories of Arty's spectacular ambulance stalking in the city. And my slamming on the breaks, almost sending Arty through the windshield. I almost had her rolling on the floor with the second story. I was getting closer and closer to my goal. She begged for more stories as the afternoon minutes ticked by.

"Did I tell you about the time my best friend and I went to Mark Twain Forest?"

She shook her head no. I told her how we left for four days, slept out in the open in the back of a pickup truck.

If she thought you could see a lot of stars here, she would be blown away by how many more you could see there. Secluded in the heart of the forest, the white light miles, and miles away, the sky lit up, like a black pincushion filled with diamonds. It had been my first time to go skinny-dipping. Cadmus condemned this story. I told him he was making way too big of a deal out of something as simple as swimming with no clothes on.

"Honestly, there is something pure about feeling the water all around you with no barriers."

Even after this statement, he told September, he had better never find out she went swimming in the nude. I winked at her and told her Pops still didn't know I had. Cricket showed up a few hours before closing, she sidled up to me behind the counter, fidgeting with an open box of wall nails.

"Where were you last night?"

"What the hell," I groaned, tossing my head back.

September came out of the bathroom, wiping her hands on her overalls. "Hey Cricket. Dee just told me how yah two went to Mark Twain forest. Super cool."

Cricket looked at me confused, "Must have been someone else, Sep. I don't think I've ever been."

"Sep, it was a different friend." I turned back to Cricket, "Why are you asking where I was?"

"Oh yeah, I forgot to tell yah, everyone at Jo's was talkin' about how yah started yer partyin' back up. Said there was some shindig down on the lake last night and they saw yah walkin' back hung. I told 'em all they was nuts. Yah went on a run with Arty and slept at his place. They all looked at me like I was the stupidest girl ever born." She paused. "We were there cause Archie makes the best milkshakes. Did yah know that?"

We all stood flabbergasted, looking at Sep.

"What?"

"Go wait outside, September," Cadmus ordered. She knew better than to argue with him when he used that tone. She walked out the front door mumbling something.

Cricket drummed her fingers on the counter. "I'm sorry."

"I did go on a run with Arty. We didn't get back until almost two in the morning. I stayed at his house." I defend myself.

"I believe you!" she played with one of the nails. "But if it's all over town you are back up to your old tricks... I mean, I even thought maybe Aaron wore you down."

"Are you serious?" Cadmus asked, raising his hands exasperated. "All because I asked one kid if you already ordered breakfast?"

"Well," I almost told him about CeCe but changed my mind last minute. "Hell, it worked on Cricket." I gave her a pointed look.

Cricket cleared her throat. "Uh... Makayla Fowler has been complaining about how Aaron ditched her yesterday afternoon. She's told anyone who'll listen. There's usually only one reason for Aaron to ditch her." Her dark curls fell on her face, covering her eyes. She looked down at the nails in her hand. "And the whole town knows what reason that is."

"And then I give the impression of you missing... Shit." Cadmus muttered.

And CeCe Cooper saw me with a beer walking down the street alone. Dad hadn't even shown up for work, another sure sign of my absence all evening. My shoulders squared and jaw set. "Let the games begin."

14

Cricket offered to take me home while Cadmus locked the store up. We rode in relative silence up the mountain. I watched the sunset, wondering what tomorrow would bring after today's debacle. I felt miffed at Cadmus but could not hold it against him. After all, when my troubles began seven years ago, he was not a part of this town. It would take him two years, one year into my real trouble, to show up. The thing was that was how it began when I was thirteen: the nights of me not going home, Dad calling around, trying to find out where I was. A year later, he could not control me at all. Makayla and I were running amuck. Well, Makayla did not do much. She mostly followed me around, covered for me when she needed to. I started drinking and hard. Makayla started getting cold feet around me.

We were still inseparable, but she did not want to cross that line. It sucked us into a different crowd of trouble-makers, a crowd I quickly realized she needed protection from. I knew I needed to get her away from them. The only problem was she wasn't going to leave my side.

"You don't think people will be nasty, do you?" Cricket piped up.

I turned my head from the window to look at her. "Huh? Oh... I don't care. I could care less what those people say."

"I don't know why they are so hungry for you to fail," she replied, gripping the steering wheel a little harder.

"It makes them feel better about themselves." I chewed on my finger before stopping myself.

"I guess so," she said. When we pulled down the drive-way, we saw every light in the house on. "What in the world? Is your dad having a party?"

"Have you met my Pops?" I replied, sarcastically.

"Want me to come in?"

"Nah, I'm sure it's nothing."

"You know what, I'm coming in." She threw the car into park and swung her door open.

"Cricket, what are you doing?"

"I miss your pops. Get over it." She tossed her key ring into the cupholder and smiled at me.

I shook my head at her. We walked up the steps and through the front door. "The rumors aren't true! Don't believe what you hear on the streets! Everyone is clean here!" I started yelling out after Cricket closed the door behind us.

She giggled as we rounded the corner, only to stop dead in our tracks. Dad was standing at the island, looking out into the family room. His face was grave, irritated really. I noticed his hands clenching the sink. His knuckles were white. There was a tall, lean, woman standing on the other side of the island, facing him. Her long hair flowed freely down her back; it was the lightest blonde, going gray around the top. Her hands rested on the tops of the stool backs. They were sun-kissed and wrinkled. She turned when we came around the corner. Her face lit up in a large, bright, white, smile. It crinkled the skin around her emerald eyes.

"Dandelion!" she said with a shrill voice.

I was sure my face was a look of deer in the headlights. She bounded the few feet between us, her multicolored, crocheted, shawl flowing behind her. She enveloped me in her arms. I could feel tears from her cheeks rolling onto my forehead. My arms hung limply at my sides. I could not see Cricket's face, but I could see Pops, his eyes were darting from her to the scene of enormous one-sided affection before him. The fury of his eyes terrified me. I tried to wriggle away from her. Eventually, she allowed me to be successful in my attempts to escape and released my body. I took a deep breath. I could feel Cricket's eyes boring into me.

"Oh Dandelion, do you know I think about you every year on this day? My heart just bursts wondering what you are doing." She reached for me and touched my cheek. My eyes grew wide and I pulled away from my deadbeat mom. "And today, here you stand before me; a beautiful, talented, twenty-one-year-old girl. All ready to celebrate your birthday with your friend." She cocked her head at Cricket. I heard Dad's first pound the counter.

My look of surprise, replaced with disgust. "Today isn't my birthday, Daisy. And I turned twenty months ago."

She laughed. She had the audacity to laugh. "Well, shoot." She put her hands on her hips to steady herself. "At least I tried, right honey?" she glanced back at Dad.

For the first time in my life, I wondered if I would see my dad turn violent. It took my brain 2.5 seconds to realize I did not want to see that. It took me another 3 seconds to calculate the best move to stop the heat of the moment in its tracks. "It's true," I blurted out. All eyes were back on me. "You tried, I mean, you've been gone for so long, how could you keep track?" I strained my voice to sound genuine. "I suppose the important thing is you're here now." I could see Dad over Daisy's shoulder. His jaw clenched, and he shook his head.

"Exactly!" Daisy exclaimed. "I'm here now; ready to spend some time with my girl."

Before she could hug me again, I shuffled over to the couch, "Want to sit down?"

Cricket followed my lead and firmly planted herself next to me on the couch. I made a mental note to kiss her for that later. The last thing I needed right now was my absent mother crammed next to me on the furniture.

"Did you have fun yesterday? Mel told me you went to St. Louis with friends," Daisy asked, settling across from me in the armchair.

I shot Dad a look. He refused to sit down or come out of the kitchen for that matter. "I did. I went on a run with Arty. We stopped by Forest Park."

"Oh." She looked surprised. "Arthur was never a fan of mine. I didn't realize Mel let you go on runs with him. Melvin, doesn't that seem like an odd thing to let your twenty-one,"

"Twenty." I corrected.

She kept talking over me, "year-old daughter do?" she turned her body around to get a look at my Dad.

I clutched Cricket's hand.

"It's some of the cleanest fun she's had in her life," he replied, avoiding my look. I clamped my jaw shut, trying to not laugh or even smile.

"What? What did you say?" Daisy asked confused. "Oh, never mind. I suppose if that is something that makes you happy, it's fine." She turned her attention back to Cricket and me.

"What made you show up now?" I blurted out.

"Well, I may have the day wrong, but I do think about you, you know." Her hands moved in front of her when she talked. It was a light, graceful movement. It reminded me of a child who held a streamer in front of them and moved it gently over the breeze.

"You could have called."

"That's not really my style."

"You've got that right," Dad grumbled, loudly.

Daisy paused, her eyes fluttered closed for a moment before she decided to proceed. "I really thought it would be a pleasant surprise. Believe it or not, Mel and I have had a nice day catching up."

"You've been here all day?" I asked, my brow furrowed.

"Mostly, your dad wouldn't let me leave. He kept insisting you would be home soon."

Dad was trying to contain her to the house. It had never bothered him what people said in town about him or us. It bothered him that they said anything at all. Dad valued privacy and had always respected the privacy of others. If Daisy went parading around town, it would be all abuzz with talk of our family. I often wondered if the town talking about my drinking had drained him more than my actual drinking.

"I never got around to asking, how are Roy and Zinnia?" Dad asked from the kitchen.

Daisy inhaled, her face looked pained as she answered, "Roy passed the year I left here. Zinnia went quietly earlier this spring."

"I am sorry to hear that."

It was not until Dad gave his condolences that the names of my maternal grandparents registered in my memory. Dad had mentioned them a few times growing up. The summer I asked him if I could plant zinnias in the front yard, he had replied 'no, because they reminded him of an old bat.' At the time, I was too young to understand what he was referencing. A few years later when I was older and asked about my grandparents, the reference made sense. It often made me curious what Zinnia was like and how often she and Pops had interacted.

Daisy nodded.

"Where have you been for the last sixteen years, Daisy?" I asked. I tried to compose my face, but I could feel my eyes narrow at her.

"You could call me Mom." She smiled.

"I'm fine calling you Daisy."

"But I am your mother."

"And your name is also Daisy."

We stared each other down for a moment. Beneath this free spirit, hippie, get-up, I could sense a manipulative personality. What would make a fifty-something-year-old mom show up unannounced? She would be wanting something from me, us. The tension grew while I tried to figure out what it could be, and she tried to figure out how to get it.

"Have you been traveling all this time?" Cricket piped up.

She beamed at me before directing her response to Cricket, "Here and there. I like to take the open road wherever it will lead me. When I find a place I like, I settle in until I get bored. I can't handle staying in the same place for long, unlike that old log over there." She waved her thumb in Mel's direction with a laugh.

"Where were you last?" Cricket pressed.

"New Orleans. I loved it. I've been there for about two

years. But, you know, it was time to move on. I'm thinking of going back out west. I love the west." She fiddled with a strand of her frayed jeans by the knee.

"Fantastic," I replied, "So, you're just passing through, ready for your next great adventure. We sure wouldn't want to slow you down."

"Yes and no. I would like to spend some time getting to know my daughter." Her eyes locked on mine.

"There isn't much to know."

"I'm sure there is plenty. Mel has been sharing how you went away to college, that you play the piano. I would love to hear you play."

"Not gonna happen," I snapped.

"Dandelion," she almost cooed at me, "I understand you are upset with my behavior. But your toddler years were better spent with that old dog. I needed to have space and stretch my wings. I always planned on coming back when you were older and more interesting. I knew you would turn out to be too much for that old log to handle; you would be like me, wanting to see the world and experience life. So here I am, fresh, new, and ready to help you escape from these old fuddy-duddies. No need to be angry with me, I had a plan for us all along."

The feeling of rage to the point of violence towards a person was a new sensation for me. I could see myself rising from the couch and slugging her in the face. Yet, at the same moment, I felt complete pity for her. The paradox left me immobile to react. She really believed what she was saying was harmless. Her actions of my youth erased from my mind with her presence now.

"Sorry Daisy, you missed her interesting years already. You should have stuck around and put in your relational rent. There isn't a place for you here now," Dad spat at her as he walked over towards me.

The look of confusion on her face was mystifying. "Clearly there is a lot of history here I need to catch up on."

My head wagged back and forth. "Uh, no, you really don't. Dad has taken great care of me. I don't feel the need to run off and stretch my wings. I have my life together. There's a plan. We're good. You should just go out west and keep living your life."

"I highly doubt you have a plan. That doesn't fit with your personality." Daisy leaned back in the chair casually. I did not like the familiarity of it all.

"What do you know of my personality?"

"A mother knows," she cocked her head.

"You aren't my mother. You gave birth to me and left me when I was four. I have two dads, a brother, and a sister. I don't need a mom." I stood up next to Dad and folded my arms across my chest.

"That settles it." Daisy stood, "I'm staying. I'll get a room at the hotel for the night. We are going to spend some time together and get reacquainted." Her colorful shawl swung back and forth with her arm gestures.

"I don't need to get to know you." I began.

"You aren't staying at the hotel." Dad sighed. I glared at him, fire in my eyes.

"Why not?" Daisy asked.

"Because you can stay here in the guest room; I'm just asking for everyone to say their goodnights now." He kept his voice calm. His eyes caught mine. They were steady, just like the ocean's rolling waves.

"I can honor that request. I will say my goodnights and get my bags from the car."

"I'll walk out with you," Cricket offered, she shot me a look of apology. Once they were out the door, I turned on Dad.

"What in the world?" I felt my voice break.

"Let's let her stay the night. See if we can get her to leave tomorrow morning." Dad threw his hands up defensively.

"I'd rather live with more gossip than her in our house." I tried to keep my voice down. I started to walk towards the steps. Dad followed on my heels.

"What do you mean more gossip?"

I stopped on the landing and turned to face him. "Long story short, everyone in town thinks I'm either on drugs, drinking, or sleeping with Aaron again. I don't want to talk about it."

Dad's hand held onto the banister at the bottom of the steps. "Are you?" it was a question that sounded like a sigh.

If I had any fight left in me, I might have turned and slung back choice words. In reality, he needed to ask the question. I let the air out of my lungs, "I'm not. I promise. I love you, but I'm going to bed now."

"I love you girl, we will get this fixed tomorrow."

Once I closed the door behind myself, I yanked the bottle of whiskey out of my bag. Thank god, I had the presence of mind to snatch it this morning, not knowing how much I would need it. I slung back a few shots before corking it and hiding it in my closet.

15

The grooves in the wood floor caught my toes while they swung back and forth off the side of my bed. I lay prostrate looking at the ceiling. Was it a surprise to walk in and see Daisy or had I been expecting it? Yes. Was I mad or ambivalent about her not remembering my birthday? Yes. Was I appreciative or irritated by her sleeping a door down from me? Yes. My fingers ran through my hair tugging it while my lips twisted.

I heard my door open, "You, out of bed."

I sat up, my fists falling to the mattress with a thud. "I'm already up."

"You want to talk about it?" Dad asked. He was rummaging around in my dresser.

"I don't even know what to say or how I feel." My swimsuit smacked me in the face. Dad had tossed it at me before starting another search in the bottom of the closet. "What's that about?" I asked, angrily.

"We're keeping on track around here. Just because Daisy is here doesn't mean we need to interrupt the routine. You are going for a swim, I am making breakfast, when you come back we will hash this out."

"Would you get out of my closet?" I protested, keeping an eye on my boot that held the liquor bottle.

Dad found my canvas shoes as the words left my mouth, "Just looking for these. Here," he put them on the bed, "You. Swim. Got it?"

"I don't want to hash anything out with that woman."

"Dandelion, she's your mother, one day you're going to have to face her. Might as well do it now and save yourself a trip later in life."

"Can't you just get rid of her while I'm swimming?"

"Some battles have to be fought."

The urge to scream welled up in my chest. I swallowed it down before it escaped. It could wait for the woods or better yet, it could wait for the depths of the pond. I ripped my t-shirt and boxer shorts off, leaving them in a heap on the floor while I tugged the tight swimsuit up over my body. A pair of shorts lay on the floor close to my feet I yanked them up before going to my closet. The bottle of booze felt light when I pulled it from my boot. I uncapped it, emptying the contents in one quick motion, burning all the way down my throat. After I carefully hid the bottle, I went to the door, opening it quietly as I could. Mazy lay in front of the guest room door, her large brown eyes locked onto me, she raised her head, her tail wagging lightly on the floor.

"Let's go for a swim," I whispered to her. Her body did not move a muscle. "Are you guarding her?" She blinked at me, laid her head back on her large front paws. "Good dog."

"It's late; you should eat before you leave," Dad told me from the kitchen when I came around the corner. The clock read 9:00 am behind him on the microwave.

"I'll get something when I get back," my stomach felt nauseous.

"Here, eat this. You didn't eat dinner last night." Dad tossed a protein bar at my face. I managed to catch it.

"Thanks," I exited out the back and went for the trees.

Through the tops of the branches, I could make out the blue sky. There weren't any clouds that I could see. I sucked in the air, looking back in the woods. The wrapping on the protein bar crinkled when I ripped open the package and took a large bite. The heat was already melting the thin layer of chocolate onto my fingertips. I took another large bite. My mind buzzed with possibilities. What could Daisy want? What would she ask for? What was I willing to give her? I closed my eyes tightly, trying to clear the thoughts. It was no use they were relentless. My feet turned, taking me away from the pond and towards Cadmus's empty cabin. The black truck that sat in front was gone when I broke through the tree line. I walked around to the back door, it usually sat unlocked. The off chance I would find it latched didn't matter, the extra key sat hidden in the rain boots on the side of the house. I tried the handle, the door opened easily into the kitchen. Murphy hissed at me and jumped off the counter by the sink. I grabbed a chair, pulling it over to the cabinet. I climbed up and rummaged in the back behind the pots. A bottle of whiskey sat closest to the front, further in were various brands of beers. I knew Cadmus was less likely to miss these. I grabbed two and jumped off the chair, careful to put everything back the way it was before closing the door behind me.

The heat of the sun bore down on my back while I made my way towards the woods. The metal tab pulled against my finger when I popped the top of the beer. The fizzing following the pop was a welcome sound. I took a drink while the previous evening's charade ran through my mind. When Daisy had turned around, I knew who she was. There were more lines on her face, her hair was lighter, but she looked the same otherwise. Her energy still felt the same. I forgot how anxious she made me feel when I was a child as if I were on pins and needles. There was no telling what she would say or do next. I had forgotten about that.

Dad was so even, predictable, steady. Once she was gone, my life felt calm. He gave me security to sail my ship on smooth waters. Now it felt rocky, just with thirty minutes of banter with her, just from seeing her face to be honest. Dad and I both knew, even though we were not going to say it, there was no way to get rid of her.

The woods felt still, hot, with no Mazy chasing the wildlife away I could hear the birds singing above me, the squirrels tossed nuts from the trees and landed on the soft ground below. The beer can felt empty in my grasp. I smashed it against a tree trunk, flatting the metal under my fingers. A rotting log sat close by, I shoved the smashed can under it. The reflection from the pond water shone through the thinning tree line. The second can popped under my fingers, fizzing I took a drink. The chaos in my mind had begun to slow and mellow. I stepped out into the opening. Stripping my clothes off, and pulled my goggles onto my eyes, I waded out into the water, leaving the beer by my clothes. The water felt more like bath water. I dove down into the depths and shot back up to the surface. I could stay out here all day, which was what I intended on doing. I was sure Dad had informed Cadmus of Daisy's appearance. He would not be expecting me in for work. It would be better for everyone if I wasted the day out here in the sun, not heading home until late.

The water surrounded my torso, coming up to my armpits. Inhaling I dove down into the depths. My legs kicked and pumped, propelling me further down.

The bottom of the pond came into view sooner than I expected. Most of my dives were in the lake where it took minutes to reach the bottom, not seconds. The dirt felt squishy and gritty as my hand sunk down in it, grabbing a handful and bringing it to the surface. When my face popped back out into the air, my hand released the mud, letting it fall back to where it came from. The odd little ritual had gone on for years. Dive to the bottom, collect dirt to prove I had done it but never let it break the water's surface. I never showed anyone. At the last moment, I always freed it, letting it fall through the water in a cloud of muck. I fell into a brisk stroke, swimming back and forth across the expanse of the water. With each lap, I felt the tension give way in my shoulders. For as long as I could remember, I had spent time in confrontation with people. Confrontation did not bother me. It had always been about the curiosity, the entitlement, the idea that because they thought they knew something they could hold it over me. The way people made you feel owned.

The ache of tiredness started in my limbs. I knew it was time to call it quits and go lay in the meadow. Mazy sat on the brink of the water, watching me.

"Make your escape from guarding the prisoner?" She barked. I patted her head when I walked onto the shore. "Good girl, ready for an afternoon nap? I sure am." I peeled the suit off, laid it flat on the boulder, before walking to our grassy spot where we liked to sprawl in the sun. I threw my arms behind my head and quickly drifted off with

Mazy pressed against me. My body felt heavy and warm, deep in slumber, dreams of a little girl in pigtails swinging on a swing set skipped in my brain. The feeling of the air rushing past my face, reminiscent of the water flowing over my body. The sound of her giggle filtered through my mind. If only I could reach back in time, back to that last summer of my innocence, and give myself new choices.

"Dee, Dee, wake up," his voice calm and quiet, pulling me out of my sleep.

I felt my body jerk, the voice, remembering where I was, remembering I was naked. I sat up, grabbing Mazy around her neck to hide my body behind hers. She was already sitting up, her tail wagging against my bare leg. Aaron was lying in the grass next to her, he held my beer above his head, and he rocked the can back and forth teasingly. He started to laugh. My face went from panic to annoyance. A string of curse words flew from my mouth. I grabbed the beer from him, finishing off the flat beverage. There was a long piece of green grass hanging out of his mouth, his hair was exceptionally messy, and his plum colored t-shirt made his skin look even lighter. The can fell from my hand and I hugged Mazy a little tighter. He stopped laughing and smiled. I noticed the redness around his eyes and the dryness of his lips.

"Aaron," my body wanted to ask him if he still had a joint. Looking into the deep calm of his eyes, I felt the urge to inhale the sweet smoke of tranquility. Arty telling me not to make promises I couldn't keep snapped me out of it before the words left my mouth. "Why are you walking through my dad's property?" I changed gears in the conversation.

"Are you telling me you've forgotten the shortcut from The Barn?" he eyed me with the experience of an addict watching an addict resist. "I heard some juicy gossip about us in town the other day. Seems a shame to waste all that hot air, don't you think?" he cocked his head to try to look around the dog.

I hugged Mazy a little tighter. "Not gonna happen. We never cared what those people had to say anyway."

"True." He sucked on the grass sticking out of his mouth.

"Why'd you stand M up? You know that sort of thing will always bring you grief." I hated the gladness I felt over his high. Only with him like that could I talk to him again.

"Well, I had to. Once I found out who was coming and the fun they were bringing, I couldn't take her out anymore. A promise is a promise, after all, Dee. Wouldn't you agree?"

His words stirred up emotions in my chest I could not name. Guilt for all of my broken promises. Beyond that, I sensed, gratitude? Appreciation? Thankfulness? They seemed too straightforward. It was more complicated than that. If you mixed gratitude, disgust, and aching, all together that was what I felt for Aaron at that moment.

"I would agree." I buried my head in Mazy's fur.

"Want me to grab your swimsuit for you?" he pushed himself up and walked over to the boulder. The black and aqua suit lay bone dry. He tossed it in my direction, and then kept his back to me while he skipped rocks into the pond. I shimmied into the suit and went to stand next to him, my hair hung over my shoulder.

"Want to know the other gossip that will be flying soon?"

He shrugged his shoulders.

I picked up a flat stone and flicked it across the surface. It caught a good four skips before going under. "The woman who gave birth to me showed up last night."

"Shut up," he turned and looked at me, startled by this revelation.

We just stood there, looking at each other for a long time. He was not nineteen-year-old-high-on-weed-hung-over-Aaron to me right now. He was just that twelve-year-old kid in a black suit standing by his mom. He was looking at me and I was that twelve-year-old girl with braided pigtails, tears rolling down her cheeks, apologies on her lips again. I was not sure how we had fallen so far from those two. I felt uneasy standing there, staring at him. I turned and tossed another rock across the water.

"How long do you think she'll be here?" he had not

stopped looking at me.

"No idea. I wanted to get rid of her last night. Somehow, she ended up sleeping in the guest room. I snuck out of the house early this morning and haven't been back." I bent down and yanked up a small flat rock.

"Mel was always good at bringing those strays in, wasn't he? Your family never could let anyone fall flat on their face. You do know you have to face her, right? You can't outrun everything, Dee."

"I thought that's what we did. Run." I started to walk around the shore, fingering the rock.

He threw a large stone out into the middle of the pond. It landed with a plunk.

"I guess you're right. Maybe I should head back and face the music."

He turned quickly on his feet to catch up to me. "Speaking of music... You ever going to start playing again?" he shoved his hands in his pockets.

"Who says I'm not?"

"I do."

I stopped and glowered at him. "How the hell would you know?"

"You're different when you're playing. Calmer," he smiled. "It softens your edges." There was that twelve-year-old boy again.

I turned on my heels and started to walk away from him. The curve of the pond brought me around to where I could look across the water and see the meadow. I watched Aaron bend down and pick up my empty beer can. Mazy lingered close to him. I let out a whistle for her, her ears perked up, and she darted around the water for me. Aaron looked across the expanse; he gave one quick nod of his head before turning towards the lake, walking back to his house.

16

When I emerged out of the woods onto the lawn I took note of the trucks parked on the drive. I remembered it was Thursday. For the last four years, Thursday night meant family night followed by a meeting. It seemed curious to me that Dad would not have called the evening off.

"Stay," I ordered Mazy before she could run up the steps and announce our arrival. She sat on her haunches and looked up at me. I drummed my fingers on the railing leading up the steps to the deck. If I wanted, I could still tuck tail and run. I knew for a fact that Arty kept his keys in the sun visor. I could just hop in his truck and take off, leave the state, go back to New York, find Ruben. On the other hand, I could do what Dad told me to do, keep putting one foot in front of the other. As Aaron said, I could not outrun this one. God, I wished I had another drink, I was jealous of Aaron's high. I could hear raised voices. I crept up the steps, holding my palm flat behind me, to keep Mazy sitting and waiting. I stopped close to the door where no one would see me.

"You can't stay, Daisy. You need to leave tonight." Arty's voice was firm.

"Arthur, it is none of your concern what I do. Honestly, why are you even here?" Daisy's airy voice floated through the door.

"Why am I here? I'm here because I never left! I stuck around for the last sixteen years of her life. That's a hell of a lot more than you did. I have a right to be here."

"I am not justifying my actions to a jealous old man."

The silence cut through the air like a knife.

"Daisy, what are you trying to accomplish in coming back?" Cadmus's voice of reason entered the discussion.

"You make it sound like I have an agenda to fill while I'm here."

"Don't you?" Dad asked.

"I'm her mother. I just want to know my daughter."

"You gave up your rights a long time ago, Daisy. Dandelion doesn't want you here and I can't blame her. I think it would be best for everyone if you packed up and left."

"I'm not going anywhere."

"Of course, you aren't." Arty's angry tone rose again. "You have to stick around long enough to see if you can cause more damage. Hell, if I stand by and watch you send my Dandelion into a spiral."

"She doesn't belong to you, Arthur."

"She doesn't belong to you either! She's her own person, no one owns her. Just because she isn't my property doesn't mean I won't guard her with my life."

"You always were so dramatic."

"If you loved her, you wouldn't press into her life like this. You would step back and wait for her to come to you. Coming into her life and causing chaos is not going to bring you any closer to your daughter than you have been in the last sixteen years." Cadmus told her.

"Thank you for the free advice from the other fatherless bachelor in the room."

"Free," I called to Mazy. I slid open the door and walked in, she darted past me and up the stairs. I felt the three men collectively brace themselves. I glanced around the room; Cadmus sitting in the armchair, Dad at the kitchen table. Arty standing, arms folded across his chest. Daisy perched on a stool by the island. She flashed me the biggest, brightest, fakest smile I had witnessed in a long time. A vision of me walking over, slapping it off her face, and walking away rushed through my mind's eye. I took a deep breath.

"Where's September?" I asked Cadmus.

"She's upstairs reading in your room."

Daisy waved at me from her perch, her silver bangles clinking against one another. "Honey, where have you been all day? I thought we were going to hang out and,"

"You need to shut up," I cut her off.

"That isn't really necessary," she argued.

"It is." I folded my arms across my chest, my heart rate increased. "These two men," I glanced at Dad and Arty, "have raised me. And Cadmus," I paused. "Cadmus means more to me than you ever will." I swallowed down the lump forming in my throat. "If you refuse to listen to them, you may not stay in my house. If you don't want to take their advice and leave for everyone's sanity, that is on you. But I'm telling you to get out of my house. I'm going upstairs to sit with Sep. When I come down you all better not be arguing about me anymore, and you," I glared at Daisy, "You better be miles down the road." Silence filled the room. I used it for an escape, going up the steps, leaving them to all make their own choices.

I walked to my room and pushed open the door. September sat cross-legged in the middle of my bed. Mazy's head resting in her lap. There were a few of my books sitting around her. Clearly, she had tried to hear the conversation downstairs though.

"Who's that lady?" she queried right when I entered.

"Someone my Pops used to know,"

"That's what they told me. It ain't completely true though, is it? She's yer momma."

I scrunched my mouth up, the term seemed too personal to use for Daisy Rivers. "She is indeed the lady who gave birth to me." I picked up a few articles of clothing and tossed them into the hamper.

"Why aren't yah excited to see her?"

"Because I haven't seen her in many, many years, and it was quite a shock."

"Well, I haven't seen my momma in four years, and I would be excited to see her." She challenged me with her glare.

I sat down on the edge of the bed by her. "That's a little different. Your momma was a good lady who loved you lots."

September mulled this over for a moment.

I pushed the hair away from her face.

She gave Mazy one long sweeping pet down her back before turning back to me. "Have yah ever been in love, Dee?"

"That's a big question. What's making you think about that?"

She cocked her head and bit her lip. "Well," she thought some more. "No one we knows ever been in love. Do yah think we're all cursed or somethin'?"

"September Marie, we are not cursed. And what do you mean no one we know has been in love?" I wished I could pry open her mind and peek inside.

"Name one of our friends whose been in love."

"Well," I fell silent. I ran down my closest relationships, starting at the top. That would be my dad. There were no women in his life that he ever confessed to being in love with. There was lust and passion between him and Daisy for one night, but after that, it was survival. The only reason he let her in was because of me. There was a great sense of relief when she walked away. No, he had not loved Daisy. Then there was Arty. There would be no children showing up claiming him for a dad ever. No men were coming forward to profess their love to him. Arty was tough, and he wasn't someone to fall in love easily. That brought me around to Cadmus. Although he was very capable of love, he was not one to waste it on anyone. I had a feeling Sep and I took up his whole heart.

"See, we don't know what it looks like." She broke my long pause. There was a tinge of sadness in her voice.

"Why are you worried about this?"

"What if there's someone I'm supposed to fall in love with an I miss it? Because I don't know what it looks like, what it feels like?" her green eyes were wide and innocent.

"First of all, you are only twelve-years-old. You have plenty of time to fall in love. I wouldn't lose any sleep over missing out on it yet. Second, you do know what love feels like. We may not all share a romantic love for one another, but we share something deeper. You, me, Cadmus, Arty, we all share a love called philia. Some have said the love of friends is the highest level of love one can know. We don't need friendship to reproduce, but we choose friends because we need them more than lovers."

She smiled at me, pleased with this answer. "Yah never answered me though."

"Have I ever been in love?" I clarified. She nodded her head 'yes'. I paused for a long moment. It felt pregnant, filling the space between us. "I'm not sure. There was one person I felt very deeply for at one time."

"What happened?"

"Life," I grabbed one of the books sitting on the bed. It was my copy of Anne of Green Gables from when I was seven. "Did you read this yet? You should read it next. Anne taught me that tomorrow is always a new day, a day without mistakes. It's all about friendship and family. You remind me of Anne."

Sep took the book from me, disappointment played around her lips. "I'll start it tonight. I'm famished. Do you think we can go downstairs now?"

"The coast is probably clear. Let's do it."

When we entered the family room, the energy felt calmer to me. The table, set for dinner, Dad pulling chicken and rolls out of the oven. Cadmus and Arty were sitting down, talking, and drinking water.

"Do we have anything harder than that in the house?" I asked, pointing to their glasses. The men stopped talking and shot me a look. I could not tell if it was exasperation or annoyance.

"Lemonade?" Arty asked in a teasing tone.

"One drink is not going to throw me over the edge."

"Let's just stick with water for now," Cadmus offered.

"Oh hell..."

"You could just go grab my whiskey from your room," Arty added dryly.

I shifted my weight. September looked up at me; disapproval in her gaze. "What?" I replied, keeping my voice neutral.

"Don't play dumb with me. Do I look like I was born yesterday?"

I shoved my hands in my pockets. "Arty, I didn't steal your booze."

September left my side, sitting between Arty and Cadmus.

Arty let my statement hang in the air. Dad was just at the corner of my vision. I could sense the tension in his shoulders. Cadmus's face seemed to be willing Arty to be wrong, even though we all knew he wasn't. "My mistake then, seems I'm more of a lush than I thought."Dad slammed the chicken on the table and shot me a look to harness it. I pulled my hands out of my pockets and sat down. "Alright..." Dad grumbled, standing behind his chair. He looked at each of us for a moment before folding his hands and closing his eyes. I had grown used to him praying over the last month. It did not feel disingenuous, just not natural. "Please give us the strength to endure this situation, and to find the blessings and lessons it contains. Please give us the endurance to continue ahead. Please guide our thoughts, words, and actions, so that we walk your path of peace and love. Amen."

Everyone replied with his or her own 'amen', except for me, "Path of peace and love? Are we hippies now, too?"

"Dandelion Jane, I will not have you starting more drama than we can contain for an evening. You cannot take your anger out on us. If you want to vent and share your feelings, feel free. Don't harp on me though," Dad answered, coolly.

"Got it, Saint Francis," I stabbed a chicken breast with my fork and dropped it onto my plate.

17

The next week passed about as quickly as a slug through salt. Dad told me to take the week off work. The last thing he and Cadmus wanted was her cornering me in the store. When she left sixteen years prior, she hadn't left any friends behind. Arty railed the night I kicked her out that she would integrate herself back into town. Dad agreed she would have no trouble making herself comfortable and getting people to talk. I was sure she was making a spectacle of herself at the hotel and local restaurants. I went swimming every day, walked in the woods, and ate dinner at Cadmus's cabin when I needed a break. He had removed his liquor from the top cabinet. I cursed Arty when I discovered its absence. Cricket came around a few times. Mostly I was alone, with my thoughts, with no company but Mazy. I felt like a caged bird.

"Didn't one of your favorite authors say that the deeper your roots are the less likely you are to die from storms? Just because Daisy is here doesn't mean you have to let her get to you. You've got deep roots here, your dad, Arty, Cadmus... It'll pass. Whatever this is with her, it'll pass." Cricket had given me this speech the last time she came to the house. I hardly believed her. It was the kind of speech that could only come from an inexperienced friend. Cricket's mom became Principal of the high school my sophomore year. We were both outsiders, both musicians, both needing a friend. Something in me always held back from her. I suppose it was my mistrust of anything female. It wasn't Cricket's fault, she could never understand what Cadmus knew, that the storm of Daisy had the power to destroy me. I was a weed without shelter, a girl without a plan.

The AC kicked on for the hundredth time that day. The temperature had risen to the 100's and would stay there for the rest of the month. July always felt like we lived in hell. The humidity felt like a wet blanket draped on your back. It did not subside until eight at night when the sun went down. The cicadas chirped all day long, drowning out all the other noises of the country. I opened the pantry, grabbing the bag of white bread and the butter dish. I tossed them onto the counter and went for the strawberry jelly in the fridge. I searched the door where I always kept it. Ketchup, yellow mustard, half-and-half, pickles, everything one could want, but no jelly. I pushed containers around on the shelves searching. I straightened up, hands on my hips, and glared into the cold tundra before me. No jelly. I walked over to the trashcan and flicked the lid up. Right on top, sat the empty jar. I grumbled about my father under my breath while the lid slammed closed. A girl could not live without her strawberry jelly. The glass doors leading to the deck reflected my disheveled appearance back to me. Pantless, dirty over-sized white shirt, my brown hair sticking out of my blue bandana. It looked as if I had just rolled out of bed, only it had to be pushing four in the afternoon. I ran up the steps and found some cut off jean shorts, slipped them on while I stepped into my Chucks. I grabbed the keys to my scooter off my dresser and bounded back down the steps. The town had seen me looking crappier than this.

The hot air felt bearable while I sped down the mountain. The scooter hugged the curves, picking up speed after trudging up the hills. Riding down into town was the fun part, heading back up the mountain, not so much. I dashed through the fork in the road and down the main drag. Technically the speed limit was 25 in town, but Sheriff Ritter had better things to do than give me a ticket. I raced through Main Street and around to Fowlers, hoping to fly under the radar, be in and out in five minutes or less. I parked, running up the steps and through the front door. I did not bother to see who was working today. I could care less. The strawberry jelly perched on the top shelf by the peanut butter and honey. I grabbed two jars and moved towards the register.

"Hitting it pretty hard these days?"

"Shut up, M. I'm not in the mood." I slammed a five-dollar bill on the counter.

Her coppery hair glinted in the light. She squared her shoulders, leaving the bill on the counter. "Sharing the extra jar with your mommy?"

"I'm not sharing anything with anyone. And that woman is not my 'mommy'," I replied, irritated with her. A few of the patrons had stopped shopping and were watching us.

"I'm still your mother, even if I haven't been around." Daisy's voice came from the back of the store. She was standing by the soda fountain. I had not noticed her in my hurry.

I closed my eyes and inhaled deeply, leaning onto the counter. "You keep telling yourself that." My eyes opened, "Give me my change M." I could feel the crowd press in around me. They could sense the fight and would not want to miss a word.

"Quit hollering at me,"

"Makayla, I'm not in the mood. I want my change. I want to get out of here."

Daisy was walking towards us now; she was only a few feet from my side. "Dandelion, can't we talk?" she asked.

I shoved my hand under Makayla's nose, if she wanted to move any slower I wasn't sure she could. "Change!"

"Here, bitch." She dropped a dollar and three pennies in my palm.

"You know what? I'm not the bitch in this relationship. Get the hell off your high horse." I grabbed the two jelly jars, "And you!" I turned on Daisy, "Stay the hell away from me!"

"What is wrong with you two girls?" Daisy asked Makayla, it stopped me in my tracks. The glass jars felt cold against my sweating palms. The heat rose to my cheeks.

Makayla laughed. "What's wrong with us? That's a loaded question."

"M, keep your mouth shut,"

A look of pure malice spread across her face. She reveled in the crowd watching the scene. "Didn't you know? Your daughter is the town's fuck up. Just ask anyone. Everyone has a list of things we know she's done." She nodded towards the other patrons, a few nodded back.

Daisy's eyes went from Makayla to me. I steeled myself for the onslaught that would unleash next. I hoped she would be happy after it ended.

"She's slept with every boy in town within two years of her age. Some were for fun, some to fill that hole in her heart from when you left, and some for drugs. Oh yeah, you didn't know? Your daughter's a dirty little addict. She's snorted it, smoked it, and injected it. She just couldn't get enough. She'd do anything to get another hit. She's not only the town druggie and slut; she's also the town thief. She was banned from the other grocery store in town because she's stolen so much property from them. The only reason my parents' let her in this place is because they remember when she used to be sweet and innocent. Most people forgot about that little girl. Of course, she wasn't much better when she was a kid. You couldn't actually call her a murderer but she sure as hell isn't a hero. Best damn swimmer in the county and she stands by while a little baby drowns. Could have jumped right in and saved her. Of course, you asked a more personal question. You asked what was wrong with the two of us. That's a story all its own. The cliff notes would be this: she was my best friend in the whole world, and then she slept with my boyfriend to get drugs."

I tried to open my mouth to protest, but she would not allow it.

"Shut up Little Weed, no one cares what your side is. You were probably too drunk and stoned out of your mind to even remember."

A tear rolled down my cheek. Daisy was looking at me. I could not tell if it was pity or disgust on her face. Everything distorted through my water-covered eyes. "Happy now?" I murmured, pulling myself together enough to flee the store.

The engine on the scooter revved to life. I heard Daisy shout my name, but I did not stop, I flew back through the town. The street was hard to navigate through my tears. There weren't many words Makayla said that weren't true. After all, the best lies were ones with an ounce of truth in them. Like the story of standing by, and letting Kathryn drown. I was there. She did drown. And I could have saved her. We were kids. We were just dumb kids, and it was a dumb accident. It was Fourth of July weekend. Makayla, Aaron, Thomas, and I were playing on the Abbot's dock. Mrs. Abbot told us to keep an eye on Kathryn, but we did not really hear her. The little two-year-old toddled right off the edge into the deep, dark water. Makayla and Aaron were making such a racket horsing around it took us all a moment to register there was a splash. Thomas, who was only six or seven at the time, was the one to realize it. He tried to get our attention. I was the first to hear him, but I did not jump in after her. My body froze. I could not even scream. About time Aaron jumped in, she had sunk to the bottom. It was not my fault. Maybe I could have saved her.

Then there was Makayla's version of what happened between her boyfriend and me. The one time I tried to be a hero and screwed it up. I hated myself for it. For all the stealing, drugs, drinking, even all the boys I had slept with, none of it I regretted more than that. It was the one memory I had tried to bury but never could. It was the decision that left the most destruction. The one time I tried to save someone and the version she believed about it was a lie. The only part of Makayla's story that was true was that I slept with her boyfriend.

My scooter began to lag, sounding like a sick animal with each push of the gas. The mountain seemed to overpower us. I gave it more thrust but heard it splutter. I came to a dead stop.

"What the hell!" I shouted. I slammed my fists into the console and saw the fuel gauge firmly planted on E. "Dammit! Piece of shit day!" I screamed into the air, dismounting, and kicking the wheel.

I couldn't tell what was sweat and tears on my body anymore. Every part of me felt wet and sticky. I yanked the key out of the ignition and the jelly out of the seat. I started walking. I was a good half mile away from where I stopped when I heard a truck coming up the mountain. Relief flooded my body. Anyone coming up the hill would stop and give me a lift back to the house. I turned to watch for it while it came around the bend. The Abbot's silver truck came into view. I turned on my heels and kept walking. No Abbot would give me a ride.

"Hey! Hey!" Aaron shouted at me through his window.

"What?"

"Is that your scooter down the hill?" his truck moved slowly next to me, keeping my pace.

"Yeah, clearly."

He revved the engine and passed me, stopping in such a way to block my path. In one quick motion, he was out of the vehicle, "Word on the street is that you just got verbally smacked down by M." He leaned against the truck, his arms hanging at his sides, cigarette in his hand.

"Yep," I kept walking towards him.

"Having a great day, huh?"

I walked up to him. "No. I'm not. I just want to get home. Now let me pass." For a brief moment, I stood in front of him, looking up into his face; I wondered if he could be that boy he used to be. If I threw my arms around his neck and cried, would he hold me close and tell me he would fight off the monsters?

"I'll give you a ride back." He took a drag off his cigarette.

The light changed, the moment had passed, and there was no going back. "Not willing to pay the price." I started to sidestep around him.

Aaron threw his arm out to block my passing, "Even if it's cheap?" His face was close to my hair, looking down on me.

"That's not a word ever associated with you, Aaron. I'm not in the mood for harassment." I tried to push past him, but he grabbed my wrist. I dropped the jelly, the glass jar shattered on the asphalt.

"Come on Dee, we used to have a lot of fun. It wasn't the worst thing in the world. Come on out and make my birthday the happiest it has been in a couple years." He pulled me in close to his chest. The smell of cigarettes was strong.

I forced my face up. I looked him in the eyes. The fear melted away to anger, "You are my biggest regret."

He flipped my wrist out of his hand and took a step back. "The hell I was."

"We were best friends. I loved you. You used it all against me. Not a day passes that I don't feel regret for what we did. How it hurt Makayla. How you hurt me." A million memories passed my mind. The three of us sitting on the store's steps, Aaron telling us he was going to have a little sister in a few months. Passing the summer evenings in town, playing a game of sardines with the other kids. Aaron sticking up for Makayla and me when the other boys would pick on us. Aaron nick-naming me Dee.

"Don't you ever say that to me; you never loved me. You were just the town slut," He spat back at me, the hurt in his face was palpable.

"I like you better high." I pushed past him and around the truck. I prayed for him to turn the truck around and head back down. The first prayer of mine ever to have an answer, I heard the engine start and disappear behind me.

I had not slept with Aaron to get drugs and Aaron never dated Makayla because he liked her. After Kathryn died, Aaron stayed away from us. I was never sure if it was from anger or guilt. The truth was it was probably both. Just how I could barely look at him and not cry, he could barely look at me and not see his baby sister in a casket. It drove the three of us mad. A year later when Sean McCall asked me out and soon after asked me to bed, I gladly said 'yes'. It seemed like a great way to escape the pain of that summer. The problem was it did not help. It just made my life worse. I had to start sneaking around and lying to my dad and Arty. I hated myself. I broke it off with Sean, but next, it was Billy and then Rob. They just never stopped coming around. I once tried to say 'no'. It was not a well-received response from Graham. After that, I decided it was better just to give in than to have your control taken from you. When we started drinking, I thought I had found the answer. Once I was drunk, nothing hurt. Soon it started to fade. It just made me angry and ugly. It did not take me long to realize the kids who were drinking in The Barn weren't just drinking. I stumbled across Aaron, high on weed. He asked me out, and I told him 'no'. I broke my own rule. It seemed like a safe thing to do with him, I knew him, and I trusted him. Something had twisted inside of him though. He pretended to be okay with it, to walk away. A week later, he had started dating Makayla. I knew it would only be a matter of time before he had her doing drugs. I could not let that happen. I hadn't saved Katie, I couldn't save Aaron, but Makayla was still mine to fight for. One night I went to his house, I begged him to break up with her, to leave her alone.

"Oh Dandelion," he crooned in a drunken slur. He pushed my hair over my shoulder. "I promise to leave Makayla alone."

"Really? Thank you, thank you, don't drag her down with us." I knew I could still trust him to save us.

"I just ask one little favor."

We went down to the lake. He told me to do a line of coke first. He promised it would make the whole thing that much better. I hated myself. When I found myself back at his house a week later asking for more drugs, I knew I could not sink any lower.

I was no hero and Aaron wasn't a nice boy. I suppose we really deserved each other.

When I got home, drenched in sweat, exhausted, and sick to my stomach. I placed the jelly jar on the counter by the bread and butter. Mazy licked my hand before I started up the stairs to my room. I kicked my shoes off, stripped my clothes, and climbed under the covers. Dad tried to get me up when he got home that evening. The sun was setting, I could tell from the golden rays coming in through the window. He was shaking me and telling me to get up. I moaned and rolled over, falling back asleep. The next morning, while it was still dark out, he tried to rouse me again. I refused to give in to his demands. By noon, he sent Arty over to check on me.

"Dee, you have to get up, Babe. I'll make you some food. Just get up."

"No," I told him firmly, throwing the cover over my head.

I stayed in bed for days.

18

On the third day, Mazy came into my room after Dad left for work. She grabbed the edge of my blankets and pulled them away from the bed. It left me exposed and naked to the room. She sat a few feet away from my face and started growling at me. I opened one eye and glared at her.

"You think you can force me out of bed?"

She barked.

I did not break my eye contact with her.

She barked louder.

I rolled over to the other side of the bed.

I felt her jump up next to me. I expected her to give up

and lie down. She was stubborn like the rest of us. I felt her cold, wet, nose push under my back and side. She began shoving my body with her head.

"Mazy! Stop it!" I shouted. If a dog over a hundred pounds decided that it wanted to push you off something with their large head, you really couldn't stop them. After one more shove, I flipped onto the hardwood floor with a thump. She snorted at me, jumped down and stuck her face in mine, licking me twice. "Fine," I pushed her face away from mine. "I'm up. Happy now?"

I picked up my aching naked body and walked down the hall to the bathroom. I turned the hot water on and stepped into it. The water ran down my face and chest for what felt like an eternity. The blue bath puff hung in front of me, taunting me, my hand felt heavy at my side, too heavy to pick up and grab the sponge. My eyelids closed, the water rushed down my face. The aching in my back lessened with the heat while my legs grew tired of standing. I grabbed the soap and scrubbed down my greasy body. I finished, patting down with a towel, and wrung out my hair. I left the towel on the floor and went back to my room. I found some gray sweatpants and a sports bra splattered with color. I slipped them on and let Mazy usher me down the steps. When I came to the landing and looked into the family room, I saw Cadmus sitting in his normal spot, a book in his lap.

"Traitor," I murmured at Mazy. She snorted at me.

Cadmus did not break his gaze with his reading, "There

are bagels freshly toasted in the kitchen."

I came down the last three steps and walked to the kitchen. I grabbed half of a cinnamon raisin bagel and went to sit on the couch across from him. I quietly picked tiny pieces of bread and popped them in my mouth.

After five minutes of this, he closed his book and looked at me for the first time. "Have you eaten before now?"

"Nope."

"Been out of bed at all?"

"Nope." I pushed my wet tresses over my shoulder.

"Is this how you wish to finish out your existence?"

"If I'm only here to take up space then why not? Let's just make it as short and painless as possible."

"You were created for a great deal more than this."

If someone else told me this, like Arty or Cricket, I would have hurled some sarcastic response back at them. It would not be true coming from them. They loved me, but if they were honest, they could not tell me beyond a shadow of a doubt that my life meant something. It was not part of what they believed about the world. Cadmus, though, Cadmus did believe it. I heard him preach it to September; I heard him talk about it with my dad. The core of Cadmus believed that we were created to do great things, and he believed he was part of helping us find out what it was.

"You need to remember that. You should go for a swim, get outside, refocus your mind."

"Stop making me swim! Why is your answer and Pops answer always, 'go for a swim', 'go on a walk', never feel the pain, just wash it away with the pond."

"Dani, you know that is not what I'm telling you to do. I want you to get your head back in the game. Why don't we go to a meeting tonight?"

"I don't need a meeting, Cadmus. I need to feel safe in my own house."

"I'm sorry Daisy showed up."

"It isn't about Daisy."

"What then?"

"It's this town, this place. I should've never come home. No one here will ever see me as anything different than a screw-up."

"Make them see you for who you are now."

"They don't care, Cadmus. No one here cares. They decide who you are by the time you're thirteen, and it will never change. The people who hate me will always hate me."

"Those are not the people who define you though."

"Aren't they? It sure seems that the things they expect

from me are what they end up getting in the end." I twisted my mouth around in a scowl.

"Perhaps you are looking at the wrong people."

"Your standards, your expectations, they're too high for me." I pushed myself up from the couch and retreated to the deck.

"Dani, the only thing I have ever expected from you is for you to be the best version of yourself," he called after me, "to love yourself and to love your music."

I did not stop walking until I made it to the woods. I let his words fall behind me. If I was honest I did not love myself, hell, I barely liked myself. I seemed to be a contradiction. One moment I could hold my resolve and stand up to the Daisy Rivers of the world, while the next I fell to pieces. There was talent in my fingers, but no drive in my heart. One moment I craved spontaneity and fun, but all the while, I wanted to know what it all meant. Most days I just wanted to peel away my skin and cast the world aside. To be frank, I was not sure what to do with myself.

The maple tree stood in front of me, the same one I hid in when I was fourteen. I grabbed a hold of the lowest branch, feeling the thick, rough bark against my skin. I pulled my torso up, feet scraping the trunk of the tree, legs trying to throw themselves over the bough to secure my spot in the branches. It was less than graceful and for two split seconds, I thought I would pitch myself over the branch and land on my head. Once my body positioned itself on the limb, I scooted my back against the trunk of the tree. I would not suspect my dad to remember this hiding place, and Mazy was not able to get at me. I hugged my knees to my chest.

Daisy. It was close to two weeks since her arrival. I hoped she had eaten at the diner. Archie would have given a good report of me. Her showing up, demanding to know about me, it made me sick. At least the town was a part of my life and thus entitled to know most of my story. Popping in for the cliff notes was just insensitive. The lining of my stomach felt thin. It could break at any moment from the thought of it all.

Weed would make this all better.

I waited in the boughs until I heard Cadmus leave in his truck a few hours later. I jumped down to the grass and walked back to the house. Mazy was sitting inside the door waiting for me. If dogs could smile, I swore she was, pleased with her work of getting me out of bed. I grabbed another half of a bagel and inhaled it on my way up the stairs. Before I made it past the landing, Mazy's bark startled me. I turned, bending down to peer out the front window. I could make out Cricket's tall figure walking down our lane. My eyes rolled, I jumped down the three steps and opened the front door, leaning on the jam.

"What brings you down my lane?"

"Cadmus called."

Of course, he did.

"He said you needed a friend."

"I'm fine. I'm pissed but I'm fine."

"Doesn't misery like company?"

She had made it up the steps and stood in front of me, her black ringlets hung loosely around her face. "I was just on my way out to run an errand."

"You aren't going to go running to Aaron and get drugs."

"Who said I was?"

"Your history," her gaze locked onto mine, the way Cadmus's would when he told me not to drink or to go to a meeting. My eyes averted towards my feet. "I swear I'll let you drink, but I'm not letting you get high today."

My chin titled up, a smile spread on my face, "Drinking sounds fantastic. Only problem is there isn't a drop of liquor in the house."

"Well, maybe that's providence."

"Thanks, Marilla Cuthbert."

"Who?"

I opened my mouth to respond then thought better of it. "Never mind. Are we stealing from your mom? I always wanted to steal from the principal. God. The guy before your mom was an ass. If he hadn't moved away I would say we should go steal from him."

"Dani, I'm not stealing from my mom."

"Well, I've already taken from Arty and Cadmus."

Cricket shook her head, "I can't believe this."

"What? How else was I going to take the edge off when I've been stranded in this town?"

Cricket rubbed her eyes.

"We could take my scooter into town and you could chat up Makayla or Mrs. Fowler while I nicked some."

"Because we couldn't just buy it?"

I tilted my head. Cricket was adorable in her innocence. "Remember how neither of us are 21 and everyone in town knows that? They won't sell to us. It would be easy to lift."

"No."

There would be only one way to get my hands-on booze without stealing it or leaving town. It meant making a call and paying more than I wanted for beer. Cricket and her moral compass were really putting me in a bind.

"Fine. We have one choice left. I'm gonna have to make a call."

"I already told you, you aren't allowed to go to Aaron."

My fingers quickly pulled up the contact on my phone and hit the call button. I slipped it up to my ear, "Aaron isn't the only dealer in town, Cricket. Aaron would never sell me beer anyway." I heard his raspy voice on the other end mutter a hello. Not even mid-afternoon and he seemed stoned out of his mind already. "Hey, Sean."

"If it isn't my favorite little weed. What can I do you for?"

"I'm in a bind and I need some beer. Can you meet me at the docks in an hour?"

"It'll cost ya."

"I figured. See you soon." I slipped the phone away from my ear. "Happy?"

"Not really."

"You get to call Arty."

19

One call from Cricket and Arty agreed to let us use his boat for the evening. Sean McCall showed up around the docks an hour later, he had always been true to his word. His curly red hair made him easy to spot. I pushed a wad of money into his palm and he passed me a case of beer. He slipped the money into his pocket and pulled a plastic bag out of the other.

"Can I interest you in some other merchandise?"

My hand went for the bag, but Cricket stopped it mid-air. "She's good with the beer. Get lost Sean."

He put his hands up defensively. "Whoa. Just checking in with old clients. No need to get testy. You've got my number if you change your mind."

We were lying on the steer in our bikinis with empty beer cans around us. I was ranting about every mistake I had made in my life up until today. Cricket listened, nodded, and offered sympathy at the appropriate times. The thing I loved most about her was her gentle way of listening and never offering advice. The boys all tried to fix me. Cricket just let me talk.

"I swear to god, I don't know what to do with myself. I'm just one big fuck up."

"No, you aren't." She replied. "Those are Makayla's words, not yours."

I sat up; tossing my empty can into the trash bin. "But seriously, what the hell am I doing? What am I going to make of my life?"

"What does Cadmus say?" she sipped her drink.

"He tells me I can do anything I want. I have the power to change the course of my life. That I just need to have love for myself. Bull crap."

"Why's that bull crap?"

"Because, why would anyone love me? You just heard all the reasons why no one should touch me with a ten-foot pole. If someone on the outside can't love me then why the hell would I love me? I have to live inside this mess."

"Well, we love you." She sat up and smiled at me.

"You all must be delusional." I laughed, grabbing another beer, and popped the top.

"You'll figure it out. I know you will."

A few hours later, I dropped Cricket at the dock closest to her house. She wanted to go with me to Arty's dock to drop the boat off; I convinced her I was fine. Once she was out, I opened another beer and threw it back while I navigated the black water and skies. The light on the end of Arty's dock shone brightly when I pulled up. I cut the engine and drifted over to the side. I leaned out and grabbed for the rope hook. My blurry vision and fuzzy head miscalculated the distance and without warning, I had tipped myself over the side of the boat and into the water. When I broke through the surface under the dock, I burst into a laugh.

"Dammit Dee," I heard Arty grumbled.

I paddled my way out from under the dock, "Why are you here?"

"I was worried about my boat. I pulled in a few minutes before you got here. Glad I did so that you don't drown yourself like a damn fool." He leaned over the edge of the dock and grabbed my hands. I could not stop myself from laughing. I was not sure what I was even laughing at. He didn't try to pull me onto the dock. Instead, he dragged me by my hands over to where the water met the land.

I fumbled my way up and out while Arty went back to tie his boat up.

"Don't tell Pops, okay?" I told him between laughs. I was lying on the grass, holding my stomach.

"I won't need to tell him. You think he's some kind of dupe. Come on," Arty pulled me up to my feet. "You're coming home with me for the night."

"You are the best," I slung my arm around his neck and kissed his cheek.

"I'm something alright," he grumbled.

"Who needs a mom when I've got you?"

He opened the truck door and deposited me onto the leather seat. "Indeed."

I stopped laughing when we were a few miles from his house. All the sudden the world did not feel funny but cold. "Do you have a blanket?" I asked him.

"We're almost home. Don't throw up in here."

"I'm not gonna throw up," I told him angrily. I slumped down and fell asleep on the seat.

I woke up the next morning in Arty's guest room. The sheets felt scratchy, the lighting was much too bright, and my head, pounding. I sat up slowly and realized Arty had laid me on top of the covers on an old bath towel. No way he would strip me out of my wet clothes, I supposed he did not want me soaking through the bed either. Typical. I closed my eyes and rubbed them with the heel of my hands. I had not felt this hungover in years. I did not even have any good stories to make it worthwhile, like a stranger asleep next to me. My eyes opened. I realized I wasn't in clothes. I was still in my bikini. I groaned. I had wanted to walk to the hardware store and borrow someone's vehicle to go home and clean up.

"Dammit Arty," I heard myself complain while I groped my way to the bathroom.

"Don't you start cursing me, Snot. I saved your ass last night," He yelled at me from the other room.

I stopped walking. I tossed my head back and moaned. "I didn't know you were here."

"What was I supposed to do? Leave you half-naked in my house? Do what you need to do in the bathroom then get out here. I have a special drink for you." I detected amusement in his voice.

I curled my lip up in a snarl. Arty's hangover remedy was the worst. There would be no way around drinking it though. One time he literally forced the hot liquid down my throat. I never asked him what he put in the concoction, but if I had to guess, it was a lot of hot sauce and raw eggs. The horrible part about it all is that it worked.

Ten minutes later, I emerged into the kitchen. "Where's my glass?" I asked.

Arty slid it over to me. "Drink up you lush."

I closed my eyes and chugged the contents down, forcing them past my gag reflux.

"Can you please tell me this will not start to be the norm again?"

"You and I both know I'm not much good at promises." I sat down at the kitchen table.

Arty came and sat across from me. He pushed a bag of saltines in my direction. "That is something you could change. Start now it's a fresh day. Make a promise, and then keep it."

"I hate to break such a good record." I nibbled the corner of a cracker. A look would come across Arty's face once in a blue moon. The muscles in his jaw would set, the wrinkles on his forehead would deepen, and the glint in his hazel-gray eyes would fade. When it happened, I knew I had crossed the line. I knew when I looked at him and watched every muscle change in his face, that I had crossed that invisible line today. I swallowed my cracker and looked down at the table.

"Dandelion Jane, I love you like my own daughter. I love your spirit, your spunk, and your love of people. Could you please tell the rest of the world to f-off and learn to love yourself? To not care what they all think of you."

"Can we save the lecture? My head is pounding." I put

my head in my hands, my hair falling around my arms.

"Fine, I just don't think I can do this anymore." I heard his chair squeak across the floor.

"Don't think you can do what? Inconvenience yourself by making me a crappy hangover remedy?" I looked up at him, spite on my face.

"I don't think I can watch you self-destruct anymore. Now get up and go get in the truck. I'm dropping you off at the store and going in to work."

"Fine by me. I didn't ask for an audience." I stomped out his front door like a three-year-old throwing a tantrum, eating my crackers the whole way.

When we pulled up to the store, Arty did not even put the vehicle in park. He idled a few feet from the curb. I hesitated before opening the door, I knew I should apologize, but my lips would not open. I pushed the door open and hopped out, slamming it behind myself, and did not watch him pull away. I walked into the store where September, Cadmus, and Dad all looked up at me from across the room. September's face dropped when she saw me. She had seen me in this state before. Dad just shook his head and pulled his keys out of his pocket. He tossed them across the store at me.

"You can't stay here like that. Go home. Don't come back unless you can work."

"Yes, sir," I caught the keys and Cadmus eyes at the same moment, "Hey."

"Dee, I don't care right now. Just go home and change," he told me, and he went back to stocking shelves.

I glanced around at the three of them. They were still doing the same things they had done before I came back. I may have stepped into a role for a month or two, but my purpose, my existence, absorbed into nothingness. Cadmus was even back to calling me by my old name. Not the name he gave me after I cleaned up. I hung my head and walked out of the building. The truck door squeaked when I pulled it open, the engine turned over, loud and rumbling in my ears. My stomach suddenly felt hollow and ravenous. Craig Fisher caught my attention. I was backing away from the store, he was on hands and knees with a bucket of soapy water, a scrub brush in his right hand, and he began scrubbing the cracks of his driveway. I wondered when he would ever stop trying to keep that piece of concrete clean. The scene was still playing in my head when I walked up the steps to Jo's Diner.

"Hey Dee," Archie said. "We've missed seeing you around." He pulled his pen down from his ear and clicked it open, "What are you ordering for everyone today?"

"Just here for me. Can I get a burger and fries to go?"

"Sort of early for that, Dee. How about some breakfast food?"

A sigh passed my lips, my eyes scanned the mostly empty diner, and they landed on the last person I wanted to see today: Daisy. She sat towards the back, in a booth, magazine in front of her face, and a cup of coffee next to her.

"How about some hash browns and bacon?"

"Coming right up," I heard the pen click closed, Archie stuffed my order in the window. I found myself walking towards Daisy.

"Let's get this over with. What do you want from me? What will appease your curiosity enough to leave?"

She looked up startled. Her green eyes were round and wide. Her lips broke into a smile, a smile that looked familiar; it was like mine when I smiled. "Sit." She waved her hand towards the empty booth across from her.

My arms folded in front of my chest, "I'm good, I'm waiting for my food, so I can get back to work."

"Melvin allows you to work looking like that?" her eyes scanned my haphazard appearance. "I know it's a hick town, but wow, I thought Melvin had better standards."

"Don't ever say anything bad against my father or this place."

Daisy looked at me with as much motherly instinct as she could fake. "What if I don't want to leave? What if I want to come back and rebuild a life with you?"

"Bull shit."

"Why would that be 'bull shit'?"

"If you wanted a life with me you wouldn't have left. You would have called. You would have sent a letter. You don't give a crap about me and you never have. That's why you came all the way from St. Louis to this pokey little town. You had to pawn me off on someone, so you could go live your life. What the hell do you want from me now?"

"Honestly, Dandelion, I want to get to know you. Everyone in this town seems to know all about you. They have all been generous in their sharing of their tales of you. My, my, you have had a colorful life, haven't you? I always knew any child of mine would be a free spirit. But wow. You take the cake, sweetheart." She picked up her coffee and took a sip.

"Dee, your order is up!" Archie called to me from behind the counter. My eyes could not pry themselves away from Daisy. She sat composed, drinking her coffee, watching me. She had no idea that what she said could hurt me. My stomach lurched.

"Just remember, there are two sides to every story," I told her, turning on my heels to grab my order.

"Every story has two sides and there is truth in both." I heard her voice carry through the building towards me, my hands clamped onto the Styrofoam container and I made my way out the door.

20

When I arrived home, I should have gone straight in and cleaned myself up. Instead, I parked the truck, leaving the container of half-eaten food on the seat, and left for the docks. If you walked past the pond, you would come upon the northern bank of the lake. Even the people who did not own property on the shorefront owned docks. The only family in town who had a house close to the water was the Abbots.

The northern end of the lake scattered with them. Dad had let quite a few families build on his property and did not charge much rent. Some of the other families were more particular about who could build and who could not. There was our dock, Arty's was farther off to the east, and Makayla's was between our house and the Abbot's. Cadmus had a dock close to ours. I always thought it was odd that Dad kept his private one when we hadn't owned a boat, ever. I supposed he wanted to hold onto it just in case.

I walked to the edge of the rickety wooden planks and sat on the edge. The water stretched out before me for miles. The rolling hills seemed to cut into the water, plunging into the depths. The water churned and swirled with the wind. The skies were dark gray. They looked ominous with the rolling clouds. A storm was just what I needed to wash this all away.

The skies opened with a slow drizzle. I kicked my feet back and forth in the water. I heard someone step onto the creaky wood and turned, expecting to see Cricket or even Arty. When Thomas Abbot came into view with his gray zipper hoodie pulled over his messy hair, headphones on his ears, it didn't surprise me, even though it should have. He raised his hand in a shy wave when I looked at him. I smiled back. He took his headphones off and sat next to me, cross-legged.

"Hi Dee," his voice sounded like it had dropped another octave since we last met.

"Hey Thomas," I replied, turning my focus back to the water.

We sat silent, watching the waves, feeling the cool rain on our skin. It should have felt uncomfortable to sit here with him, but it didn't. Something about it felt natural and familiar.

"So… I realize I shouldn't ask you this…" he began.

You are safe. You are fine. I told myself.

"Aaron needs help…"

"Thomas," I looked over at him, my eyes were pleading with him to stop there and not go any further.

"I know." He held my gaze. "But… you're the only person who actually cares about his wellbeing next to me. He's not listening to me. I'm just his little brother. Maybe if you talked to him."

"Thomas, I'm not any better than your brother." I shook my head. The idea of me saving Aaron sounded like a comedy.

"Yes, you are, Dee." He cut me off. "You were always the strong one."

I paused. I hadn't thought of myself as strong in a very long time. "I don't feel so strong anymore, kid. This summer crapped on all of us."

"Well," his chest filled with air while he pulled himself straighter. "Don't let it win. Fight back."

I repressed a smile. Thomas trying to act tough was like watching a puppy attack a beetle. "I'm sure Aaron will be fine. I mean, everyone goes back to school in what, two weeks. He will clean back up and go get his straight A's. He always comes out on top."

"I don't think you understand," Thomas pleaded, "he hasn't used since before rehab. I don't know that he can clean up without someone telling him to."

I looked back at Thomas. His face was sincere, concerned, there was something in his eyes like a tired panic. The same look September gave me that morning. "If I go talk to him it'll only make it worse. You should go beg Cadmus."

"I know he's a dick to you, but your opinion is the only one that matters to him."

"Well, he's sort of up a creek then. Because you're right, your brother treats me like trash. My opinion of him is that he is a dick. If I could never see him again, I would be happy. Let him kill his brain cells and drink his pain away. That's what the best of us do, kid."

Thomas watched me. He had a way of making me feel exposed with those piercing eyes. "You don't mean a word of that."

I pulled my back straight. "Yeah, I do."

He stood up. The drizzle turning into drops on my head. "No, you don't. You've always wanted the suffering and lies to stop." He started to walk down the dock away from me. "Dee," he turned around, and I looked back at him. "I never blamed you for Katie. I just want you to know that."

I winced. He walked to the end of the dock and jumped

down into the wet grass. He went back towards his house, headphones on, hands tucked in his hoodie. I turned back to the choppy water. "Fudge," I sighed. The last thing I wanted to do was go see Aaron. The pleading of a teenager was too strong a pull for me. If Cadmus had not saved me, I would be dead. Hell, Aaron would be dead. There was no way in good conscious I could not go and try to right this wrong. I should have just gone, gotten dressed and gone back to work.

The clouds had opened completely now. The rain became uncomfortable. It would take me longer to go home, change, and then head to The Barn. What did it matter? I would just go there first, yell at Aaron, feel at peace with my half ass attempt, and then go home. I promised myself I would only stay for five minutes. I needed to prove my family wrong and make it back to work. Thomas was right; I could fight this.

The Barn, the popular place to get high among the kids in town, an abandoned barn on Tim Brewer's property in the middle of the woods. If you were looking for a stoner, you knew they would be there. I started walking east back into the woods. The cover from the trees gave me some reprieve from the storm. I treaded lightly through the densely covered forest floor. There were not any well-worn paths in these parts for my bare feet to navigate. It was a short walk before I could see the dilapidated building. I didn't hear any voices or stirring sounds; I may luck out and find it empty.

Luck and I were perfect strangers today. When I come up to the front, I saw the door left ajar. I walked up to it, gave it a good tug, and entered. The floor littered with bottles empty of their alcohol. The smell in the air was unmistakably marijuana.

"Well, well, well, look who's here." I heard Aaron say. I surveyed the scene. He sat towards the back, a cigarette hung out of his mouth. He looked terrible. His jeans were dirty from sitting on the ground, his shirt stretched, his dark hair disheveled on his head, and his usually clean-shaven face had a five o'clock shadow showing through.

I frowned. When I entered the sight of Rob and Graham passed out off to the side gave me a start. The rain hitting the tin roof intensified. The inside of my brain could feel each pelt of water. I tentatively stepped around them. "You look like hell, friend."

"You've looked better yourself." He patted the ground next to him.

I sat down by him, keeping a wary eye on the boys, and exhaled. He offered me a cigarette. I waved my hand, "You know I hate those things."

"People change."

"Apparently not."

He grinned. "Why are you always right?"

"Thomas came to see me."

"I bet he did," Aaron complained, his face lost that mischievous grin I loved.

"He's worried about you."

"Everyone is worried about us, Dee. They always have been. They always will be." He took a drag from his cigarette.

I fell silent. I glanced around at all the bottles, hoping to see one still full. Just my luck, they were all empty. "What are we gonna do about it?"

"No clue." Ash fell from his hand.

"Can you answer me one thing?" I flicked a piece of hay across the barn.

"Shoot."

"Why this summer? Thomas said you have been clean for years. Why now?"

"I could ask you the same thing." He exhaled smoke into the air.

I went to reply, but he cut me off.

"Don't say Daisy. And don't lie and try to tell me you've been fine. I see your eyes. You haven't been fine in weeks." He would not relinquish his gaze. "You know the answer just as much as I do. The question was what are we going to do about it? Or rather, what are you going to do about it?"

I would have liked to tell him I did not know what he meant; that the last straw for me was Daisy. I could not hold my finger in that dam any longer. That without a plan everything fell apart around me. However, he was right, that would be a lie. All I wanted to do every time I saw him was numb the pain. Every interaction with Makayla made me want a drink.

"What do you want?"

He reached across the space between us, brushed my hair gently away from my face. "What I've always wanted. For the pain to go away. The memories to fade."

I knew what memories he wanted to fade. They were the same twisted ones I had nightmares about, even years later. The drinking and drugs had twisted everything that was good between us and turned it to cinders and ash. "Aaron, I can't make your pain go away. God, I wish I could."

"No, you can't," he conceded, tossing his cigarette butt.

I stood up; brushed the dirt and straw off my bare thighs. "I just wanted you to know that Thomas is worried about you. Hell, I'm worried about you. We could still make a plan you know." I tried to sound brave, but my shoulders sagged, and my voice sounded tired. I moved towards the door, past Rob, and Graham. I made it out into the rain before he grabbed my wrist.

"Dee."

I turned back to him, "What?" the rain was splashing from the leaves onto our skin and hair. The sound of it falling on the ground, hitting the bark of the trees, churning the water of the nearby lake, it was like a symphony to my ears.

"I hate myself for everything I've done to you. I thought it was all over, that I was over it all. Seeing you again just made it all too real. Fuck, none of this is any fun without you." He looked tired around the eyes.

"Aaron, don't do anything stupid," I pleaded with him.

"I'm not going to do anything stupider than I normally do."

"That doesn't make me feel any better. Why don't you come home with me? Those two are not going to be awake for hours. Hang out; sober up, then head home. Go hang out with Thomas tonight."

"Nah. There's only one reason I would go home with you, and that's not part of the deal."

"Aaron."

"I promise not to do anything stupid, Dee."

I realized he had let go of my wrist, but our fingers had become entwined, it grounded me to the spot. Everything around me faded away, I felt his smooth skin pressed against mine. "Just," I hesitated, "come with me." I pulled his hand with mine, turning on my heels to go through the woods.

"Don't do something stupid," he told me, letting me drag him through the forest.

"I'm not."

He squeezed my hand, "Yeah you are."

I continued to drag him through the woods with me.

"In an hour I'm going to be sober and mean. You told me yourself you only like me when I'm high."

"Well, stay high for a while then. I'm not leaving you in the woods like this."

"You'll regret it."

"I know."

21

We walked up the deck hand in hand, soaked to the bone. Mazy was sitting inside the kitchen watching us come up. Her tail waged excitedly back and forth. I slid the door open, and we walked in, dripping all over the hardwood floors.

"Hey Maze," Aaron said while she licked his hands.

"Mazy, stop," I scolded her. She would not leave him alone.

"It's fine, Dee. I've missed you girl," he crooned at her. She was going wild over him.

I watched him standing there, soaked, smiling at my dog, and my dog loving on him. It felt like we were two little kids coming in out of the rain. My arms broke out in goose bumps from the cool AC air hitting my skin.

I rubbed them frantically with my hands. "Ok, I need to go put clothes on, and we need to find clothes for you."

"I'm fine." He scratched Mazy's ear.

"Aaron, you can't sit anywhere while you are soaked. I'm sure Dad has something you can wear for an hour. I'll toss your stuff in the dryer." I told him matter of fact. "Come on, let's go find you something." I started up the stairs. He patted Mazy's head and followed behind me. We went into my dad's room, I started rummaging around in his dresser. I found some gray sweatpants and tossed them at him. "Here put these on," I walked over to his closet and started looking for a smaller size t-shirt.

I found a white shirt stuck in the back of the closet. Dad was more of a jeans and a dark-colored shirt kind of guy. I turned around to hand it to Aaron. He was standing behind me in the sweatpants and no shirt. I had seen plenty of boys half-clothed or not clothed at all, but something about it embarrassed me. I could feel my cheeks go red. I walked over and handed him the shirt.

"Here," I said, he took it out of my hand. "I'm going to go change." His hand slipped under my downcast chin and raised it up. My eyes met his. I did not feel like a kid in his presence anymore. My arms wrapped around his neck, I stood on tip-toe and pressed my lips against his. It was our first kiss not coerced in a long time. He pulled me closer, and I kissed him harder. In the past when my lips met his, I filled with self-loathing. It became a familiar feeling of trepidation. This felt different. It felt private. No strings attached. Spontaneous. Wasn't it? What had Aaron said in the woods, that I would regret taking him home? How could he know what would happen? Was I that predictable in my unpredictable behavior? His palms pressed against the small of my back, my fingers played with the hair close to his neck. I heard Mazy barking downstairs. He pulled away from me, leaving me wanting more.

He leaned his forehead against mine, "You should go get dressed."

I pulled away from him, "What?" Of all the boys in my past, there was never a history of one of them not pushing for more. There were no passionate kisses left unexplored. No warnings for where things could lead. Just that it would always push further, faster, rougher, and lonelier in the end. I found myself angry with him. Of all people to put the brakes on, of all people telling me I wasn't worth it. He had been the one taking for far too many years.

"You don't want to do this. We both know that. You have never wanted that from me. Go put your clothes on." He reached his hand out to touch my cheek, but I pulled away from him. I could still hear Mazy barking downstairs.

"What are you doing?" the words fell from my mouth mingled with disgust.

"You're still just kissing me for a drug."

My hand raised and slapped him right across his cheek. His skin went red. There was a flicker of fire in his eyes before he laughed and rubbed his face.

That cold hard look replaced the softness of his face. "Of all the things I've done, getting slapped for that one is surprising. You are a piece of work Dandelion Sanders."

"You have no room to talk."

"I don't think I have ever pretended to be something I'm not. You always knew what you got with me. Right now, though, you are a completely new kind of low. I tell you not to sell yourself out for a hit, and you get mad at me for not delivering." He paused. If I didn't know him better, I would have thought he was collecting his nerve, "You will never see me, as anything, but your dealer. Whatever it is you want you will expect to get from me."

"That wasn't what that was about."

"It wasn't?" he looked at me with mock surprise. "Oh baby, you really are delusional. If it isn't a beer, it's gonna need to be some drugs, and if those don't work, you'll bet all your money a boy will. Well, I'm not that boy."

Mazy came running into the room, barking her head off, "Quiet!" I yelled at her. She went behind me and started pushing me towards the hallway. "What the hell?" I yelled at her, she continued to shove me towards the steps.

I ran down them and met Daisy standing in the foyer. "Get out!" I screamed at her. Aaron had come down the steps to see what was going on.

Daisy ran her eyes up him and down me. "Sorry to interrupt the afternoon fun and games."

My blood boiled. "Why are you breaking into my house?"

"The door wasn't locked, I knocked, and no one answered. Now I can see why." She watched Aaron.

"You didn't interrupt anything," Aaron replied coolly. He pushed past me with his wet clothes, he had not put the t-shirt on, "I'm throwing these in the dryer while you two catch up."

I wanted to slap him again.

"I came by to see if you wanted to talk more." Daisy was saying to me.

"Did I leave you with the impression I would want to chat again?"

"I went by the store and Melvin told me you had come home. I thought that maybe you were sick or something. You didn't look too wonderful at the diner this morning."

"I'm not sick. I had to run an errand before I came back to work."

"Run an errand?" Daisy's eyebrows flicked up, "Is that

what the kids are calling it these days?"

"The door is behind you, feel free to use it. I need to go get dressed and get into work." I turned to leave.

"I thought maybe you could tell me your side of the story. You didn't seem very pleased that I had heard it from everyone but you."

My body slowly turned back around, "I'm sure there is nothing more colorful I could add to their stories of me."

I heard Aaron come up from the basement and start to rummage around in the fridge and pantry. She was trying to peer around the corner to see what Aaron was doing. He sat down at the table with chips, bread, peanut butter, and some pickles.

He glanced at me, "Don't worry, I didn't touch your damn jelly."

"Why don't you just help yourself," I complained.

"Thanks, I will." he popped open the bag of chips and crunched down on one as loudly as possible.

"Is there anyone in town you get along with?" Daisy mused.

Aaron laughed. I frowned at her.

"She's not a real 'best friends' kind of girl."

"Shut up, Aaron." I came down the steps and stood

between them. "Daisy, this isn't a great time."

"It never seems to be a good time for you."

"Well, you're the one who just showed up out of the blue."

A light bulb seemed to flick on inside Daisy's brain, "You're Aaron Abbot, aren't you?" She pushed past me.

"The one and only."

"Thank god," I muttered.

"You seem to be a perpetual theme. In all the stories about her," Daisy told him.

"I bet I am." He shoved a chip into his mouth and grinned at me.

"I haven't figured out what you are to her. Best friend? Boyfriend? Enemy?"

"We're all still trying to figure that one out."

The two of them together was my worst nightmare come true. It was like my reoccurring dream from when I was four and fell into the creek. In my nightmares when my lungs choked on the water spilling into them and I wanted to yell and scream but couldn't. I wanted to run and hide, but my body would not move. My head felt like a fishbowl sloshing with water. They continued to banter back and forth about me while I waited for a savior. That was not real life though; people did not come to your rescue when you had made your bed.

"Have anything to add to that?" Daisy asked me.

"What?" I mumbled.

Aaron laughed at me.

"Oh goodness," Daisy said under her breath.

"I... I..." My hands broke out in a cold sweat. "I can't do this," I found my legs and took off out the front door. I jumped into Dad's truck and peeled out down the driveway. I had no idea where to go, anywhere but here.

I drove for three hours before stopping. The needle on the gas gauge was nearing empty. The first gas station with attached convenience mart I saw, I swerved off the highway and pulled in. I rummaged around in the glove compartment until I found Dad's emergency money he kept. It was a plastic bag taped to the top of the compartment. My fingers found the edge. I stuck my nail under the corner and started to work it away, I pulled enough off that I was able to yank the bag down. I pulled out the wade of twenties and counted it up, over a hundred dollars. Dad did not play when he stuck that in there. I pulled out forty and went inside. I walked to the back of the store where some t-shirts with deer heads in camo silhouettes hung. I yanked off a small and looked around for shorts, no luck. I walked to the front where the cashier stood eyeing me like a crazy person.

"Twenty on the pump with the truck, do you have any shorts?"

"Uh, no, not really a clothing store." He replied, taking my money.

"Whatever." I got my change from him and stomped out of the store, throwing the t-shirt on over my head.

After the tank filled, I pulled back out onto the highway. I continued heading north with no real destination in mind.

22

The highway wound through the rural countryside of Missouri. I pushed the accelerator down farther, watching the needle move closer to eighty. Here and there were dots of civilization, for the most part, it was fields, cows, and hay bales. I glanced at the clock it was past seven in the evening. Soon the sun would dip down on the horizon. I decided I needed to find a place to crash for the night and figure out where I was going and what I was going to do. I passed a sign telling me I still had twenty miles to go to Kirksville. Surely, there would be a small motel outside the city. I slowed my speed to keep a lookout for anything promising.

After another ten minutes of driving a green sign with

Motel written on it and an arrow pointing right popped up. I hit the brakes and made the turn. I followed the country road until the motel from the 60's came into view. There were three cars parked in front of the building. The main office lit up with lights, and a TV played on the wall. I looked down the row of rooms, about fifteen in total, it looked mostly empty. I grabbed the cash out of the glove box and marched to the front desk.

"Hello," the man behind the counter greeted me. I took note of a woman sitting on the couch, watching TV, she looked me up and down, frowning.

"Hi, can I have a room for the night?" I asked.

The man behind the desk hesitated, watching the woman on the couch, "Uh, well, we are sort of booked up."

"Are you sure you don't have one room? I'm only staying the night," I asked again, setting my bag of money down on the counter.

I watched him eye the money and then shoot the woman another glance. He looked back at me, "I'm sorry Hun, I don't think we have anything. Maybe drive into Kirksville."

I slammed my fist on the desk, "Are you serious?"

"Honey, we don't rent to your kind," the woman piped up from the couch.

"My kind?" I snapped. "So, females? You know what, whatever." I picked up my money and went out the door.

I floored it out of the parking lot and down the road. I made a left onto the highway before I realized my mistake. I slammed on the brakes and did a U-turn in the middle of the road. The red and blue flashing lights caught my attention in the mirror a moment later. "Fudge," I pulled the truck over to the side of the road. I rolled the window down. The trooper came to the side of the truck.

"License and proof of insurance, miss," he said to me behind his sunglasses, "You pulled an illegal U-turn back there."

I forced a smile on my face, "Hi, sir, I'm really sorry. I know I should not have done that. I got turned around and went for the easy fix. I promise to not do that again." I gripped the steering wheel.

His lips went into a thin, stern, line, "Are you trying to get out of a ticket, miss?"

I swallowed hard, "No, sir."

"License and proof of insurance then." He held his hand out.

I opened the glove box and found Dad's extra card for insurance. I handed it over to the trooper. He kept his hand out and looked to be losing patience with me. "Funny story," I took a breath, "I just realized I left the house without my driver's license. Must have left it in my other bikini." I chuckled, nervously.

He glanced at the insurance card, "This is registered to a Melvin Sanders. You don't look like a Melvin to me. Doing a little joy riding, miss?"

"No, sir! That's my Dad's. This is his truck. My name is Dani, I mean, Dandelion Sanders."

"Dandelion?" he pulled his sunglasses down on his nose to look at me better. "Who the hell names their kid after a weed? Does he know you're driving the truck?"

"He gave me the keys." My eyes felt so wide I'm scared they will pop from the sockets. Every interaction with Sheriff Ritter from my teenage years flooded my mind. He had always told me things had a way of coming around and biting you in the butt when you least expected it. I would sit at his desk, reading my D.A.R.E. manual, rolling my eyes, mouthing 'screw you' every time he turned his back.

The trooper studied my face for what felt like an eternity, "What is your social security number, miss?" I rattled the nine-digit number off to him, "I'll be right back."

My head fell back against the headrest. "Fudge..." I exclaimed as I remembered the ticket I received in New York and never paid. My hands covered my face as it fell towards the steering wheel. The only time I had driven in the entire two years I was away. Ruben and I had rented a car and taken a drive around the state. It all started when I had the urge to get out of the city, I told him I couldn't breathe anymore surrounded by buildings. On our way home, a cop pulled me over for speeding. Why hadn't I just paid that damn ticket?

After ten minutes of waiting, I heard the tread of his boots walking back over to the truck, "I'm going to need to ask you to step out of the vehicle, miss." He told me. "You made an illegal turn, you are driving without a license, and you have a suspension on your licenses for unpaid tickets out of state." He waved his fingers at me, motioning for me to come out.

"What the hell? No! I am having the worst day ever. All I want to do is find a motel and get some rest," I pleaded.

"Miss, you need to exit the vehicle for me."

"Why? Why is this my life? Why can't I just have something go right?" I felt myself unraveling.

I watched him reach his hand down and put it on his holster, "I'm going to ask you one more time to exit the vehicle, miss."

"Oh crap," I reached for the door handle and climbed out of the cab. I put my hands up instinctively.

The trooper turned me around and put my hands behind my back, cuffing me and walking me towards his car. "You have the right to remain silent. Anything you say can and will be used against you in a court of law..." He continued, pushing my head down to clear the door jam.

The only question going through my head was who

would be my phone call: Dad, Arty, or Cadmus.

The feeling of familiarity as I sat in a cell no bigger than 10x9 feet wide raised a great deal of resentment in my chest. A sense of déjà vu floated in the air. A cot attached to the concrete wall with iron chains, the toilet made from steel, hung on the wall as well. The top of it was a sink. It reminded me of a very odd drinking fountain without a spigot. I sat on the edge of the bed in yellow prison pants and my white, camo, deer head shirt. The officer told me I did not need to wear the matching yellow shirt from the jail, but my bottom half needed to cover up. I folded my hands in my lap while I waited for him. The trooper had not been so much a dick as someone who saw the world in black and white. I tried to calm my mouth down on the ride to the jail. I did not need to dig my hole any deeper.

The officer in charge, Officer Lewis, finished paperwork at his desk and came over to the cell with his keys out. "Alright, you get a phone call." He told me while he unlocked the door. I stood up and shuffled over to him. "Come on," he led me over to his desk and made me sit on the chair by the phone. "Tell me the number."

I bit my lip and thought about this for a moment. Logic told me I should call Dad, he would need to sort the truck out. My heart wanted to call Arty because I didn't think he would lecture me this time, he would sit quiet in his disappointment. I knew in my head that the best compromise would be Cadmus. I told the officer his number and waited for him to hand me the receiver.

"Hello," Cadmus said.

"Hey."

"Where are you? Are you alright?" his voice rose with panic.

"I'm fine. I'm really fine."

"Where are you?"

"I'm in a jail outside of Kirksville. I need someone to come bail me out, probably Dad because they think I stole his truck."

"Why didn't you call him?" Cadmus asked with a tinge of frustration in his voice. "Are you on anything?"

I rubbed my forehead, "You know why I didn't call him. Can you please tell him and come get me? And no, I'm…" I glanced at Officer Lewis, "fine."

"Dani, it is going to take us six hours to get to you, and it's already well past eight. You are going to have to stay the night."

"Cadmus!"

"No, Dani, you did this, you're going to have to live with it for a night. We'll be there in the morning." His voice calm but firm. "Try and get some sleep." He hung up the phone.

My jaw dropped in frustration. The officer raised his eyebrows at me and took the receiver out of my hand.

"Not what you wanted to hear?" he asked.

"Not exactly," He walked me back to my cell and locked the door behind me.

"Maybe it'll be good for you. Maybe you need some tough love."

"Thanks, Dr. Phil," I let slip before I could stop my smart mouth. He had a good sense of humor and chuckled at me.

"I'll turn some of the lights off. Try and get some sleep kid."

I grabbed the paper-thin pillow on the cot and tried to fluff it up. A useless endeavor. I laid back and stared at the white tiled ceiling. This would not be my best story when I was a grandma.

The next morning, I woke up to a new officer putting a tray of oatmeal and toast in my cell. I had tossed and turned most of the evening if I had to guess I had only managed a few hours of sleep within the last wee hours of the morning.

"Rise and shine," he told me.

I grabbed the tray from him, "Thanks," I pushed my hair out of my eyes.

"Officer Lewis informed me you have someone bailing you out today. I'm Officer Green, by the way," he walked back over to his desk.

I picked at the toast for a while before dipping the spoon into the oatmeal. It was bland and tepid at best. I decided not to complain, it didn't seem like my place to. I managed to eat most of it. Worse than the food was realizing that I had to pee out in the open. I watched Officer Green for a solid two minutes. I decided the paperwork had engrossed him completely. I dropped my pants and squatted. My nerves making it, so I could hardly urinate. My eyes bored holes in the back of his head. When I stood up and pulled my pants up, I vowed not to drink any more water until my ride came. Dehydration I could deal with. After an hour of staring at the wall, I asked Officer Green if he had any magazines I could look at. He told me jail wasn't supposed to be fun. It felt like a violation of my rights, but I did not argue with him. Lunch tasted worse than breakfast, chicken noodle soup out of a can. I began to wonder if their microwave worked or if he purposefully left it sitting out for ten minutes before handing it to me. Around two, I fell asleep out of pure boredom.

"Dandelion Sanders, you are being released. Get up," said Officer Green.

I heard him unlocking the cell. I sat up and rubbed my eyes. Across the room, on the other side of the counter, I saw Dad, Cadmus, and September looking back at me. I grinned. They just glared back. No one said a word when we walked out to the parking lot. I hesitated between walking to Cadmus's truck or Dad's. "Thank you, both of you, for coming to get me, for bailing me out, again."

"Dandelion," Dad's face looked tired, the wrinkles had deepened in twenty-four hours. The sea in his eyes looked calm and composed. "I'm sorry. I haven't figured it out yet, but I believe I have somehow punched a hole in you that makes you the way you are. You keep trying to fill it up and every time you do, you wind up even more empty."

The proposition that I ticked the way I did because he built me wrong, my brain could not process that now. I wanted to tell him how mistaken he was, that he never did anything wrong by me. I had been born broken.

"I'm taking Sep with me. You ride with Cadmus." He walked to his truck.

September threw her arms around my waist. "I'm just so glad you're okay," she said before running after Dad.

I stood speechless in the parking lot with Cadmus. We watched Dad pull out before he told me to get in the vehicle. I obeyed, silent and humiliated.

23

The first hour of riding in the truck together we spent silent. After Dad's speech, the thought of opening my mouth scared the shit out of me. I could not figure out if he was angry, disappointed, or just tired of me. The best option seemed to be to wait until he decided he wanted to talk.

When the second hour had slowly ended and ticked into hour three with still no words spoken, I thought about asking him to start yelling at me. I managed to bite down on my tongue before I did.

However, by hour five, I could not stop myself from breaking the silence.

"Cadmus," I began.

"Dani, I don't understand why you came home and decided to throw all your hard work out the window. I knew seeing the old gang would be hard. Daisy showing up really threw a wrench in everyone's life. Those things didn't need to make you tuck tail and run or go get drunk. That's why we wanted you to make a plan. You can write a new story for your life. You don't need to keep repeating the past and the mistakes you've made. You can keep moving forward. You need to let us in to help you."

Clearly, he had this speech planned for most of the trip and had been waiting for his cue to speak. "I know," I replied.

He glanced at me. I realized he had prepped for a fight.

"You're right. I should have had a plan. I shouldn't have been naïve about it all. I should always plan for the worst." I tugged the shirt down around my thighs.

Cadmus rolled his shoulders, "I should have pushed you more, I wanted to give you space."

"Cadmus, you know you can't push me. It isn't anything you guys did or didn't do. It's me. I'm just great at falling apart."

He pulled against the steering wheel. "You don't have to be. You don't need to keep repeating the old pattern. You are worth more than that. I know you don't believe that. I know you don't act like it. You sell yourself short."

"I don't actually. I really am not worth that much. Do you want to know what happened yesterday afternoon?" I could feel my fuse ending, "Aaron rejected me."

Cadmus winced.

"Yup, I don't know that I can sink much lower than that. What do you think?"

"I don't think you should be offering yourself to Aaron."

"Why not, what does it matter? Everyone in this town has had a taste of me. What's wrong with offering myself to someone when I just want to feel something? I just want to feel something good instead of chaos. The last month has felt like an unraveling. I just wanted to feel something familiar. I wanted a little bit of home." I hugged my sides.

"Your home is filled with much better things than Aaron."

"True, but he doesn't expect anything good from me. He sees me for what I am. When he looks at me, he can see the pain, the guilt, the addict, and he doesn't flinch. You know why? Because when we look at each other we're looking in the mirror."

"I'm not going to go along with that. You can be so much more. Yes. Those things are part of your story, but they don't need to be your whole story. Let the past stay behind you. It doesn't have to define who you are tomorrow or the next day. Don't etch that persona in stone."

"My personality flaws aren't going anywhere. It's who I am. We can't all be perfect." I turned my face away from his.

"I never asked you to be perfect. I only asked you to strive for more."

"Striving for more backfired."

"No, no, it did not. You had a setback. Everyone has setbacks, what makes people great is when they keep striving forward." His palm beats against the wheel.

"Maybe I don't want to be great. Maybe I just want to have fun."

"Don't say that. We both know you want more than that."

"Do I? It seems like the more I try to make more of myself the farther I sink under the water. I was abandoned to a small-town life. Maybe it's time to accept that." I watched the cornfield out the window, each row blurred into one long muddle of green. The individual stalks blended in with the crowd.

Cadmus paused for a long while before responding, "I'm done arguing with you."

"Good."

"Dani, be more."

He always had to have the last word in an argument.

I let it drop. Thirty minutes later, we pulled into town. The streets were mostly deserted. There were a few kids running out in the front lawns trying to catch fireflies. We passed the hardware store, and I noticed Craig was sweeping his driveway off across the street.

"Can you drop me at Cricket's?" I broke the silence.

"No."

"What?"

"I said no. When was the last time you showered? You've been in nothing but a bikini for how many days? You can see Cricket tomorrow."

"Fine Dad," I spat back. He did not respond.

We drove up the mountain. I watched the trees pass quickly out of my window. Every few yards I caught a glimpse of the town below us. I let out a yawn, realizing how exhausted my body felt. I wanted to crawl into my bed and stay there for a few days. Cadmus pulled down the gravel drive to the house, the rocks crunched under the wheels. He stopped behind Dad's pistachio green truck. September came bounding down the front steps with a sandwich in her hand. I hadn't realized we had fallen that far behind them on the drive.

"In the truck, Sep," Cadmus called out his window.

She frowned at him but knew better than to argue. I slid out of the passenger's door without a word. I patted her on her head when she walked by. They did not say a goodbye; I did not give him the satisfaction of looking back before I went into the house. I expected to hear Dad in the kitchen. The house was quiet and the small light at the foot of the steps was on. I sighed and flipped it off, stomping up the steps. I knew the message, but tonight, I did not care. Dad's bedroom door sat ajar when I came into the hallway. I walked over and pushed my way in. He sat on his bed, his reading glasses perched on the edge of his nose, a book in hand.

"What do you want, Dandelion?" he did not look up at me.

"I thought maybe we could talk." I stood in the door-way.

"I said my piece at the station."

"Pops…" I shifted my weight. I knew how to do this with Cadmus and Arty, not with Dad, we didn't share our sentiments.

"Let's sleep on it. Emotions are running high tonight."

I could feel my chest heavy with each breath. "Fine," I started to pull the door closed when he spoke up.

"I expect you to be back at work."

"Yes sir," I shut the door.

The next morning, I woke up with Cadmus's words ringing in my ear. "Dani, be more." I slung my feet over the edge of my bed. I grabbed some shorts and a tank top off my floor. I knotted my hair, on the top of my head, slipped my shoes on, and stomped down the stairs. Dad had already left for the day. There was a plate of waffles on the counter wrapped in plastic wrap. I popped them into the microwave and drummed my fingers on the counter, losing myself in my head. When the machine beeped, I jumped and cursed under my breath. Mazy rubbed up against me, trying to help me settle my nerves. "Go away, Maze," I complained, pushing her away with my thigh.

I slammed the plate down on the counter and picked at the edges of the food with my fork. My stomach felt hungry and nauseated simultaneously. The idea of filling it with all this dense food was exhausting. After the first waffle, my stomach could take no more, I tossed the remaining two in the trashcan.

The idea of hanging out with Cadmus and Dad for an entire day was not giving me the warm and fuzzies. I yanked my satchel off the hook by the door along with my keys. I pulled my hair down, shoved the helmet on, and fastened it under my chin. My scooter took me down the drive and out to the road where it should turn left to head out of the valley. Instead, I found it going right. I was going to need some help to make it through the day.

The driveway at the Abbot's sat empty. Not surprising.

Mr. Abbot was never home. He spent all his time out working on projects or checking up on his properties. Mrs. Abbot had hardly lived in the house for the last four years. I wondered if Thomas stayed around or went out doing whatever it was he filled his time with. I hoped he would not be here. I parked my scooter by the steps and walked up onto the wraparound porch of their log cabin styled house. The front door seemed to glare down at me. I stood hesitating in front of it. I still had time to change my mind and leave. Before I could decide, I realized my finger had already pushed the doorbell. I turned on my heels to bolt, but before I could make it one-step off the porch, the door opened. I turned around sheepishly and smiled at their housekeeper. I forgot they had hired help. Of course, they did. They were the Abbot's after all.

"Hi, Miss, can I help you?" she asked with a wary look.

"Is Aaron around?" I took a step closer to the door. I wished I could hide my face.

"He's upstairs, sleeping."

"Right," I gritted my teeth.

"Do you need me to show you where his room is?"

"Nope, I got it." I jumped at the chance and walked as quickly as possible around her and up the large staircase behind her. I made a left and hurried down to his room at the end. I did not bother to knock on the closed door. All I wanted was to be out of sight before anyone else knew

I was here.

His room, almost as large as the first floor of our house. The floors were wood with ornate rugs scattered under the bed, by the closet, and under chairs, that sat by the window. The flat screen TV hung on the wall opposite his bed, a good 75 inches wide. Clothes scattered all over the floor and furniture. His ceiling fan whirring over my head, blowing my hair around my face and neck. Aaron sprawled on his stomach under his sheet on his bed. The top half of him visible, his skin was bare, his leg dangled off the side of the bed. I gently shook his shoulder. He groaned and swatted at me with his arm. I shook him harder.

"Go away, bitch."

"Not until I get what I came for."

His head jerked up. His hair stuck up haphazardly. His eyes were bloodshot. A deep crease ran down his cheek from his pillow. "What the hell?" he sat up on the side of his bed and the sheet fell away. "Why are you here?"

"Hi to you too," I backed up and sat down on the window seat. I glanced out into the backyard. I threw rocks at this same window years ago.

"Did you have fun taking off the other day?" he rubbed his face trying to wake up.

"Not really." I fiddled with the frayed edge of my shorts.

"I wouldn't think so. You looked like a lunatic running

out of your house." He ran his fingers through his hair, shaking his hands, making it stick up everywhere.

"Thanks. Did you and Daisy have a good time after I left? You seemed to hit it off nicely."

He smiled at me. "Your mom is a real piece of work." He stood up and went to his bathroom. He left the door ajar. "Why are you here, Dee?"

My palms felt sweaty. I rubbed them on my shorts. The inside of my mouth seemed to fill with cotton balls. It seemed like a good idea to come, but now that the words needed to leave my mouth, I was not sure I could do it.

"Didn't I tell you you'd be asking for it by the end of the summer? You held out long, it won't be long before everyone leaves." I heard the toilet flush and water turn on. When he came out, he was wearing that mischievous grin.

"I almost made it," I agreed.

He walked over to his nightstand and pulled out a bag of weed, "This is all I have. How you paying for this?"

I grabbed the plastic bag from my dad's truck out of my pocket.

"Wow, real currency. I haven't sold to you that low in a long time."

"Well, if I'm not buying coke I'm not sleeping with you for some weed." A ting of disappointment came out in my words. I pushed the money into his palm.

"You want some coke?" he wet his lips.

"You got any?" the words left my mouth like lightning. My heart rate accelerated.

He shrugged, "I can get my hands on more."

We stood in silence. I shifted my weight on my feet. I stood on the edge of the rabbit hole staring down into the darkness. I knew this plunge well. The taste of euphoria on the tip of my tongue.

Aaron wagged his head, "It's been a long time since you did any coke."

"Yeah," we grew quiet again watching each other nervously. If I told him 'yes', I was agreeing to more than drugs. The hesitation in his eyes mirrored mine.

"Why do you need the drugs, Little Weed? Mommy getting under your skin too much?" the thought there, the taste in my body, and the seed planted. I knew it would not need any watering to grow. We both knew where this would lead. I grabbed the bag of pot out of his hand and went for the door. He slapped my butt when I walked out.

"I'll see you soon," he called after me.

I closed the door behind me and ran out of the house. When I made it to the top of the mountain, I stopped my scooter. My hand shook while I opened the plastic bag.

Aaron had left his papers in with it. I took one out with enough weed to roll and lit up. Every thought in my mind came to a sudden halt. Every nerve in my body relaxed. I exhaled and closed my eyes. Now I could face that hardware store full of men.

24

The outside of the store looked vibrant - the red door brighter than a fire truck, the white on the windows crisper than a bleached bed sheet, the paint peeling around the windowsill looked sharper, the texture deeper. The smell of potting soil, wood chips, and grease hit my nose in full force when I opened the door. It was overwhelming in a way that left me wanting more. Cadmus was stocking seed packets while Dad rearranged the wood. I did not see September in her normal perch. I could hear the silence. What everyone else was missing, the scratch of my feet on the floorboards, the rustle of the seed packets, the soft touch of Dad's palm against the plywood, even the dust settling on the windowsill had a sound. Why had I ever given this all up?

"Good morning, Dani," Cadmus said without looking up.

"Morning," I replied, a giggle on my lips.

He stopped with the seeds and looked over at me, his stare narrowed. It reminded me of a cat when they were trying to decide if they should pounce or not. I tried to hold back a laugh unsuccessfully.

"Where's Sep?" I asked, walking back to the counter.

"She went swimming with the Cooper kids," he replied, watching me walk down the aisle.

"Dandelion, come help me with this," Dad said while he struggled with a large piece of wood.

I walked over to help, concentrating on what it was he needed me to do seemed impossible, there were distractions all around. I ended up standing there just looking at him, my head cocked to the side, confused, while he fumbled around with it. The texture mesmerizing. The light in the air captured the dust flying.

"Dammit girl, give me a hand!" He hollered.

"Okay..." I muttered, shaking my gaze away from the dust. I put my hands out to steady it, the wood felt coarse and gritty under my palms.

Dad managed to slide the wood into the slot with minimal help from me. He turned around. His face was red from the effort, "What is wrong with you?"

The seemingly sudden outburst caught me off guard.

I supposed the anger he felt towards me about the truck and the whole getting arrested thing hadn't subsided yet; although, that felt like a lifetime ago, and I did not understand why he could not let it go. I suddenly realized his face looked rather like a beet with the color it was. I burst out laughing. "I'm fine. I think something is wrong with you though."

Dad shot Cadmus an exasperated look. Cadmus walked over. His palms took up my face gingerly while his eyes studied my face. Dad threw his arms in the air and walked out the backdoor cursing while he went.

"Dani, are you high?" Cadmus put his dark palms on my shoulders.

"I'm fine. I feel better than I have felt since before Juilliard."

"Let's sit down. I'm getting you some water." Cadmus pushed me onto the stool behind the counter. He came back with a glass of water that he insisted I drink.

"Cadmus, I'm really fine." I took the glass of clear liquid, enthralled by the bubbles floating to the top of the cup and popping. "I'm better than fine. I'm fantastic."

"You really aren't. When was the last time you smoked?" he pulled over another stool and sat in front of me.

I took a sip of water. It tasted like purity, clear, cool, purity hitting my lips. "Dunno…"

Cadmus leaned in. "Did he give you anything else?"

A smile broke out on my face, "Not yet."

He sat back, "Dani, you don't have to do this. Daisy will leave soon, I promise. Aaron is leaving for college, in what, a week. We can hang on for that long. You'll get back to swimming, working, maybe you should start playing that piano Arty bought you." He talked in a warm, even tone.

"But now I remember how much fun we can have around here. Why did I ever let you convince me smoking was so bad? It isn't. I don't want Aaron to go away and leave me alone again." I took another sip of water. I could hear the trucks on the street outside, the low rumble of their engines.

Cadmus put a hand on my shoulder, "He doesn't have your best interests at heart, sweetie. He enjoys watching you fall apart. It makes him feel better about himself."

I shook my head at him, "I'm not falling apart right now. I told you, I'm fantastic. Now, Aaron, Aaron is falling apart, not me."

"I'm going to take you home now."

"What? Why? I don't know why you would ask me to come to work if you didn't really need me." I sat the glass down on the counter harder than I anticipated. The sound of the glass hitting the thickly polyurethane wood reverberated through the shop. "I'll drive myself back."

Cadmus laughed, "Dani, you can't work when you're high. And you certainly are not driving yourself home."

"How many times do I have to tell you I feel great? I'm taking my scooter home." I found myself walking down the middle aisle and out the front door.

Cadmus trailing behind me, "No, you aren't. Get in my truck. Step away from that scooter." By now, we were standing in front of the store, my hand on the handle of my scooter.

"Whatever," I let my hand fall and turned to his truck, climbing in, I slammed the door closed. "Can you do me a favor and stop babying me?" I asked. He pulled the truck out on the road.

"Now that is something I don't think I have ever been accused of," he said humorously. "I usually get yelled at for the opposite, you know, having a stick up my butt, or acting like a drill sergeant. I need to remember this day."

"Don't make fun of me."

"I'm not making fun of you."

"Ok."

"Ok," he shook his head and looked back at the road.

We rode the rest of the way in silence. The peace flooded my brain again. When we pulled up to the house, Cadmus watched me go up the steps and into the house.

He grabbed the phone out of the kitchen and set it next to me on the couch.

"Mazy, keep an eye on her," he patted her head. "You," he looked at me. I tried to focus on his face but something about it looked funny. "Stay put. If you need us, the phone is right there. I have to go back to work. Just, stay in the house, alright?"

I nodded.

Cadmus shook his head and locked the door behind him. I listened to the truck pull down the driveway and leave. I was suddenly ravenous and walked into the kitchen. An hour later, I had plowed through most of the junk food. I found myself lying on the couch, eating strawberry jelly straight from the jar, my head pounding with a headache. I inserted my earbuds and cranked up the music on my phone. I closed my eyes and dozed off.

I woke up to Cricket sitting across from me reading a book. I sat up and rubbed my pounding head. "Hey," I muttered pulling out the earbuds, "When did you show up?"

"Cadmus called me, asked me to come check on you."

"Right," I stood up and went into the kitchen.

"I think you ate enough, there was trash everywhere when I got here. What do you want now?" she called over her shoulder at me.

The kitchen looked immaculate. Cricket loved to clean when angry. "Thanks, I need some aspirin and water." I opened the cabinet by the sink and pulled out the bottle of medicine. I put three into the back of my throat and chugged down some water. I walked back to the couch and lied down.

"So, that was a stupid choice," Cricket told me.

"What, eating the junk food? The boys want me to get fat, so I'm not too worried about it." A grin broke out on my face.

"Don't play dumb with me. Why do you need to start drugs again? You totally had your crap together. Remember? The last two years of high school were good." She emphasized the last word.

"They were a lot of hard work." I slung my arm over my eyes.

"It was a lot of hard work that paid off. Not everyone gets to go to Juilliard, you know. God, I was so jealous you got in, and I didn't. If I would have put in the work, you did... Maybe... just maybe... All I'm saying is when you put your mind to it you can do some pretty amazing things, Dani."

I pulled my arm away from my face and looked across at my friend. Her hands were running through her hair, pulling it away from her face in frustration. "Notice how I couldn't cut it at school? My miracle years are over.

I'm ready to take that hardware store over from Pops, just how everyone in this town predicted. Don't dump your crap on me. You want Juilliard that bad, try again."

"I'm not. You know I am not. I am happy where I am. I just don't want to watch you throw away your life because of your stupid mom being a bitch and Aaron using the opportunity against you."

"She's not my mom and don't talk about Aaron." I pushed up on my elbows.

Cricket's hands fell to her lap, "What is it with you two? What is the draw for you? I don't get it. I never have. He is just this manipulative little prick. Yet, you love him. Why?"

I shrugged.

Cricket exhaled loudly.

"Ugh," I rubbed my arms frantically, "I haven't felt this anxious in years. I want to crawl out of my skin."

She leaned back in her chair, "Well, maybe you should make better choices with your life and start with real anxiety meds."

I pointed to the door, "You can leave now."

"Fine," she stood, grabbing her bag from the floor and slinging it over her shoulder. "I did my duty to Cadmus; I made sure you hadn't choked on your own saliva or anything." She started for the door.

"When are you going to confess your love to him?" I added in a spiteful tone.

"What?" she stopped and glanced down at me.

"You are so fast to do whatever he asks. Just get it over with and jump him. Be done with it." I felt ugly, but my mouth ran on.

She opened her mouth to say something then shut it quickly, thinking better of it. She shook her head and went out the door.

Mazy came over and laid her head on my lap. I scratched behind her ears. "At least you still love me," I cooed at her.

25

The weekend passed uneventfully. Cricket sent me a message, she was sorry for yelling at me. I managed to apologize for my words, a feat in and of itself. The house sat quiet during the day while Dad went to work on Saturday. He spent all of Sunday at Arty's house. Monday, he told me to stay home, take some time off, until the kids went back to college. No one spoke of Daisy, I was not sure if she had decided to leave town yet or not. I craved a break from the monotony. Instead, I filled the days sitting on the deck or laying in the meadow getting high. I rationed out the bag of weed to last for days. I contemplated making a booze run.

The August heat equaling unrelenting, like July. The air full of the sounds of insects. The skies dotted with white and gray clouds. The breeze carrying a storm on its shoulders. It whipped my hair around my face, bending the wildflowers to the ground. The humidity stuck to my skin while I laid in the meadow coming off my morning high. The last smoke from my stash.

The year before I was in Central Park with Ruben, a day similar to this. The humidity not what it is here, nevertheless, the heat radiating off the buildings was just as merciless. We had found a nice, open, grassy spot and laid our blanket out. He read to me for hours. We drank iced coffee from my favorite little coffee house down the street from the school. At the end of the first school year, I had moved into my first apartment. I started waitressing at an upscale restaurant. How I would keep up with working full time and do school was weighing heavy on my mind. Ruben twirled my hair around his finger. He continually told me that it would all work out, just the way it should, that the cosmos would be good to me if I was good to them. The problem with that, I owed too much back debt to the cosmos.

I sat up, grabbed a Black-Eyed Susan, and broke it off at its stem. I twirled it around in my fingers, letting the fragrance waft off and hit my nose with each turn. The water on the pond choppy, the wind picked up. It felt like a lifetime had passed since I left New York and came home. It felt like years had passed since I had heard Ruben's voice. Cricket had told me to call him, at the time it did not seem wise. Now though, maybe he had started to miss me. Time was a healer of pain and mistakes, right. I should go home and call him. I thought, letting the flower drop out of my hand and I stood up.

The insects in the woods seemed to be growing in their noise, awaiting the oncoming storm. It drowned out every other sound while I walked on the moss-covered path. Mazy had stayed behind today, allowing me to tread discreetly past the wildlife filling the woods. A doe even met me at the pond when I had arrived. A few squirrels skittered when I came upon them. My eyes watched them run up the maple tree. My mind darted to wondering what Ruben would say when I called him. The worst he could do was hang-up on me, I decided. I could live with that. I would at least know where we stood.

The skies looked angry and gray about time I came out of the woods. I was sure a storm would start at any moment. I began to run towards the house.

"Dee," called a deep rough voice.

My head jerked around. I stopped in my tracks. I located the voice on the east end of the woods. Rob was heading towards me. My back stiffened. I scanned the area for Graham. They rarely traveled without the other.

"Aaron sent me," He continued, stopping a yard away from me, "He wanted you to know he's got it. Party time is tonight." The skies opened, and rain beat down on us. He gave me one last look before darting back into the forest.

I ran up the steps and into the house.

The sound of the rain on the roof faded to white noise while my brain fought with itself. Smoking weed again was one thing. Surely, it was not my smartest play, but it certainly was not that harmful in the grand scheme of things. Did I dare show up tonight and plunge back into that world? The town would be clearing out, leaving me in peace. Maybe one night of a good party would not hurt that much. It would just be one night after all. With him leaving, I would not be able to get my hands on anything easily. It did not mean I would start a habit again. It was just one more hit. One more hit until next summer. Who knew where we would all be in a year. I might not even be here. It could be our last bang before parting ways. I started to hear the voices of the men in my life, telling me why it was a terrible idea. There was no fighting their logic. The thing was I knew it was a bad idea, but it could still be fun. That's what they did not seem to understand. None of them seemed to remember what it felt like to be young. To live safe brought you no closer to adventure, you should live fast, hard, and dangerous. That's what made the good stories. That's what living was all about.

Thursday, which meant family dinner. Even Cricket came. I supposed she really was sorry for our argument. The house smelled of grilled cheese. Dad had grumbled all late afternoon about how he could not grill with the storm. I got tired of listening to him and offered to run to the store for different ingredients. Pops began to raid the pantry and refrigerator, coming up with the alternative without sending me out. It started to feel like lockdown around here.

"Come play with me!" September begged. She sat on the piano bench.

"Fine, fine." I obliged by sitting next to her and playing the accompaniment to "Heart and Soul". It was the most I had pecked out of the keys in weeks. I felt a tinge of regret for not taking advantage of the gift from Arty.

"Now, play something real." She grinned at me when we hit the last note. I felt the house go quiet around me.

"Oh Sep, I'm so out of practice. You don't want to listen to that."

"Yes, I do," she insisted.

My heart quickened. It felt like a lie. To sit with them, to smile, to know tonight I would leave and party for one last time. It did not seem right to give them hope by touching the pearly whites.

"I'm sure you remember your favorite piece," Cadmus told me.

I did. I knew I did. I could hear each note swirl in my head. The feel of my fingers running along the keys. It was still in there. I swallowed hard and turned back to the instrument. My hand trembled and I reached for the notes. It began quietly, my fingers moved slowly across the keyboard. It grew in sound and strength. It felt like a release to let it out, like a deep sigh of breath I had been holding in for too long. When my fingers came down on the last note, I second-guessed my choices for the night. I could easily stay home. The room erupted in applause. I never felt like a phony after a performance until now. I could feel the heat rising in my cheeks.

"Excuse me," I darted up the steps to the bathroom. I closed the door and sat on the floor against it. "Deep breath," I told myself. Trying to slow my quick breathing.

"Dandelion! Dinner's up!" Dad called to me.

I splashed some water on face and told my reflection to keep it together. There did not need to be any drama tonight.

Everyone had gathered around the table, hands folded in front of them. I tried not to roll my eyes. Dad's new-found love of praying before family meals had started to get old.

"Okay," he said, clearing his throat, "Have patience with all things but first with yourself. Never confuse your mistakes with your value as a human being. You're a perfectly valuable, creative, worthwhile person, simply because you exist. And no amount of triumphs and tribulations can change that. Unconditional self-acceptance is the core of a peaceful mind. Amen." Everyone pulled their chairs out, squeaking against the floor, and sat down.

"Pops that isn't a prayer. That's a motivational poster," I told him and grabbed a sandwich.

"Well, I turned it into a prayer. We need some self-acceptance and worth-while-personhood in this family." He slung a spoonful of canned green beans onto his plate.

"You can't just make something into a prayer."

"Why not?" Arty interjected.

I turned my attention to Arty, "It's silly. Saint Francis didn't say that meaning it to be a prayer." I looked back at Dad, "And I'm tired of you not telling me what you think but "praying" it in front of everyone." I added air quotes to annoy him.

"I tell you what I think on a daily basis, girl. It is your own choice to turn a deaf ear to us all. We have told you for years, months, days, hours, that we love you and believe in you. It is your own choice to continue letting yourself feel worthless and not try harder. Your emotional stability is not my job. That would be your job." He took a sandwich off the plate and slammed it down.

"Thanks for telling me how you really feel, Pops." I gulped down some sweet tea.

"You're welcome. Need I continue? Anyone else want to get in on this?" Dad looked around the room. I noticed September squirm in her chair.

"I think you hit the nail on the head," Arty replied.

I shot him a death glare; he returned it full force.

"I just love family dinners." Cricket broke the ice with a nervous giggle. Cadmus tried not to smirk but failed.

I let them take over the rest of the conversation for the evening. When everyone finished, I started to clean the table off. I was not in the mood for conversation and coveted the chance to stay in the kitchen alone. Of course, it did not work. I rinsed the plates; Cricket came and stood next to me, pushing my hip with hers, playfully.

"Are you okay?"

"Not really." I took a handful of cutlery and put it in the basket on the dishwasher door.

"What's wrong?" she handed me a plate to rinse.

I scrubbed the plate with a bristle brush, "I feel like I'm going to crawl out of my skin."

"Because?"

"I don't know how to do this; to be home, to not get in trouble, to not want to run away."

"You just need to find some peace. Go for a swim tomorrow. That always helps to clear your head." She put her arm around me and kissed my cheek. "Even though you drive me bonkers, I still love you."

I smiled at her. I was not looking forward to disappointing them all again, but I also knew it was inevitable.

The only light in my room came from the moon filtering

in through the window. Mazy snoring loudly next to me. It had been an hour since Cadmus and Cricket left, Dad fell asleep hours before that. I lay in my bed fighting within myself about what I would do. My brain had known since the words left Rob's mouth that I would go tonight. It was my heart putting up a good fight. I told myself it would be a harmless last hurrah; I knew it was a lie. Nothing good had ever come from any of this. After another few minutes, I gave up the fight. I rolled off the edge of my bed, silently as possible and dressed in the dark. I did not worry about waking Dad. I did worry about Mazy. I knew if she saw me leave the house, she would start barking. The window scraped when I began to open it, I stopped, biting my lip then started again. My head peered out. I forgot how much of a drop it was from my windowsill to the awning on the back door. I swung my legs out, turning onto my stomach. Holding onto the window with clenched hands, I lowered my body until my feet touched the top. A sigh passed my lips when I let go of the window and dropped, jumping from the awning to the deck in one quick motion. I knew I could not drive, that would wake the house for sure when the motor started. The path cutting through the woods had always been the fastest route. I steeled my nerve and began to trek, through the woods, past Cadmus's cabin, September's small light shown out in the pitch black. I glanced up to her room, wishing I could have been more for her. I turned and kept going all the way to the Abbot's drive.

If I could have gone back in time, I would have stopped

myself. That one choice of going to Aaron's turned into a domino effect. At least, that's what it felt like in the days after. In reality, it was not just that choice; it had been the hundreds of choices I had made over the last twenty years of my life. A culmination of every bad turn, folding in on itself and blowing up in my face.

Obviously, Mr. and Mrs. Abbot were gone. I hoped they had had the presence of mind to take Thomas with them and not leave him in the den of vipers. There were trucks and cars scattered on the lawn. I could hear people down at the docks and voices coming out of the barn. I knew I would recognize the faces of each of them, but I knew I would not know them. We had partied alongside each other for years, but I did not know these people. I walked up the steps and into the house, scanning the massive family room for a familiar face. A couple wrapped in each other's arms, making out on the sofa, a girl passed out in a chair, a cluster of boys smoking in the corner. I proceeded up the stairs to Aaron's room. Aaron hated parties.

The closed-door at the end of the hallway had light seeping out under it. I braced myself, hoping not to walk in on him having sex. He sat on his bed, shirtless, watching TV. A bottle of vodka sitting next to him.

"Hey friend," he said when I came in. He patted the bed next to himself. "I knew you'd come."

I climbed up onto the bed next to him. "You know me. Who invited all these people?"

"Rob and Graham, you know how those two goons are." He offered me the bottle of booze.

I yanked the cap off and took a swig. It burned my mouth and throat when it slid down. My whole body went warm.

"You alright," he laughed at me. My eyes winced. "Haven't had vodka in a while have you?"

"Not anything good. God, that tastes amazing." I took another swig.

"Dude, I got some good stuff. Are you even ready for this?" he looked almost giddy, reaching across me to the nightstand. He pulled out a package filled with white powder.

"Have you tried it yet?"

"Nah, not this batch. I was waiting for you." He reached around me again; musk and citrus hit my nose. He pulled out another bag from the nightstand. He dumped the contents on the bed, a tourniquet, and needles.

"Are you out of your mind?"

"Come on, you know you want to."

"No way, no way." The dangers of the drug were an ever-present warning in my mind, there were a few thresholds I knew I should never cross.

He took a swig of vodka and started to unroll the tightly packaged white substance.

"You can't be serious," I heard myself laugh. "I'll snort it. I'm not shoving a needle in my arm. You are out of your mind."

"Fine, be a wuss and go snort your coke, you bitch." He handed me a package.

I hopped off the bed, massaging the plastic between my fingers. I snuck a glance back at him; he seemed tranquil, sitting there, putting the powder on the spoon. I turned back around and started to cut mine with the razor blade he'd handed me. "You got a hundred?" I teased him.

"Don't you? How you paying me?" he replied sitting on the bed with a lighter, heating the spoon.

"How I always do." I glared down at the perfect white powder lined up on the table. My mouth dried out while my hands shook, not from fear, from anticipation. As if it was already in me, I could not stop myself from chasing that high down. I rolled up a receipt that I found in my shorts and snorted up the line in one quick motion. My head spun, and vision blurred for a second. Then the euphoria hit.

26

I turned back to Aaron when he inserted the needle into his arm. He laid back and sighed. My mind alive, firing in a million directions. My heart accelerated. I felt impetuous stripping my shirt off, hopping onto the bed and straddling him. I leaned down and kissed him hard on the mouth. His hands grabbed my hips, and he pulled me down. I came up for air a minute later. I felt his body start to tremble under me. I grabbed for the liquor bottle.

"You okay?" I asked absently, taking a swig of alcohol. When I looked back at his face, his pupils blown; they looked like black glassy marbles while his whole body convulsed. "Aaron!" I screamed, sputtering liquor. He was unresponsive. His torso writhed and shook. "Aaron!" I screamed again. The high left, faster than it had come. The fear overloaded my brain. It hurt. I watched his body convulse and his eyes rolled back into his head.

I tried to hold his arms down my thighs felt him tremble under me. His movements stopped suddenly. I jumped off him, not letting go of his arm. I heard him moan, and I took it for a good sign. I started to pull him out of the bed. First, his legs dangled over the edge, and then I pulled him up by his arms. I leaned him against me; it felt like an impossible feat, his solid frame pushed into mine. Slowly he came to stand on his feet, his whole weight out of the bed and leaning on me. I grabbed my shirt off the end of the bed walking towards the door, dragging him next to me. It was no good. I moved my body out from under his arm and side. I braced myself while his limp body came down on my back. I held onto both his arms and tugged him towards the steps. He moaned again.

"Aaron, just, just try. Try for me. I have to get you down the steps." His breath felt hot and labored on my neck. I twisted around to face him, his arms slung over my shoulders. I bent my knees over his legs until his backside touched the floor. I straddled him again, and his eyes opened a slit.

"Dandelion..."

"I've got you. We have to get down these steps. I'm gonna pull you down. Like when we were kids. Ready?" my brain ablaze and popping in a million directions. It felt like a battle going on. I climbed around him and sat behind him, pushing his body down the stairs, one loud thumb at a time. None of the other partygoers seemed phased by watching me. They were all too drunk and high out of their minds to care what I was doing. With the next thump, the door at the top of the steps opened tentatively. Thomas's shaggy head poked out, looking for the sound.

"Thomas!" I called, my voice sounded frenzied. His eyes fell on me.

"What the hell?" He raced down to our side. One look at his brother and his complexion went white as a sheet.

"He isn't dead." My speech quick, panicked, "Gotta get him in a car. Hospital." Thomas helped me carry him down the stairs without a word.

"Little Flower..." Aaron moaned.

"Come here," I told him yanking him up by his arm. He pushed up weakly on his legs, throwing his arm around me again. Thomas grabbed his other arm, putting it around his shoulder. Aaron seemed not to notice his younger sibling's presence. We stumbled out the front door and onto the porch. It hit me that I hadn't driven.

Maybe someone left their keys in the visor? "Car?" I spoke frantically. "Car?" Thomas let go of Aaron for only a moment to go in search of a vehicle. As he left us, we fell down the steps into the grass. I landed on top of him. Citrus and woods struck my nose. His breath tickled my neck. Aaron moaned again. I tried to pull him up, my hand brushed his chest, I could feel his heart, it wanted to beat out of his chest.

"Don't die on me," I told him. I pulled him up and scanned the yard, looking for Thomas. He was running from car to car looking for keys. I saw a car I recognized, it made no sense that it was here. Cricket's Civic. I decided to ask questions later. She always left her keys in the cup holder. "Thomas! That one!" He looked where I pointed then came back to help me with his brother. We hauled him towards the car. His feet must have felt like dead weight to him. I pulled open the back door and we laid Aaron down. Thomas went on the other side and climbed into the back with him.

"Dee?"

"Not now," I replied. I slammed the driver's door shut, and started the engine, peeling out down the driveway. I saw Cricket's phone sitting on the passenger's seat. I grabbed it and pounded in 911.

"911. What is your emergency?"

"My friend OD'd on coke. He injected it. I don't know how much." I crammed the phone into the crook of my shoulder. I turned the wheel down the curve onto the road.

"Where are you?"

"In a silver Civic coming down Mountain Road from the valley." I floored the gas pedal up the incline of the mountain.

"I have an ambulance in route. Is he breathing?" her voice calm. How could she be calm right now? Didn't she understand that he was going to die, and it was my fault?

"I don't know. Thomas! Is he breathing?" Silence. "Thomas! Is he breathing?"

"I want you to stop the car and check on him. The ambulance will be there soon."

"Dee! He's, I don't know! He won't stop shaking!"

I stopped at the top of the mountain in the middle of the road and jumped out of the car, the phone clutched in my hand. When I opened the back door, my eyes landed on his still body.

Thomas' eyes fixed on his brother; he looked like he was in shock, "Is he turning blue? He stopped the shaking."

I brushed my hand under his nose and across his open mouth. No airflow. "He's not breathing!" I screamed into the phone.

"Do you know how to do mouth to mouth?"

"Yes." Countless hours of CPR training for lifeguarding came back to me instantaneously.

"You need to give him mouth to mouth until the ambulance gets there."

I dropped the phone on the floor of the car, "Get out!" I shouted at Thomas, he did not move a muscle, "I need him flat, get out!" Thomas snapped out of it, opened his door, and tumbled backward out of the car. Aaron's head flopped onto the seat. I began to pound on his chest, counting before pressing my lips against his. They felt clammy instead of soft and warm. I was willing him to wake up with every fiber of my being.

"Don't leave me," I whispered in his ear while I shoved on his chest. There was no change in his appearance. I breathed more air into his mouth filling his lungs and forcing his chest to rise. "Come on Aaron!" Alarm rose in my tone. More compressions, more air from my lungs to his, more memories racing through my mind. I started to lose count. With each breath, I cursed the ambulance drivers. "You can't leave me," I told him, my voice was getting louder while I watched him slip away from me. His pallid complexion and his lips an abnormal bluish gray. I forced my hands down on his chest again and I exhaled all my breath into his lungs, feeling I had nothing left to give, "Get your damn heart beating again!" I yelled at him. "Don't you dare leave me in this shit hole alone! I need you!" My lips felt wet and tasted salty. I pushed them against his again. I could hear the sirens coming up the mountain now. I forced his lungs to compress. "Wake up Aaron!" I screamed. Listening to the sirens and wondering why they weren't already here. I stopped and looked down at him; I touched his cheek with my palm. "Please, please, don't leave me, you can't leave me. You can't go like this. I still need you."

Suddenly, like a miracle, he coughed. Thomas let out a cry. I brushed his hair away from his face. His eyes opened a slit, "Why didn't you let me go?" I shook my head at him then his eyes rolled back in his head.

"No!" I screamed. Someone grabbed me from behind, pulling me off him, I felt like a wild animal, I screamed, kicked, and tried to pull away from their strong arms.

An hour later Don and Julia Abbot came rushing into the ER. I had not sat down since arriving. Pacing back and forth waiting to hear if he was alive. Don charged into the hospital like a bull.

"What the hell did you do to my son?" he screamed at me.

Thomas sprang from his chair, pulling at his dad's arms, "She saved his life! She didn't do anything!"

Don swatted Thomas away like a pesky fly, "Shut up, Thomas!" He kept charging for me. I backed up until I felt a wall. He was in my face yelling obscenities at me. I heard the hospital staff telling him to get away. His large frame blocked out any view from my vision. I cringed against the wall, waiting for him to hit me. The security guard pulled him away from me. Cadmus, Arty, and Pops entered the room.

"Leave my daughter the hell alone!" I heard Dad bellow. Then I heard the crack that was Dad's fist breaking Don Abbot's nose.

"You crossed the wrong man, Melvin Sanders!" Don yelled. More security guards flooded the waiting room. Arty grabbed me and pulled me away from the fighting. Both men were wrenching away from security guards trying to get at each other again.

"It's that damn son of yours!" I heard Dad get in the last jab before security separated them.

"Are you alright?" Cadmus asked me, I shook in Arty's arms.

"He's gonna die. He's gonna die, and it's all my fault." I couldn't stop the panic now. I crumbled onto the floor in a ball of hysterics. Arty wrapped his body around mine, trying to force my brokenness back together. It did not seem possible I would ever be complete, not if Aaron left me now.

If Don Abbot stayed a hundred feet away from me, he could remain. My Dad wasn't so lucky. They escorted him to jail for assaulting Don. I knew Don would press as many charges as he could against my dad. He was just that kind of man, malicious.

When I had given up all hope, a nurse came out and told us he was stable, hooked up to a ventilator, and family could come back to see him.

"I have to see him," I blurted out.

"Like hell you are," Don replied.

"Are you family?" the nurse asked.

I shook my head 'no'.

"I'm sorry miss, only family." She held my eyes, "He's going to be okay. You did the right thing. You got him here, and he's alive," she added. I caught a glimpse of Thomas following his parents to the back, watching me watching him with that sad look that never left his face.

It took Cadmus and Arty another thirty minutes to convince me to leave. Really, they drug me out of the hospital. No one said a word the entire forty-five-minute drive back to the house.

"Will you be okay for a little while?" Cadmus asked. We were sitting in the driveway of my house in Cricket's car. Arty followed us in his truck.

"I'll be fine," I told him when we exited the vehicle.

"We will be right back. I just want to go check on your dad." Arty told me, his head sticking out the window.

I started to walk towards the house.

"Call us if anything happens," Cadmus hollered while Arty pulled his truck away.

I trudged up the steps and opened the front door. The house, dark, with dawn nearing. The pale white light from the sun leaking into the room. Mazy licked my hand. The weight of the world had descended on my shoulders. I buckled onto the floor and cried. She curled up in front of me. When my tears finally subsided, I looked up and saw a funny shape sitting in the armchair. I rubbed the tears away from my eyes. Cricket. Her legs pulled up on the chair, her knees under her chin, something about her did not appear right.

"Cricket?"

She did not reply. Her eyes look glazed over she stared out the front window.

"Cricket, what's wrong? I'm sorry I took your car. Aaron almost died." I stood a few feet from her, but her eyes never left their fixed point.

She did not respond.

"Cricket, what's wrong? Did you hear me, Aaron OD'd; I had to take him down the mountain. He's okay though. Thank god he's okay." I moved across the room to the couch. I suddenly realized what was wrong with her face; her cheek and lip swollen on the left side. There was a bruise forming around her right eye. "What happened?" my heart dropped, my body sank down onto the furniture.

Her eyes appeared dead when she met my gaze. "Mel woke up, and you were gone. He called Cadmus; Cadmus called me, and I went to Aaron's. I knew there was a party there tonight." She fell silent for a moment. "I never made it in the house."

"Who did this to you?" I already knew the answer.

"They came up behind me and grabbed me. I couldn't even scream." Her pain, her numbness, they seeped into my skin.

"We have to call Sheriff Ritter."

"Don't," she said in a forceful whisper, her eyes snapping onto my mine.

I felt I had run into a brick wall, "We have to."

"Did you?" she replied, almost venomously. "Did you ever tell all your secrets? It won't help. It'll only make it worse."

"You can't let Rob and Graham get away with it." I pleaded.

"You did."

"That was different. I was a druggie, who was going to listen to me."

"No. No, you weren't. Not then. Someone would have listened. You ran away. Leave it alone, Dani." She stood up. "Is my car here?"

"Yeah... But... I can't let it go..." I let the air out of my lungs.

"Why not? Isn't this how girls live? With our mouths stitched up, our cheeks full of secrets never to be told. It's just white noise, Dani. No one cares what happens to us."

I could not argue with her. I could not apologize to her. I could not seem to let another word slip from my mouth. I just sat there watching her walk out of my house.

Made in the USA
San Bernardino, CA
13 March 2019